EVE'S RIB

Also by C.S. O'Cinneide

Petra's Ghost

The Candace Starr Series

The Starr Sting Scale

Starr Sign

C.S. O'CINNEIDE

EVE'S RIB

Publisher: Scott Fraser | Acquiring editor: Jenny McWha | Editor: Dominic Farrell
Cover designer: Laura Boyle
Cover image: shutterstock.com/KHIUS

Library and Archives Canada Cataloguing in Publication

Title: Eve's rib / C.S. O'Cinneide.
Names: O'Cinneide, C. S., 1965- author.
Identifiers: Canadiana (print) 20210368934 | Canadiana (ebook) 20210368942 | ISBN 9781459749801 (softcover) | ISBN 9781459749818 (PDF) | ISBN 9781459749825 (EPUB)
Classification: LCC PS8629.C56 E94 2022 | DDC C813/.6—dc23

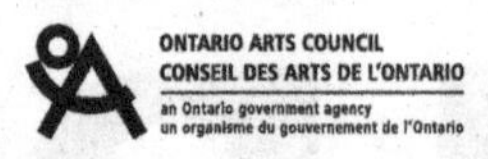

We acknowledge the support of the Canada Council for the Arts and the Ontario Arts Council for our publishing program. We also acknowledge the financial support of the Government of Ontario, through the Ontario Book Publishing Tax Credit and Ontario Creates, and the Government of Canada.

Printed and bound in Canada.

Dundurn Press
1382 Queen Street East
Toronto, Ontario, Canada M4L 1C9
dundurn.com, @dundurnpress

For Mom and Dad.

Thanks for not feeding me to the wolves.

PROLOGUE

Eve sat at the kitchen table and waited for the life to drain out of her.

She had called in sick at work, knowing what was to come. The cramps that would start off weak and low, rising to a crescendo that would eventually twist and expel. The spark of life within her had already begun its all too familiar flicker. It would soon go out. A tiny sun gone supernova. It left a black hole inside her every time. Eve could not predict the future, nobody really could, because there was always more than one. But she had been here before and knew the signs. She was, in this way, like any other woman who had suffered similar disappointments.

She knew she should count her blessings. Her career was at a high, her marriage of three years was as solid as the house Richard and she had just bought — a three bedroom with a wraparound porch that hugged them snugly at the edges. But those successes only seemed to mock Eve as she continued to fail in this one regard. She felt as if she were to blame, somehow careless with the fruit of her husband's seed. A rotten gardener, not deserving of a child.

She rose from the table and went upstairs, stood outside the brightly decorated nursery. Dust had settled on the mobile above the solid wood crib, tarnished the shine of its silver stars. Eve reached out with her hand and sent the mobile spinning without touching it. The dust flew into the air to sparkle in a beam of morning light. She had greater powers than this, was able to move not only objects but circumstances with her will and a practised incantation. Eve could see for miles using only her mind's eye, whisper suggestions that allowed others no choice other than to follow. She could do all this, but she could not keep a baby inside her for nine months. Despite all the spells she knew, despite medical technology, that magic escaped her. Even IVF, that modern-day womb conjurer, was not an option. Eve had no trouble getting pregnant, only staying that way.

Eve had never asked to be a witch, if that's what she was. The word was only a close approximation of her nature. Most people, she supposed, did not get much of a say in who they were. The act of becoming was an organic process rather than a conscious choice. What we want has to percolate in the atmosphere along with what was meant to be before it is distilled enough to rain back down on the world as destiny. If you've ever stuck your tongue out to catch a raindrop, you know wild things don't taste the same as the contrived, and fate was a wild thing.

It had been her friend Janet who'd first seen the gifts within her, back in high school. She'd taken her to Nanny, Janet's Jamaican great-grandmother, so they could perfect their skills together under her greying tutelage. Nanny would sit them down at the base of her frayed green-and-white lawn chair and pass on her ancient wisdom. About the white and the black of magic, and the line that lies in between. Nanny had been the first one to tell Eve the story of the Ragman. That's what she used to call him, after the tinker who came around the house when she was a young girl, sporting his jacket full of wares. *You don't want what he's selling, little girl*, she'd told Eve late one night as she and Janet sat with her at the old farmhouse Nanny kept at the lake. *You got to promise Nanny you won't answer the door if the Ragman calls.* Eve had nodded her ponytailed head that sultry evening and promised. But that had been a long time ago.

Eve closed the door to the nursery and made her way to the bathroom. Sitting down on the toilet, she watched as the first drop of blood fell into the bowl, blooming in the water like a rose. Soon it was joined by others, making the crimson bouquet complete. It didn't take as long as the last time.

When it was over, she cleaned herself up, showered, and put on a sanitary pad. Then she went downstairs to the kitchen table and got the box of chalk she'd bought that morning. Pulling on the rope that brought down the stairs to the attic, she climbed them with heavy steps, like a woman mounting the gallows.

As Eve drew the pentagram on the floor of the attic, tears mixed with the dust of the chalk. She stood and surveyed her handiwork, trembling. Then she lay down with her flat belly at its chalky apex and bought everything the Ragman had to sell.

ONE

Eighteen Years Later

Eve tried to rest her book on the rib that wasn't broken. She looked around the emergency waiting room, saw the cop stationed at the door, the nurse behind the bulletproof glass. A man with one shoe snored softly in the corner, cradling his hand in a blood-soaked T-shirt like a red, angry newborn.

"This is quite the place, isn't it?" the elderly woman in the plastic chair next to her said. She was well dressed, with salt-and-pepper cropped hair. Eve and the older woman sat in a lineup of grubby orange seats placed against the wall across from triage.

"Yes, it is," Eve said. She knew the older woman was only trying to be friendly, looking for conversation to pass the time, but Eve was hurting too much for small talk. She returned the friendly lady's smile while simultaneously attempting to silence her with an incantation of muteness. Unfortunately, the woman's Coke-bottle glasses were too thick. Eve couldn't initiate enough eye contact to get the spell to personalize and stick.

"I was in here last week." Salt and Pepper shook her head. "And it was something, let me tell you. People screaming — and the language." The woman made a short series of tuts, possibly as a form of Morse code for the language she was too dignified to repeat.

"Hmm." Eve winced in lieu of another smile as she turned back to her book, hoping the social cue would work better than the incantation. She was usually a kinder person than this, but the pain was making her less of one. Despite looking down at the book, she managed to keep track of what was going on around her with a well-developed mind's eye. This was one of the few gifts she could still execute with any mastery. Through the window to the triage room, she watched a nurse question a sleepy-eyed prostitute who slouched in a chair. A yellow, viscous liquid that looked like an egg thrown at Halloween had dried on the bulletproof glass. It distorted the nurse's and the prostitute's faces, so Eve couldn't read them for signs.

"Don't you think I know that!" The prostitute's raised voice reverberated against the smeared glass. Eve looked up from her book. The woman was perched on the edge of her moulded seat as if she were afraid of catching something nasty from it through her short skirt. When she leaned too far across the desk toward the nurse, a burly orderly arrived, causing her to crumple back into the chair. She cried softly. Eve turned both her primary and secondary sight away, not wanting to pry.

"They shouldn't have a window like that," the woman beside Eve said. "People deserve their privacy."

Eve nodded, but she knew why windows were necessary. The hospital staff were doing their work in a fishbowl so no one would think they were out for a smoke break or getting laid on a gurney somewhere. A wall could hide the possibility that there was no one behind the wizard's curtain, would prevent them from discovering that they were all waiting for nothing and no one. Such situations tended to breed anarchy. That was why the world developed religion, as well as witchcraft. They were both ways to help punch through the wall to get a better look at what was on the other side.

"I'm here for a urinary tract infection. Can't seem to get rid of it. My daughter's got a bad chest cold." Salt and Pepper indicated a woman a bit younger than Eve in the chairs reserved for those already processed by triage. The woman's daughter managed a weak smile in their direction before coughing into her sleeve.

Eve shifted in her tacky bucket seat of plastic. The slight movement sent a searing pain from her lower rib into her spine. She wished she could wrap it in some healing magic, but she wasn't powerful enough. She was once. But a witch's power was only as strong as her spirit, and hers had been broken five years ago.

"I feel like I live here," the woman beside her continued. "My husband died this spring and then I had a stroke and then this." She peered over at the book that Eve had balanced on her lap. It was a murder mystery set in Glasgow. A lot of *fucks* stood out on the page. She wondered if the chatty lady would notice and complain about language again. Eve was a writer. A few years ago she'd quit her tech job to write full-time, with limited success. Her own gritty crime novels had a lot of *fucks* in them as well.

"So, what are you here for?" Salt and Pepper asked her after a short interval. "If you don't mind me asking."

Guessing what was wrong with other people was the only game to play in an emergency waiting room. Everyone tried to figure out the reasoning behind a young healthy-looking man being taken ahead of an ancient Filipina woman in a wheelchair. But judging books by their covers was rarely accurate when assessing other people's pain. Eve had tried to assess the maladies of other patients as she'd waited, but without using any of her special capabilities. She could open certain people up, but they were rarely pretty inside. She tended to focus on the covers, just like everybody else.

"Rib," Eve said, indicating her clutched side. "I fell."

The door opened on the nurse's bulletproof cage, and the young prostitute walked out with a brave smirk on her face as she tugged at her tube top. She took a seat next to the coughing daughter and pulled out a phone sporting a bright-pink case encrusted with rhinestones and ten-dollar-hand-job spunk.

"Eve Knight!" the triage nurse called through the open door. Eve stood up, stifling a gasp as her rib shifted unnaturally. She tucked the book with the bad language into her large purse, holding it to her left side where the bones behaved better.

"Well, good luck, dear," said the little lady who lived in the emergency ward.

"Thanks," Eve said, turning to look back and address her, even as her right side flamed in disagreement. "Good luck to you too."

HOURS LATER, EVE WAS LYING prone on an examination table, being yelled at by a doctor working the last thirty minutes of a back-to-back shift.

"Why are you not takin' the pain medication?"

The doctor had a heavy brogue that made him hard to understand. Scottish, like Eve's murder mystery. There were faded brown stains on the sheet of the thin mattress she lay on. She hoped it was old blood, rather than something more recent and less sterile. A pretty young med student stood by, shadowing the doctor to learn how things were done.

"They make me sick," Eve told him. "The meds." She didn't like to take pills. Medication, like magic, was uneven in its efficacy and prone to side effects. The Tylenol 3s with codeine had made her vomit. She could still hear the sound of her ribs popping as she heaved.

"A broken rib hurts like hell. There's nothin' you can do but take the pain meds." The doctor's nostrils flared like those of a charging bull in a lab coat.

Eve wished she had gotten the nice doctor. She had heard him making his rounds behind the curtains earlier, asking a young girl gently if she was sexually active and then kindly explaining to her what that was. But Eve had gotten the mean doctor who yelled, so everyone could hear how pathetic you were. She was glad he didn't ask if she was sexually active. She wasn't sure what that was either. After twenty years of marriage, Richard and Eve still had sex, but it wasn't that active.

"I know it's supposed to be painful." Eve held her side. She was afraid the mean doctor would touch her again with his sharp hands. *Does this hurt? Does this hurt?* He'd dug his nasty digits into her upper abdomen with no mercy before, only stopping when she'd yelled "Shit" at the top of her lungs like a safe word.

"You didn't see a doctor when this happened? Just got pain meds prescribed over the phone?" The doctor tutted like the elderly woman with the urinary tract infection.

"Yes." Eve squirmed on the squeaky mattress. "My doctor knows me." Eve, like her family physician, knew there was nothing to be done for a broken rib. You couldn't put a cast on it. You weren't even supposed to tape them anymore because it interfered with your breathing. Eve had wrapped an old, greying tensor bandage around her middle anyway and made the phone call to Dr. Verschuren to ask for painkillers.

People thought witches had all sorts of herbal tricks up their sleeves for healing. But the modern pharmacy grew out of the apothecary of wise women and was the natural progression of it. Only backward amateurs used essential oils infused with horsehair to treat illness and injury. Although there were still some remedies that worked as well as they had back in the Middle Ages, Eve couldn't get them at the trendy little Wicca store that had opened up on Main Street. She ordered hers off the internet and got them delivered to her front door. More modern magic.

"I was worried maybe there had been some internal damage, you know, to an organ," Eve said. The pain had been so bad every time Eve reached her arm out or twisted her torso that she was afraid one of the ribs was spearing her liver or perhaps a kidney.

"The ultrasound doesn't show anythin' of that nature," the doctor snapped, consulting his clipboard. *He can look inside people too*, thought Eve.

"You fell onto some garbage cans, you're sayin'?"

Eve tried to sit up on the exam table to answer. After a few failed attempts to roll over onto her good side and sit upright, the med student offered her a guilty hand.

"I fell *into* a garbage can," she corrected the doctor, trying to make things clear. "I was cleaning it, and I slipped and fell in." Eve hadn't slipped. But she had been trying to reach one last piece of grime on the inside of the can with a sponge when it happened. It was a huge bin with wheels on it, so tall the top was well above the waist of the cut-off shorts she wore for housework. Eve had taken the full brunt of the lip of the can on her lower ribs when she fell, caught in a hard plastic–ridged Heimlich manoeuvre. A screech had emitted from her insides rather than the cracking noise one might expect. It had sounded like a taut rope slipped from a rusted metal pulley.

"Do ya drink?" The doctor switched to a different line of questioning. Eve ran a comparison between the screaming drunk three curtains down who'd soiled himself and the recycling bin full of empty red wine bottles she had in her garage.

"Not really. A glass of wine in the evening, maybe." More like two or three glasses of wine in the evening sometimes, but that seemed like the wrong answer.

"Keep takin' the pain meds and come back in if you have any trouble breathin'."

Eve nodded, promising to only come back and be humiliated again if she could no longer draw breath. Satisfied, the mean doctor pulled back the curtain in search of another patient to yell at in the fifteen minutes he had left in his shift.

The med student lingered.

"Why did you fall?" she asked Eve.

"Dunno. Must have slipped on a banana from the green bin." Eve tried to laugh off the lie, but it hurt too much.

"It's just, you've been in here before." The med student spoke softly, perhaps she'd been learning more from the nice doctor than the mean one. Maybe she could explain to Eve what sexually active was.

"Is there someone at home to take care of you? Your husband, perhaps?" It was a veiled question, looking for a threat.

"He's away," Eve said, shutting down the conversation with another lie. "My daughter's at home. She's seventeen. She can help me." She slid her white-sneakered feet to the tiled floor of the exam room, holding her ribs in place with her hand. She reached over carefully to pick up her purse from the chair.

"I know about your son."

Eve leaned hard on the arm of the chair. The emergency room had gone silent. No machines beeped and whirred behind the curtains. No doctors yelled or reassured. The med student stood frozen with one hand in mid-air where she'd lifted it to adjust her glasses. This was something Eve couldn't control, not like her mind's eye. It happened when one of her stronger emotions manifested itself as a force with mass and substance, disrupting the space-time continuum. But it never lasted long. Soon papers started to shuffle again, machines beeped, wheels rattled along industrial tiled floors. The mean doctor was yelling at another patient. This time some poor mother who'd chosen not to breastfeed. "What do ya think your boobs are for, woman?" he shouted, his indignation accentuated by his thick Scottish accent.

How can she know about Michael? It had been five years. Michael fell too, but he'd died before he could lie about it in the emergency room. That task had been left to Eve. She'd been lying about it ever since.

Eve tried to look inside the med student's mind to see what she knew, but her inner thoughts were a mishmash of body parts and blood. The images Eve saw made her head spin like the Tylenol 3s.

"It's normal, you know," she said to Eve, "to be affected by the death of a child, even years later. To blame yourself. But you can't let those feelings become destructive. There are professionals who can help, support groups, people who understand what you've been through."

She doesn't know anything, Eve thought. Just what she's read in her file. *Eight-year-old son, dead on arrival. One surviving daughter. Mother sedated.* Clinical words on a page. Nothing to worry about. Nothing that could disrupt the delicate defences Eve had thrown up around herself and her family.

Eve abandoned the med student's thoughts. As she did, a severed arm got caught in the psychic portal between them. It threatened to become part of Eve's memories as well, but she sealed the portal shut in the nick of time. The arm had crawled back into the med student's subconscious as the portal closed, but not before it scuttled along the floor to tap Eve on the nose with one pointed index finger.

The med student thought Eve had done this to herself, and maybe she *was* somewhat responsible. But this woman was wrong to think that people would understand about her son, Michael. Or her daughter, Abbey. No one could really understand about Abbey.

"I'm fine," Eve said. "Honestly." She gathered her purse and her book up with the rest of her fictions and left the kindly med student who knew nothing behind.

BACK AT HOME, EVE WINCED leaning over to put the dirty cups and bowls in the dishwasher. Bent over, she could see her daughter's sleek young legs and the bottom of her blue plaid school-uniform kilt. The hem seemed to have lost a couple of inches from the last time Eve checked.

"You were supposed to leave the car for me today. Selena and I needed to go to the library." Abbey was beautiful in a glacial way, with her pearl-blond hair and hoarfrost-grey eyes. People often thought she was Russian. Richard said that that was because of the high Slavic cheekbones inherited from his mother's side. But Eve was afraid it was just because she looked angry a lot of the time.

"I was at the hospital," Eve said. "About my rib."

"It's not like it's broken," her daughter said.

"Actually, it is." Eve turned back to the dishwasher, set the knives upside down in the basket so they wouldn't cut anyone.

"I really doubt that. It wasn't like you were in a car accident or anything. It can't be broken." Her daughter made the statement as if it were a fully capitalized tweet that all the wrong people would follow. MOTHER ACTS LIKE RIB IS BROKEN. SAD. As with most mothers of teenagers, everything Eve said was fake news nowadays.

Abbey dropped her plate from dinner in the dishwasher and disappeared up the stairs to her room, probably to Instagram about it. Her immaculate blond hair swished behind her in an indignant ponytail. The dog, a scruffy white puffball in need of grooming, followed her daughter hopefully up the stairs where she slammed her bedroom door in his dejected poodle-cross face. He was four years old, but they still called him *puppy*.

Eve could remember when things had been different. When her daughter had hung on to her every word as if it were gospel. But then nature and hormones had come into play, and she had been forced to act out her role in the bitter tragedy known to every mother. Adolescence. The brutal pushing away orchestrated by one's own flesh and blood. When Abbey was little, Eve would stay at her bedside every night until she fell asleep. Even when she was working crazy hours at the office, they'd find time for impromptu spring picnics, lying back on an old plaid blanket to count clouds, their hands intertwined. In those days, Eve could feel Abbey's soul circling around her own like a bright little moon. But the closer a child is to you, the harder they have to work to break free from your gravitational pull. Abbey and her father didn't have a history of the same kind of bond. They could enjoy each other with much less conflict, safe in different solar systems.

But knowing all this didn't help a great deal. Because when a child moved into the teen years everything changed for them, but nothing changed for the mother. Every rejection, every sign of disrespect was still a slap-in-the-face surprise to Eve. Her love for Abbey burst the boundaries of her heart. Even though sometimes she wanted to go screaming into the night, leaving her daughter and the pain of loving her behind. If she were honest, she knew that propensity to scream started long before Abbey hit puberty. She was not like other daughters. That's why Eve needed to protect her.

Richard came in from the dining room with his own plate and stacked it on the lower tier of the machine. "You shouldn't be doing that," he scolded, nudging her out of the way to take over. Eve felt her rib grind at her liver, despite what the doctor had said. Richard didn't seem to notice. But he'd never been the most observant of men.

"You shouldn't be doing any of this stuff." He stacked a bowl directly behind a plate that would block all the water from cleaning it. "You should be in bed, lying down, resting." She couldn't help feeling that he wanted her out of sight, the stress of her injury hidden so he didn't have to worry about it. It hadn't always been this way between them. But tragedy had a way of chipping away at the glue that sticks a marriage together.

"It's depressing to be in bed all day," Eve said. Their bedroom didn't get much light through the south-facing windows. Heavy blinds blacked out what little sun reached in. Richard liked to sleep in on the weekend.

"Well, you aren't going to get better if you don't take it easy." He tried to force a spoon into the front of the overflowing cutlery basket. "I'm sorry, Eve, but you bring a lot of this on yourself."

"Are you kidding me?" Eve couldn't see into Richard's mind to figure out what drove him to make comments like this. Her best friend, Janet, had formed a binding spell when they got married. It was too tempting for a witch to use her magic on a husband, unbalancing the marital equation.

"I just want you to get better," he mumbled.

He thought her too sensitive. She knew that. And she was, but not in the way Richard believed. She'd always seen and felt the world in an uncommon way. Even before that day in high school when Janet put a name to what they both were. *A witch knows her own*: Janet had told her that, after gym class one day, when she'd caught Eve's mind's eye marvelling at the slick ebony of her skin, glistening wet from a run in the rain. Janet had been the only Black student in their school until a skinny Ugandan boy from Montreal transferred in during senior year. Everyone had expected the two to get together, as if they were a matching pair of cards in a game of Concentration. They didn't realize Janet was gay and looking for a different kind of suit. She and Eve had tried to be lovers for a while, but every time they kissed Eve would giggle, so it had put a damper on things.

"I'm going upstairs." Eve took her Scottish mystery from the kitchen table and retreated to the master bedroom, passing the dog, who remained forever hopeful curled up on the floor in front of Abbey's door. The irony that she was banishing herself just as Richard had asked her to was not lost on her.

Looking at her cellphone charging on the bedside table, she thought about calling Janet. It had been so long since they'd talked. Janet had moved a few years ago to a hobby farm in the country after a bust-up with her long-time girlfriend, Jana. She'd used her thwarted sexual energy to create frightening sculptures, fusing technology with images from the Old Masters. Her latest was a bust of *Venus de Milo* with a working radio embedded in the head. It had two dead batteries sticking out of the goddess's severed arms, acting as dials to adjust the volume and tune in the stations.

Chatsworth wasn't that far away, but it was still over an hour's drive. The two friends kept tabs through Facebook posts and texts, but often months would go by where they didn't see each other in person. Eve had some other friends, but she'd held them at a distance since Michael's death, not wanting to infect them with her grief. She didn't want to infect Janet with her latest struggle either. No one wanted a phone call from a friend who did nothing but complain.

Propped up with pillows on the bed to read her book, she was two chapters into Glasgow's crime-ridden streets by the time Richard came through the door. She kept on reading. He stared at her for a while, then sprang into action.

"How long before you stop being mad at me?" he asked while changing into a T-shirt. He'd dropped his collared casual work shirt on his side of the bed.

Eve didn't answer him. Her weapon of choice was staying mum. A stony silence, the only rock she was capable of throwing. He stood there a bit longer, trying to figure out what he'd done to upset her. But Richard's imagination often stopped short of understanding other people's feelings. Empathy was like a foreign language for him. He only understood it in broken phrases. Their teenage daughter didn't seem to speak a word of it.

"Eve?"

"Do you really want to talk, Richard?" Eve said, putting her book down. She knew Richard would rather have thumbscrews taken to him than discuss the problems they'd been having. CIA operatives could learn a thing or two from her husband's refusal to crack under such circumstances. He wasn't a bad person, not in the grand scheme of things. He cared about Eve, in his own imperfect way. But his approach to all conflict was either denial or anger, both of which caused the important things to be left unsaid.

Richard sighed, shook his head. "I've had a long day." He turned to leave, paused with his hand on the doorknob. His voice softened a little. "Just try not to do anything, okay?" He walked out, shutting the bedroom door behind him. Eve heard Abbey purr as she met him in the hallway.

"Daaadddy," she squealed, and Eve listened as he gave her his best side, his laughter and his jokes about the day. It had been a long time since Richard, or Eve for that matter, had given each other their best sides.

Abbey continued with her cooing. There was a bikini she wanted to order online. Richard told her it was more than okay and gave her his credit card number.

Eve leaned over the bed and picked up Richard's discarded shirt. She brought it up to her face briefly to inhale his scent, before taking it to the laundry hamper in the ensuite and dropping it in. Love, like any old habit, is hard to break.

On the other side of the closed bedroom door, she could see Abbey throw her arms around her father's neck, thanking him as if he'd just bought her a stable full of ponies. Richard smiled broadly, bathing in the sunny glow of his daughter's love and appreciation. He didn't know the darkness hidden by that artificial light. Nobody else did either, Eve hoped. And that's the way she had to keep it. After all, Abbey couldn't help the way she was made, that had been Eve's doing. Hers and the Ragman's. She hadn't needed his dark assistance for her pregnancy with Michael, but he'd cast his long shadow over her son just the same.

The dog let out an excited bark as Eve hobbled to the bed to lie down again on her broken side.

The pain of her rib and her secrets was excruciating.

I remember when she had a regular job. She made good money at it, whatever it was she did. Something similar to what my dad does now, but different. Anyway, I remember when she used to get dressed every day in her little black pencil skirt and blouse to go to the office, how she did her hair in this cool little chignon. Now all she does is hang around the house in a pair of nasty jean shorts and sneakers and pretend to be making a living. We don't even have enough money to send me away to university. I'll have to stay here and attend locally like the pathetic asswipes who didn't get good enough grades to go someplace decent. My parents say it's better staying close to home, but that's bullshit. They just don't trust me. They want to keep me where they can see me. Especially my mom, who sees everything but nothing at the same time.

I haven't told either of them that I've applied for the Thompson scholarship to McGill University in Montreal, a whole province away. The Thompson is based on academic merit exclusively, not all that lame extracurricular stuff. It pisses me off how many awards there are for things like being a good world citizen. What the hell is that, anyway? Wessex, Ontario, is about as worldly a town as Buttfuck, New Brunswick. We don't even have a Starbucks in the downtown. I work every weekend to get the grades I do. But some jerk who sells dried-up brownies in front of the gym for a flooded South American village no one has heard of has more chance of getting an award than me. Because my parents put me in separate school, there's also an award for being a good Catholic. I'm definitely not getting that one.

My only competition for the Thompson scholarship is Selena, my best friend, although we don't talk about it much. We've always competed since we were kids. Two days after we moved onto this street, Selena and her mother came by with a basket full of muffins to introduce themselves. I remember Selena hiding behind her mom, obviously forced to go with her. I took her into my bedroom and showed her the black dress with the spaghetti straps I'd worn to Michael's funeral. She asked me where I got it instead of telling me she was sorry about my little brother like everyone else did. Other than that, she was pretty quiet.

We got assigned to the same grade seven class that fall and I figured out pretty quickly that she was the one to beat academically. Selena didn't have many friends on account of being so shy and neither did I, so we started hanging out. We used to sit on a low brick wall at the back of the schoolyard and eat our lunches, just the two of us, even in the winter. I thought she'd have something cool and ethnic like samosas to eat, but she brought the same thing, cream cheese on a bagel with cucumber, every damn day. When I asked her why, she couldn't tell me. Selena is predictable like that.

Half the time, I didn't get my lunch until my mom showed up at noon to finally drop off some leftovers in a Tupperware. I'd try to hide from her in the schoolyard, behind a tree or buried in leaves or the snow where the hill met the fence to the old age home next door. But somehow, she always found me. I hated that. I wanted her to feel guilty for not getting up and making me a lunch in the morning, even if it was just cream cheese on a damn bagel.

I wanted her to live with the guilt that I was starving because she couldn't get her act together. This was after the cool job that made real money and before she got into the writing thing. She had nothing to do all day, except to be sad about what happened to Michael. Like I said, she likes to feel sorry for herself.

So naturally, Selena and I both signed up for the International Baccalaureate program at All Saints High School when we hit grade nine, even though it takes two buses to get there. That's where all the smart kids go, and most of the rich ones whose parents are trying to make up for the ambition their kids lack. This is our final year, and Selena's still the one to beat. I saw her mid-term average last semester. She left her report card sticking up out of her book bag when she went to go sharpen a pencil. It was 98 percent. My overall average is 99 percent. So, I'm still winning.

I've ordered something from Victoria's Secret online. I told Dad it was a bikini. He's so clueless, he can't tell the difference between swimwear and lingerie. I like wearing sexy things, letting the boys see the shadow of my black bra beneath the white ironed top we have to wear. There's no padding so my nipples are visible. The teachers can't say anything. They can uniform card you for rolling the waist up on your kilt to make it shorter, but they can't outlaw your anatomy. If any of them tried, I'd make a big deal about it — shaming girls about their bodies and all that. I know how to work the system. They're delusional anyway, thinking that forcing us all to wear the same plaid skirt and collared cotton blouse will somehow keep us safe from being sexual. Have they looked at what's on the internet, for fuck's sake? There are whole websites on the dark web dedicated to girls in the exact same outfits. Men as old as my father stare at me on the bus coming back from school salivating. Disgusting.

Of course, the uniform is meant to make us all the same, anonymous and compliant, like prisoners. But they can't control me, can't make me like everybody else. One afternoon in English class I hiked up my uniform skirt so Dylan Penske could see I had on garters. I fingered the lace at the top of my thigh-highs under my desk like I didn't know he was watching. He had to ask to be excused, holding his jacket in front of his tiny boner as he rushed to the door. He probably jacked off in the washroom thinking about me. What a loser. He's got this weird face, a pointy chin, and a huge forehead like a Neanderthal. Selena and I call him Funnel Head.

Zanax is going to be at our school on Friday night. It's for underagers, so you get to pretend like you're at a rave, but really it's just a glorified teen laser dance. I want to go, but Selena isn't sure if her parents will let her. I think that's just an excuse. Selena never wants to do anything. All the other kids in our year are puking their guts out at bush parties or going up to the old quarry to screw in their parents' cars. I mean, they're all a bunch of idiots going nowhere, but it would be fun to do stuff like that every once in a while.

My parents don't know how lucky they are with a kid like me. I don't go to parties and get wasted on Ecstasy or get busted by the cops. Maddie Johnston got arrested for distributing kiddie porn last week for Christ's sake. The joke, of course, is the kid was her. She sexted pictures to her boyfriend, stupid photos with her pushing her skinny boobs together to make them look like a plumber's butt crack. Those pictures are all over the internet now. If that's not bad enough, there are two girls in my year that are pregnant, showing off their pitiful bumps and registering for baby shower gifts at Walmart. Haven't they ever heard of *Roe v. Wade*? Then again, that lady fell apart later and became a born-again pro-lifer, so I guess she's not the best example. I don't know who I'll go to Zanax with if Selena doesn't come. But I'm going. I've got to get out of this place, if only for one night.

I can hear my mom getting ready for bed now, going downstairs to turn off all the lights, making sure the doors are all locked. Then she'll go into the bathroom and pick up the wet towels, hanging them like little soldiers over the rail. She'll bitch about it later to my father. Jesus, what else does she have to do?

People think they know my mom. They think she's all smart and selfless, writing her dumb stories that nobody reads, volunteering at the food bank and serving dinners to hideous homeless guys with piss on their pants. She hovers around the house like a shell-shocked Gestapo just waiting for me to screw up, and she calls it caring. But she's not caring. And she's not like other people. She's dangerous.

And I'm the only one who knows it.

that had been patched in piecemeal. You couldn't click on one of the icons too early, or the computer would become overwhelmed and take longer to boot up. Or it would just freeze. He needed to take it to the tech boys, get them to wipe off all the garbage, restore the laptop to its original virgin state. Richard clicked angrily on his email icon multiple times, knowing it would only make things worse. Every click sent another binary-coded message to the hard drive, confusing it further in its sleepy stitched-together state, slowing it down even more.

How could Julia be so reckless as to send him a personal email on the company server? Didn't she know they monitor those things? Although it would have been worse if she'd sent it to his home email. He never looked at that, but Eve did, picking up the unpaid bill notices and hassling him about them. He had the money to pay them, but there was too much on his mind to remember to do it on time.

He'd noticed the email on his phone this morning, recklessly titled "Tonight." Julia knew how to give a man an out-of-body experience with a bottle of olive oil and her supple hands, but about some things she was utterly clueless. He'd deleted the message from his phone, but he needed to wipe the email server's backup using his laptop as well. He couldn't risk someone coming across what she'd written. Julia reported to him, so there was an imbalance of power. Combining business with pleasure was a volatile mix.

He hadn't meant for it to happen. The thing with Julia. And when it had happened, he meant for it to be a one-off. He'd never cheated on Eve before. Oh, there was that sweet business analyst with the short skirts who used to let him sit too close to her when they all went out for lunch. But that never came to anything. Julia had caught him in a weak moment. Eve had been in one of her writing trances, closeted in her study to work on her latest novel, barely finding time to pick up the dry cleaning or make dinner. Richard wasn't a misogynist. He was capable of fixing a meal, or running errands, for that matter. But Eve was home all day, and he was pulling sixty-hour workweeks more often than not. His wife used to be in the industry. She knew what it was like. But these days, Eve didn't seem to have any energy left over for him or for much of anything else.

He could remember when his wife had been stronger, how vibrant and exciting she'd been when they first met. A natural introvert, he'd loved to watch her flit around parties like an exotic butterfly, touching her wings on the chosen ones, making everybody laugh and feel good about themselves. It hadn't bothered him, the charm of her incandescent wings touching others. He knew at the end of the night she'd be going home with him, that he was the only one who stood a chance of capturing that light in a bottle. It was as if quicksilver flowed through her veins instead of blood, and the mystery of how to tame that both tantalized and tortured him. What he felt for Julia couldn't begin to compare to his love and desire for Eve during the first heady days of their relationship. Usually a cautious man, he'd asked Eve to marry him after only dating a month, in an attempt to own what he couldn't understand. Today, his wife remained a mystery to him, but one he no longer actively sought to solve. The mercury in her veins seemed to have been replaced with lead since their son died.

It wasn't like what happened to Michael only happened to her. It happened to all of them. Although Abbey seemed the least affected. He'd worried about her lack of emotion at first, then decided it was better than the alternative. Kids were different, he supposed. But Eve carried her grief as if it were only her cross to bear. It made him furious, her insistence on retaining ownership of all the pain, like Michael hadn't been his son too. Richard had held his mourning in close, where no one could see it, but Eve wanted to talk about it. And so they had drifted apart from one other. Stranded on their own lonely islands, unable to comprehend what made the other seem so distant.

He'd hoped the writing would help, that she'd channel her heartache into the words and come back to him. But Eve ended up turning further inward instead of out, her butterfly folding up and stuffing itself back into the chrysalis. She managed the day-to-day, penning her novels in sporadic bursts, or volunteering around the neighbourhood. But she seemed to take no pleasure in most of the things she did. So unlike the woman he'd known and loved for so many years.

He knew he should be more supportive, but instead, he found himself annoyed with her, wishing he had the luxury to be so goddamned sad. It was an accident, a tragic fucking accident. Why couldn't she understand that? It was hard enough to accept the death of his son, but it hurt him to think that his wife was choosing to be buried alongside him.

He hadn't been planning to meet Julia tonight. He'd wanted to break it off, knowing he had too much to lose, both professionally and personally. But when he thought about going straight home after work, facing all those problems he couldn't fix, it made him want to punch a hole through his open door.

It was 8:59. He couldn't wait any longer for the laptop to come alive. He'd lock the office and come back after his meeting to get rid of the email. Then he'd call Julia and arrange to hook up at their usual place. There would be those who might notice the non-open door and wonder if he'd changed his management style, but who really gave a damn.

He fished the key for his office out from behind a bunch of paper clips in his desk drawer. A burner phone hidden there made him semi-hard with its associations. Julia called it his booty phone. Richard would use it to call her later, to remind her of the importance of discretion, and to confirm their date. He closed the drawer on the phone for now and got up from his desk, slipping his usual phone into the front pocket of his pants. Eve said that'd give him prostate cancer, the most interest she'd shown for his groin in months. He emerged from his office, closed the door behind him, and locked it with the key.

As Richard hurried down the hallway to the meeting with Munich and Mueller, the laptop finally came to life in his office. A dozen windows opened for his email, each one heeding the impatient clicking demands he'd made earlier. They spread out across the screen in multiple echoes of one other, with the magic of an infinity mirror, each one a testament to the things he couldn't see or understand.

FOUR

Eve leaned on the grocery cart with one hand and held her phone in the other. She was consulting a photo of the shopping list from the whiteboard on the fridge. Richard had told her to use the phone's voice memo function. But she couldn't be bothered dictating her family's needs into a soulless device. Better to freeze their requests in a picture that she could carry with her everywhere.

A man in his thirties walked toward the cash register holding a bouquet of flowers, his only purchase. The mums had been dyed unnaturally bold colours — sherbet orange, bubble-gum pink, electric blue. Eve smiled, despite her rib. There was something about a man carrying flowers in public. It was like puppies on the internet or a baby passing gas — you just couldn't help being affected. The man paid for his bouquet, then rushed off through the sliding doors, and the display of his romantic gesture was swallowed up with an electronic swish.

Eve hadn't meant to answer the phone call from her mother but had accidentally swiped the icon when trying to enlarge the grocery list with her thumbs. So summoned, her mother's voice now rose up from the depths of the screen.

"Did you get an X-ray?" she said in lieu of hello.

"Yes," Eve sighed. "The lower right rib is cracked." Eve chose her words carefully. Cracked sounded less dramatic than broken.

"I tried to call you earlier, but you weren't at home." They didn't have a landline anymore. Richard, Eve, and Abbey all had their own cellphones. Her mother knew this. If she thought about it, she'd realize Eve had purposely not answered the phone before. But it was wiser to let her mother believe she'd been out, although ironically, she was out right now.

"You're not keeping something from me?" her mother said. A rhetorical question, really. What daughter wasn't keeping half her life from her mother? And Eve had more confidences to keep than most. Her mother never did have the gift of "knowing," or she'd been too conventional to honour it. Eve answered her inquiry as daughters have for centuries.

"No, Mom, I'm not keeping anything from you."

"Well, what is the doctor doing, then?"

"He can't do anything. You just have to wait and let it heal."

"You do too much, that's your problem. You're always doing too much." Eve's mother was appalled by the bloated demands of her daughter's life. Her own life had disappeared to a pinpoint since Eve's father had passed. A visit from the dishwasher repairman would send her into a tizzy. The day before was spent in anxious anticipation and the day after in complaint. After that, she'd have to take to her bed for a week, from the extreme exhaustion brought on by other people performing services for her.

"How's the hip?" Eve asked, attempting to change the subject. Someone bumped into her cart trying to get at the organic bananas and sent the handle into her side. She had to bite down on her tongue to keep from screaming in the produce department.

"Fine." But Eve knew it was bad. Eve had tried to send some healing her mother's way. There were winds that carried such requests if you knew how to ask. But either her diminished powers weren't enough, or her mother wasn't in a position to receive them. Eve had asked Janet to speak to the winds on her behalf, but when Janet tried, her spells were flung back in little shards, catching in her hair like tiny sharp boomerangs.

"I saw Marjorie the other day," Eve said. "She said the two of you should do lunch."

"I don't know about that."

"Why don't you know?"

"Marjorie can still walk. She goes to the gym every day. I feel useless around her."

"You're not useless, Mom."

"Yes, I am. I can't do anything."

"You made this phone call."

"Pfft."

"And you can walk. You just need to use a cane."

"I can't go out walking with a cane!" her mother cried into the phone. "People will think I'm old." Eve's mother had won the genetic lottery that made her look impossibly young for her age. At an ultrasound last month, the technician had asked her what the date of her last period was. She'd told him 1998. She didn't want to be outed as a senior by something as clichéd as a cane.

"So, you can walk, but you just can't be seen to be walking. Is that it?" Eve said. The pain in her side was making her cocky. She wished her mother would go to lunch with Marjorie, or anyone else for that matter. It would be good for her to get out of the house. But instead, Eve's mother spent most days sitting in a wildly uncomfortable chair she refused to replace. A rebellious act that effectively punished her own body for betraying her.

"You'll understand," she said, "when you're my age. These things are genetic, you know. It could happen to you too."

"Thanks, Mom."

"I'm just saying."

Eve wondered if this was how Abbey felt when the two of them talked. Annoyed, yet guilty at the same time. Although Abbey didn't seem to have much time for guilt.

"Listen, Mom, I'm at the grocery store," Eve said, trying to find a way out. "I'll call you later, okay?"

"Are you getting Richard's dinner?"

"Pardon?"

"Are you shopping for Richard's dinner?" Her mother still believed the measure of a wife was her ability to put a home-cooked meal on the table every evening. When Eve still worked in the tech sector, her mother had been horrified to hear she ordered takeout after a long day at the office, or even worse, that Richard had cooked.

"Richard has a work thing tonight." He'd called Eve this morning, told her he was taking his programmers for a few beers. *Don't wait up. Don't do too much,* he'd told her, just like her mother. Richard would kill her if he knew she was grocery shopping. But Abbey had woken up to find they were out of kombucha, the sweet, fermented tea drink she liked to take to basketball practice. Eve had still been in bed when she'd come up to complain about it. *Can't you even keep food in the cupboard, Mom?* Eve felt like pointing out that an overpriced health drink laced with yeast wasn't really food but buried herself under the pillows instead.

Eve knew Richard wasn't going for beers with his programmers. Just like her mother knew when Eve didn't answer the phone it wasn't because she was out. She didn't need her second sight to suspect what Richard was really doing. He thought she was naive. But she wasn't. She was just too tired to confront him. And to be honest, part of her had ceased to care. Although she could remember the beginning of their relationship when Richard had meant so much more to her. He'd possessed a deep and dark sensuality that had set her sixth sense into a tailspin. They'd stay up long into the night discussing poetry and politics between fucking. A witch's most attuned erogenous zone was her brain. It had been a whirlwind romance, and they were engaged before she'd had the chance of a full moon to question things.

"I have to go," her mother said. "The physio is coming at three and I have to get ready."

Eve looked at the clock on the wall of the grocery store. It was 11:00 a.m.

"Okay, Mom, I'll talk to you later. Love you." And she did, despite their complex relationship. That's the thing about mothers and daughters, no matter what happens you are joined at the hip for life. Even if it's a bad hip that keeps you captive in a chair.

Eve reached up toward a too-high top shelf. The act fused her body into an elegant arc of agony stretching from her lower back along her side and up into her fingertips, where weak sparks sputtered out. Two boxes of cereal dropped down into her cart. Their shredded insides made a ragged kind of music as they tumbled in, like a pair of falling castanets.

EVE DIDN'T FEEL UP TO going to book club at Sharon Patel's. She hadn't even read the book. But the wine flowed freely at such events, and Abbey would be there, hanging out with Sharon's daughter, Selena, in her bedroom. Richard would be out all night anyway, wherever it was he was going. So Eve popped a couple of Tylenol 3s and made an appearance in the Patels' well-appointed living room down the street. Walking in, she was a bit unsteady on her feet and almost tripped over the cat in the corner.

"Of course, we were shocked when Cuchulain had kittens," Sharon Patel announced to Eve and the rest of the group. The Patels had thought the cat was male when they gave her the name of a famous Irish hero.

"Cuchulain means *hound killer* in Irish," their host explained. Sharon was descended equally from Norfolk Brits and Burmese Jews. Her husband, Sanjay, was the product of a newly immigrated man from Calcutta and a red-haired Irish girl who'd insisted he be baptized Catholic. In a country as diverse as Canada, it was hard to cry cultural appropriation when staking claim to any one ethnicity was a crapshoot at best.

"Aren't they just darling?" Sharon said. The new mother lounged elegantly in a satin-padded basket that Sharon referred to as a "queening box." Cuchulain's litter nuzzled against her, eyes tightly closed and anxiously mewling.

Abbey had pleaded with Eve to bring home one of the kittens. But Eve could barely trust her with the dog, and she had never been the type of witch to take a familiar. They could be great for adding some extra oomph to a spell, but it was a tricky business. Janet had kept a hedgehog as a familiar, and she'd ended up blowing off one of its legs while trying to develop a charm to combat snoring. She'd fashioned a peg leg for it using a whittled piece of willow and a faux leather strap from an old high-heeled shoe. But the animal was never the same. A devoted member of PETA, Janet was devastated. Eve's dog was too dumb to be a familiar, a result of poodle inbreeding. But cats were naturally attracted to magic. Eve couldn't afford to bring that kind of trouble home.

"Come take a seat," Sharon said as Eve poured herself some dark red Shiraz from the decanter on the sideboard.

The only chair left in the living room full of women holding the same book was almost as uncomfortable as Eve's mother's. She sat down with her wine, trying to keep as upright as she could. But it was a losing battle. The woman next to her offered her a pillow from the sofa. Eve accepted it gratefully and put it behind her back.

"Poor you," Sharon said, making her overly concerned face. "You always seem to have some kind of an injury."

"I guess I'm just clumsy," Eve said, trying to settle herself in the straight-backed chair.

"Yes," said Sharon, picking up a kitten for a cuddle. "I suppose you are."

The Patels had introduced themselves when Eve and Richard first arrived in the neighbourhood. They had moved not because they were looking for a newer, better home but because they wanted to escape their old one. In their first house, Eve had imagined Michael and Abbey growing up, having friends over as teenagers, their laughter and music flowing down from the second-floor loft where their bedrooms were. Close, but with a space of their own. But after the accident, Eve could no longer bear to look at the railing that ran along the hall in that second-floor loft. Michael had fallen from it when he was eight, smashing his head open on the first-floor hardwood. She'd run down the stairs taking them two at a time. But it had been too late for magic. Eve was holding him in her arms when he died. As his soul passed through her, all her powers latched on to him as she sought to keep him earthbound. And so, her essence had ridden piggyback with her son into the next realm. She'd howled as both her child and her fruitless abilities to save him were ripped away from her. She had been left powerless ever since, at least for all the things that mattered.

Sharon knew about the accident, but she didn't know what really happened that day. No one but Eve and her daughter knew that.

Abbey and Selena ran down the stairs laughing, then shushed each other when they saw the grown-ups in the living room.

"We're just getting some snacks, Mom." With her thick black hair pulled back in a long glossy braid, Selena's liquid amber eyes and full lips declared the richness of her background.

"That's fine, dear. How is the studying going?"

"Wonderful," Abbey replied formally. "We're almost finished our poetry assignment."

"I am glad to hear it," Sharon said, mirroring back the same formality with just a touch of ice. She didn't like that her own daughter hadn't been given the chance to reply.

Once the two girls had their snacks, they ran back up the stairs again at a pace, as if the horrors of middle age in the living room might infect their good looks. Eve remembered what it was like to be that young. The power that came with puberty as you walked down the street with your newly minted curves, everyone looking, often as if you'd done something wrong. All beauty, it seemed, was met with a certain degree of distrust. Eve tried to follow the girls up the stairs with her mind's eye, but her vision was too hazy from the Tylenol 3s.

"Well, I hated the book," said Pauline Henderson, dipping a dark-brown cracker the consistency of cardboard into a richly whipped white dip. "And I loved his first book. But this one was just such a disappointment."

Eve took a gulp of the bitter Shiraz. It was in one of those glasses with no stem that you could fit half a bottle in and convince yourself you were only a social drinker. On the side, written in gold letters, it advised, *MAKE GOALS, SMASH, REPEAT.* She couldn't stand it when book club started like this. *I hated the book. I loved the book.* Where the hell did you go from there? Eve liked to discuss the issues or ideas the book raised. This one, for instance, examined a runner's experience growing up in a developing nation. Eve used to run marathons herself. Well, at least half marathons. Although not as a Black man in a developing country.

"It's like he had to finish the book quickly, so he just wrote the ending in five minutes and called it done," said a friend of Pauline's. She was new to the group. But Pauline and her were in high school together, just as Eve and Janet had been. Old friends. It was nice to have people in your life who knew you from when you were young. Janet used to come to book club, making the long drive from Chatsworth even after she'd moved away. But she got into a fight with Georgina Patterson two years ago about the territorial range of the gray jay and hadn't come back since. Janet liked to say she was blacklisted from the club — a joke, because she had been the only Black one in it.

"Well, I wasn't a big fan of the book either, I'm afraid," Sharon Patel declared. "My Selena read it as well, and she thought the same way." Sharon never missed an opportunity to tell them Selena had read the book too. She considered her daughter a girl with tastes beyond the teenage vampire novels of her peers. Eve found it curious that no matter what they read, Selena always felt the same way about the book as her mother. She couldn't imagine Abbey feeling the same way about anything as her.

The women went around the room, each one chiming in as to whether they liked or did not like the book. At this rate, the discussion would be over in five minutes, which is what they all wanted anyway, so they could get to the real raison d'être of the evening, getting slightly smashed and trying to one-up one another.

"Did Abbey read the book?" Sharon asked, knocking Eve out of her cozy wine buzz. She shouldn't be drinking while taking the Tylenol 3s, but not drinking wine at book club was tantamount to social treason. Besides, it made her feel so wonderfully mellow. She could barely feel her rib anymore.

"No," Eve said. "She's been really busy lately."

"I can imagine. Selena says she's been putting in a lot of extra hours studying. Has her eye on the Thompson scholarship." Eve hadn't heard of the Thompson scholarship, but she and Richard could use all the money they could get toward Abbey's university. Abbey planned to be a doctor. That meant a full degree and then med school. Eve couldn't even fathom the cost of that.

"It's a shame when kids don't have enough time to just be kids, isn't it?" Sharon commented, taking a discreet sip of wine from a regular wineglass with a stem. "I'm so glad Selena has her basketball."

"Abbey's on the basketball team too," Eve pointed out, feeling the need to defend her daughter. She thought of mentioning the debating club and the athletic council

Abbey belonged to as well. But they didn't sound "kids being kids" enough.

"Well, of course," Sharon drawled, "I didn't mean to say that Abbey wasn't involved in other things." But this was exactly what she'd meant. "I just was thinking how much pressure some kids can be under. But of course, with you at home, you have the time to give her the support she needs."

Sharon Patel was often not at home. She was a classical cellist who performed out of town with her symphony-conducting husband. She'd missed half of the girls' basketball games. Eve took both Abbey and Selena to practice most days. She and Richard had made the decision together that she should quit her software exec job after Michael's death, to write and stay close to home so she could keep a better eye on things. The unspoken words between them being that she hadn't been keeping an eye on things before.

"I mean, I don't know how you do it, being at home all the time," Sharon continued when all she got from Eve was a terse nod. "I think I'd go stir-crazy without my work. But of course, you have your writing, don't you? It's so nice to have a hobby."

Eve swallowed down hard on the wine-tinged bile that came up in her throat. It made her hiccup, totally ruining the possibility of a classy retort.

Feeling the tenseness between the two women, Pauline Harrison started to rave about the crudités. "Honestly, Sharon, you must give me the recipe. This is positively delicious. And you even remembered the gluten-free crackers for me. You're such a doll."

Distracted from their standoff by the sudden focus on what was surely store-bought dip, Eve and Sharon backed off. Pauline and her friend got into a warm and friendly argument about what "vegan" was. Sharon smiled and explained that they were both wrong in their definitions. And so the night progressed.

Eve was starting to feel woozy from the meds and the wine. She focused on the cat stretched out so elegantly with her slick black kittens attached to multiple pink teats. Eve hadn't been able to breastfeed Abbey. She'd been colicky, always struggling and spewing against Eve's breasts. Michael had been no problem, latching on like a trooper, falling asleep in her arms afterward in a contented, passed-out milk-drunk. Eve stared down the cat in her comfy repose, so at ease with being a mother. Cuchulain didn't have to watch out for the next disaster. She didn't have to keep "a better eye on things." The cat's lids half closed in ecstasy as her milk let down and Eve couldn't penetrate them to plant a suggestion. She didn't want to hurt the animal, only make it stand up and piss in the queening box in an undignified way. She wondered if the Patels would have the cat fixed after this. Eve had been fixed, just a few years ago. The cat even had her beat reproductively.

Eve decided she would leave book club early to buy some cigarettes at the corner store. She'd smoke them on the back deck when she got home. She wanted to inhale the fire and the fury she felt at her own failings and blow them out into the atmosphere. All witches had a love-hate relationship with fires, dancing by them and dying in them equally throughout history. Every fire was linked sacredly to the First Flame, Nanny had taught Eve and Janet. And by this she had meant both the sun and its counterpart, the flaming core of the earth. Eve had given up cigarettes years ago. Mostly, anyway. But tonight, she craved the potency of that first heady hit of smoke she'd had as a teen, pulling into her lungs what felt like the cosmic dust of a forgotten star.

With the time she had left, she turned her attention to the bedroom upstairs where her daughter snacked and possibly studied with her friend. But images of the girls only came to her in blurry watercolours, sprawled out on the pastel rug of Selena's room. She was about to give up, make her excuses and leave, when a vision dropped down from the ceiling and swayed in front of her face — a dark noose fashioned from a thick black leather belt. A quick gasp escaped from Eve's mouth before she could think to hold it back.

"Are you okay?" the woman who'd given her the pillow asked.

Eve looked up and saw a slick dark shadow slowly spreading across the ceiling from where the belt had dropped. As Sharon turned to offer Pauline Henderson some more crudités, a drop of blood fell from it soundlessly into her glass of Shiraz.

"Yes, I'm fine," Eve said. She blinked her eyes repeatedly to shake off her second sight. The noose curled back up into the ceiling like a recoiling snake. The pool of blood on the ceiling receded as if sucked in by a straw.

"Are you sure?"

"No, really, I am," she assured them. The vision was probably some errant psychic energy she'd tapped into by accident in her hazy state. Such things had happened in the past. "It's just my rib," she explained.

"Poor you," Sharon Patel said again.

The cat got up from her bed without even a planted thought from Eve. The tiny kittens were shaken off her nipples one by one as she stretched and stepped out of the box. A particularly tenacious one fell off onto the carpet at Sharon Patel's perfectly pedicured bare feet. She picked it up and tossed its sleek body back in with the others, then excused herself to let the cat out the back door. The kittens writhed in the box blindly, their whole world having disappeared.

Eve pictured inhaling the sweet toxic chemicals of cigarette smoke into her lungs on the back deck, swallowed up in the darkness of the night with her eyes squeezed shut, blind to everyone and everything.

FIVE

Get this! I caught my mom SMOKING! Can you believe it? I mean, I know she used to smoke before she met my dad, but it is so incredibly low-class. Like those girls downtown in their shiny leggings and pilled sweaters, pushing cheap strollers with a butt sticking out of their mouths. I told her if she died of lung cancer I wasn't coming to her funeral. She said she didn't care if anyone came to her funeral, then maybe she'd get some peace. What a drama queen.

Selena and I worked on our next "Dear Old Funnel Head" note tonight in her room. We've been slipping the notes into Dylan Penske's locker all week. They all start off with "Dear Old Funnel Head, how I wish that you were dead." We write them on the back of a printout of Maddie Johnston's infamous kiddie-porn sexting picture, so he won't show them to anyone. And when I say write, I mean we cut out letters and words from the newspaper and paste them on the printout like old-school blackmail letters. Selena's parents still get the *Globe and Mail* on Saturdays. What a bunch of backward peasants.

"Dear Old Funnel Head, how I wish that you were dead. In the night, I will come creeping, stab you ten times and watch the blood seeping." That one was Selena's. I wrote the follow-up.

"Of my quest for blood I will never tire, around your neck goes a piano wire."

LMFAO! We watched Dylan from around the corner when he opened up that one, saw the way his face kind of crumpled up and he looked around the school hallway all nervous, like he got caught having a boner about me again. Honestly, it's just a fucking joke. Who is going to take something like that seriously?

I suggested, "I'll twist the knife and watch you quiver, then gut you out and eat your liver." But Selena said it was too intense.

"Watch your step, this isn't for fun. Don't look now, I've got a gun." That's what Selena came up with. Beyond the fact that it is really sad poetry, I pointed out that neither of us had a gun. She got all upset about that, like I meant we would actually do the things we were threatening Funnel Head with. For fuck's sake, like I said, it's just a joke. But that doesn't mean you don't have to think about realism. Then we spent twenty minutes trying to rhyme something with poison, but that is goddamn impossible.

We finally settled on, "I'll bury you alive with the other asshats, and watch you being eaten by hungry rats." Not perfect, but it'll have to do. It was hard finding the word *ass* in the headlines. I had to take an article on gas prices, chop off the *g* and add an *s* to it.

When we were done, Selena told me she couldn't go to Zanax, completely screwing me over. Her parents are going to be away, and it would have been perfect, but she has to stay home with her stupid cat. Honestly, what is she going to do, stare at that dumb animal with her kittens clamped onto her like barnacles all night? Disgusting.

That's probably why I got so angry when I came home. I was already upset. It's not my fault what happened. But with Mom sitting there in the dark on the back deck totally wasted on wine, poisoning herself with cigarettes and making jokes about her funeral, I felt like I had to do something. Save her from herself. I hadn't meant to break the wineglass, just to take it away from her. She'd had enough to drink anyway. When I threw her glass against the deck railing, she didn't even flinch. Just got up with her gross cigarette still in one hand and teetered over to try and pick up the pieces, bent over like an old lady because of her rib. She could barely stand up.

Somebody has to do something about her. I mean, I love her and everything, but I really don't like her. It's hard having to be the responsible one in a parent-child relationship. And Dad is useless. He doesn't understand what she's capable of.

That day, when Michael fell over the railing, I was there. I saw what happened. How it got all dark and the house shook, and that sound came out of Mom from somewhere else, somewhere deep, without a bottom. She thinks I don't know these things, but I do. Like I know when she tries to see into my thoughts. I can feel her crawling around in my mind sometimes late at night, tickling my brain. But then I just throw up a mental picture of that day with Michael and she disappears, fast and furtive, like a thief. I guess all moms do this, although I've never heard the other girls complain about it. So, I keep it to myself. I figure my mom is probably worse about it than others. She's embarrassing enough without me admitting to that. Anyway, I can handle the mind creeping, but the smoking is just fucked up.

I *so* have to get out of here. If I don't get that Thompson scholarship, I'll have to do something drastic. Who could stay in a place like this? I should call Social Services and tell them my mother is a drunk and trying to kill me with second-hand smoke. But they'd just put me in a group home with a bunch of freaks.

I've got to get away from my mom and her poison. Even if I can't rhyme anything with it. And I'm buying a ticket to Zanax anyway. Fuck Selena. Fuck everyone, including that goddamn cat.

SIX

Richard meant to break things off with Julia that evening, but he'd lost his nerve soon after his boxer shorts. He'd planned to say all the right things — he loved his family, he couldn't risk losing them. The usual crap. The funny thing about the usual crap was that it was so often true.

He worried about losing his job as well. He wasn't one of *those* guys, wasn't copping a quick feel off some intern in the photocopy room uninvited. But he worried others might not see it that way, thinking that Julia had been forced into a relationship with him so she could keep her job or get a promotion. Richard was responsible for hiring and firing staff, including her. But she was the one who'd started it, rubbing up against him at the tapas bar when they'd been away at a conference. She'd taken a churro off the dessert tray and licked at the yellowed cream with her little pink tongue, then put her full lips around it like it was his cock. He should never have taken that gooey pastry bait.

But she'd felt so good underneath him, so healthy and young and receptive. When he came inside her, it was like he was letting loose all the stress he had into her cunt, where it got licked up like the churro cream.

He shouldn't think the word *cunt*. It was a vulgar word, and he didn't like to think of himself as a vulgar guy. He was sensitive to women's issues. He knew they'd been cut a raw deal. He acknowledged the gender pay gap and the fact that his wife and daughter couldn't walk alone some places where he could. But when he thought about sex, he became some other kind of man, picturing women as just anonymous soft bodies with juicy orifices for him to stick his fingers and tongue and dick into. It was like those images came from a different part of his brain and he couldn't take responsibility for them. He figured most men were the same, married or not, although the good men didn't act on their baser fantasies. Richard had thought he was one of those good men until he met Julia. He was ashamed of himself for cheating on his wife, but somehow not enough to stop.

When he came home late, he saw the light on in the backyard. Eve or Abbey must have forgotten to turn it off when they let the dog out for his last crap before bedtime. He cursed under his breath, hoping Eve wasn't out there cleaning up after the dog. He'd told her to take it easy. He really was worried about her rib. But looking through the window, he saw smoke circling up from the patio table above Eve's still silhouette.

"What's going on, Eve?" Richard stepped tentatively through the sliding doors from the kitchen to the back deck. He wasn't ready to deal with his wife so soon after Julia. He'd assumed she'd be asleep at this hour. After most nights like this, he'd lie down on the couch to prolong his Julia buzz, going over all he'd done to his mistress under the crisp, white cotton bedsheets of the hotel. But something about Eve's stillness worried him. He took a step forward in the dark.

"Watch it," she said, her eyes stared into the shadows cast by the willow tree in the backyard. "There's glass."

Richard stopped where he was, just outside the sliding doors. He had taken his shoes off when he'd come into the house. He wasn't sure where the glass was that Eve was talking about.

"Are you smoking?" he asked, genuinely surprised. Eve used to smoke when they were first dating, usually at parties or bars when you could still do that sort of thing. But she'd quit cold turkey when she got pregnant with Abbey and hadn't touched cigarettes since. Or so he'd believed. He realized now that there'd been a faint whiff of smoke in her hair from time to time over the last few years. You could wash your hands and brush your teeth all you wanted, but hair always seemed to suck up the faint scent of whatever you'd been up to that you shouldn't have. He ran a hand through his overgrown French crop and wondered if it smelled of Julia or sex or the sweat he'd worked up fucking her. He'd showered at the hotel but hadn't shampooed. He made a note to book an appointment to get a brush cut.

"How was your evening?" Eve asked him, ignoring his question as she let smoke out with a hard exhale.

"Fine. Just a few beers." He needed to come up with something better than this. It was one o'clock in the morning. "One of the guys is having some marital problems. He wanted to bounce them off someone."

"Sure," Eve said, leaning her head back to blow more smoke out through parted lips. It was as if she were in a trance or a dream state. Richard remembered what that was like, to go through the motions with no real consciousness. After Michael's death, they'd both been a couple of shell-shocked soldiers, holding each other up as they struggled up the hill to the next battle. But Richard eventually woke up from that nightmare, made it over the hill, even though it had meant leaving his wounded wife behind.

"I didn't think you'd started smoking again," he said, trying to get her to look at him. Instead, she blew a smoke ring up into the air. It reminded him of when he'd first got up the nerve to speak to her outside a bar after a work thing. She'd blown the rings above her head and then pierced each one with an outbreath of smoke. He felt a faint response from his body remembering how sexy it had been.

"Do you see it," she said, pointing at the glass. Now that his eyes had adjusted, he registered the little shards twinkling in the moonlight at the edge of the deck. She must have broken something. He walked over to stand behind her at the patio table.

"Listen," he said. "I'm sorry about earlier." He *was* sorry. About her rib, about everything. He hated seeing her like this, so defeated and pale. He leaned over to give her a kiss.

"Your breath smells like pussy," she said, breathing out a sigh that was somewhere between angry and resigned. Richard froze, still bent over her shoulder. He looked at the deep pool of red wine in the glass she held in her lap and saw a reflection. Not of his wife, but of oh-so-white cotton bedsheets and a quicksilver flash of flesh. He blinked and moved in for a closer look. But Eve got up to stand behind the broken glass, using it as a barrier between them. The nail of her big toe had a chip in the varnish, so unlike the shiny crimson toes of Julia, ten perfect wet rubies dripping from the ends of her feet.

"Abbey did this," Eve said, indicating the broken glass. "You need to talk to her, Richard." She flicked her cigarette butt onto the back lawn Richard had busted his balls mowing last Saturday in the blazing sun. "And you need to do something about this woman you're seeing."

"I don't know what you're talking about," he said, wishing he'd brushed his teeth as well as showered. "Really, Eve, you're losing it. You've got to get a grip." That sounded right to him, just the perfect tone of righteous indignation for the philandering fuck he knew himself to be. "Wait, are you telling me Abbey did this?"

"Yes," she said.

Richard wasn't sure. He still thought Eve might have broken the glass herself. She looked pretty hammered now that he thought about it. And it wouldn't be the first time something ended up shattered with no explanation. Stuff seemed to explode around his wife with strange regularity.

"Do you love her?"

Richard wasn't clear whether she meant Julia or Abbey, but he made his assumption. Eve had a way of knowing things. He might as well fess up.

"I don't know," he said, his voice breaking because he knew that he didn't.

"Then figure it out." Eve turned away from him, leaning on the deck railing, the fight gone out of her. "Figure it out, and do something about it, because I just can't anymore."

He clasped and unclasped his fists. He felt vulnerable in his stocking feet, unable to cross over to her because of the glass. He didn't have a response. He wasn't even sure if he was supposed to give one. Instead, he walked away and slammed the sliding door. It rocked back and forth on the track behind him.

"Damn it," he muttered under his breath. He was a decent man, a good husband, notwithstanding this most recent situation, and that was an anomaly. Besides, he was going to end it soon. No harm. No foul.

He grabbed an extra pillow and stormed off to the guest room, threw himself down on the hard bed still in his work clothes. The hanging leaves of the willow tree hushed in the wind from outside the open window. Richard had bought Eve this house because of that tree. Its drooping branches were the only thing she'd remarked on when they toured half a dozen homes with the real estate agent. She said they reminded her of a mermaid's hair. But to Richard they only made the tree look regretful.

This room should have been Michael's. He pictured his son's bedroom in the old house. Michael had complained about the baby-blue walls painted before he was born. He had wanted them replaced with a "big boy" colour. Richard hadn't gotten around to it, like so many assignments. When the room was emptied for the move, he'd closed the door and sat on the floor looking up at the accusing pastel. He felt he'd let Michael down in his aspirations to grow up, and now he never would.

All Richard's hopes and dreams for manhood had been pinned on that little mop-topped head, all the things he didn't get to be and wished he'd been able to. Richard squeezed his eyes shut, then opened them again, trying to erase the pale blue walls from his mind. Usually, he kept his son locked away in yet another part of his complex man brain, sidestepping Eve whenever she wanted to talk about him. He'd pay for pills or Pilates or whatever else he thought would drag his wife up out of the hole sorrow had dug her, but he refused to go with her to the locked box where he kept his grief for Michael hidden away. By avoiding that grief, it made it easier to pretend on some level that his son was still out there, only waiting on new walls.

Richard closed his eyes again and tried to conjure up the snow-white hotel sheets, the sighs and the moans and the sweet slickness of his sweat mixed with Julia's coconut body lotion. Anything to banish the fragrance of that mop-topped little head. But all he could smell was the smoke coming through the open window, his wife filling the spare room with the toxic scent of her well-earned disappointment in him.

SEVEN

In the morning, Eve felt like hell.

"You okay?" Richard asked, popping his head in through the bedroom door. He'd slept in the guest room.

"I suppose," Eve said. She hid under a decorative yellow pillow. Her mouth tasted like a furry animal had crawled in and died there.

"I heard you last night — being sick. I just wanted to check on you." He paused. "About last night."

"Not now, Richard," she said.

"Okay, I get it." Richard closed the bedroom door and went to work.

Eve turned her head and breathed in the hint of vomit in her hair. Her head throbbed in synch with her rib, but she resisted reaching for the Tylenol 3s. She'd learned her lesson there.

She hadn't slept well without Richard in the bed. Reaching out at four in the morning only to touch empty sheets, she'd suffered a sharp pang of loneliness. It was amazing how a man could still be a comfort in bed, even when you knew he was visiting someone else's. Eve had to admit that she was hardly in a position to judge Richard for that. Taking the moral high ground was a tough climb when you were guilty of your own affair. Eve had broken it off with Mark months ago, but he hadn't taken it well. He kept showing up in her life like an unpleasant picture in a children's pop-up book. At the drop-in centre where she volunteered. When she took the dog out for a walk. A couple of times, he'd even come to the house. Mark was her therapist, or had been. Their relationship was proof he wasn't afraid to cross lines. She should have known he wouldn't be that easy to get rid of.

Eve rolled over and tried to fall back asleep, but she couldn't. Her phone was humming on the bedside table with an incoming call. She reached out blindly and pulled it into the bed with her to consult the screen. It was her editor, Jessica. Eve considered not answering but knew it would only delay the inevitable.

"Hi, Jessica."

"Hey, Eve. How are things?"

"They've been better."

"You sound a bit rough."

"I am a bit rough." But Jessica wasn't going to let her off the hook for something as simple as hangover.

"Listen, I'm sorry to call so early. But I'm still waiting on that marketing material for your next book." Eve had written her first novel about a tough, hard-living hit-woman on a whim. She'd never anticipated the three-book deal they would offer her to write a series, or the amount of work that small success would entail.

"There are only so many words I can use to describe a leggy brunette who busts up biker gangs, Jessica."

"I thought the latest book was about the Mafia," Jessica said.

"Same difference."

"C'mon, Eve. This woman is your alter ego. You should know her inside and out by now."

"Sorry, Jessica, but the only thing my alter ego and I share is that we're seriously flawed."

"You'll figure it out. All we need are some keywords for internet searches. Oh, and a tagline or two for the cover copy."

"How about *Buy this book, so I can get some fucking royalties*?"

"That's what I like about you, Eve," Jessica said. "You never lose your sense of humour."

EVE TRUDGED DOWNSTAIRS IN SEARCH of her laptop, determined to get some work done before she went to her volunteer job in the afternoon. She set up at the kitchen table, braced the ladder-back chair with a few pillows, and fetched a coffee. Abbey had left for school and the house was quiet. As the laptop booted up, her gaze drifted over to the picture window that looked out on the backyard. The late-spring green leaves of the burning bush along the back fence trembled lightly in the breeze. It was the only piece of foliage she'd transplanted from the old house. Many of her kind used the plant for spells, but Eve enjoyed the bush's unabashed display of vanity each fall for its own sake. Turning fiery red for all to see, it was the male peacock of shrubbery. Last night, after she'd been sick, she'd thought she'd seen something from the window, rustling in among its branches. But it had probably been a spillover from the bloody vision of the belted noose she'd seen in Sharon Patel's living room. Manifestations tended to travel in packs. They followed closely to feed off each other's psychic crumbs.

The backyard was undisturbed now, except for one massive black crow squawking from the willow tree. Eve went to get her binoculars. Crows could carry messages in the shine of their feathers. But when she stepped out onto the deck, the crow was gone, and so was the glass that Abbey had broken. She wondered who'd cleaned it up. She'd been too wobbly on her feet last night to have taken care of it.

She put her hand in the pocket of her sweater and felt the crumpled package of cigarettes, knowing there were a few still left. She should throw them out, but much like a book, a pack of cigarettes demanded to be finished, no matter if you were enjoying it or not. Although she couldn't afford to be caught a second time. It was bad news that Abbey had found her smoking. She'd never hear the end of it now. Eve wasn't sure when her daughter became the voice of her most shameful shortcomings, but Abbey always picked the right time to remind her of them.

Her daughter had not been the voice of reproach last night, though, not when she'd first returned home. She'd called for Eve in the darkened house, sounding like a much younger version of herself. *Momma? Momma?* When she was stressed or upset, Abbey still sought Eve out, curling up in the crook of her arm, where she'd share her worst worries and fears. Eve would be allowed the luxury to stroke her impossibly thick blond hair and feel the warmth of her body against hers. Her daughter, her child. But all possibility of one of those rare encounters had disappeared when Abbey saw Eve with the cigarette between her fingers.

"What the fuck, Mom?"

"Abbey … I … it's just … I … I've had a hard day."

"All your days are hard."

"But …"

"I can't believe you're smoking. Oh my god. Are you drunk?"

Abbey had picked up the glass and thrown it. The vulnerable childlike need had vanished from her face, disappeared like a card in a magician's trick, to the point where Eve had wanted to look up the sleeves of her tightly zipped jacket to see if she'd hidden her feelings there. They'd argued some more after that. Something about Eve's funeral of all things. Then Abbey had stormed up the stairs to her room, unable to stomach the sight of her mother giving in to old addictions. Her daughter despised weakness, like so many people who gravely feared it.

Eve fetched a heating pad and wrapped it around her middle as she sat in the kitchen chair and got to work. After a while, the heat encouraged the blood flow to her injury, melting the pain like butter. She focused on her task, trying to dispel the images of the night before. But some visions continue to haunt, especially if the ghost is you.

When Abbey had broken the wineglass, Eve had seen multiple shadow selves reflected back in the broken crystal. The glittering young woman she'd been when she met Richard, the harried but doting new mother after Abbey was born, and finally, the grieving sentinel she'd become as she sat on the backyard deck swallowed up in smoke. A fourth image sputtered and popped with snow like a bad TV signal. The future. But she couldn't latch on to it before it vanished, just like her daughter's need for her had. Or maybe it had all been an illusion. Eve was forever seeing metaphors in her life where there were none.

THE DROP-IN CENTRE HAD BEEN busy earlier during the lunch run, but things had settled down now. Eve stood behind the counter, wiping up deep-brown spills from the hurried serving of franks and beans. A well-dressed man with three-inch fingernails painted black and filed to sharp points stepped up and pushed a quarter toward her. Eve reached for the coffee, kept hot on the stainless-steel burner, poured him a cup, and spooned in one ration of sugar. The spoons were kept behind the counter because of the addicts — their potential to be used for freebasing made them more dangerous than the knives.

"How's it going, Harold?" Eve asked as he picked up the milk and added a dollop of dairy to the mug. The sight of his dagger nails wrapped artfully around the pitcher in an elaborate fan brought to mind a geisha tea ceremony as well as Freddy Krueger.

Harold grunted, his usual response. He was a regular here, and Eve had come to know his ways. After demanding more sugar, he took his coffee and went to sit at one of the Arborite tables by himself, opening up a newspaper so no one would talk to him.

"That man shouldn't be here," Heather said as she covered over the leftovers from lunch with an industrial-sized roll of Cling Wrap. "Those chinos are from L.L. Bean." Heather volunteered on Wednesday afternoons with Eve. Her favourite topic for discussion was which patrons deserved the seventy-five-cent lunch and which ones didn't.

A large girl pushed a stroller containing a sticky-faced two-year-old through the door and took a seat in the corner. Eve walked over and asked if they'd like something to eat.

"I seen the sign, we're too late," the young mother said, pointing to the thick bold writing on the chalkboard, *Lunch Served at 11 and 2 Only.* She smelled of smoke. Perhaps Eve did too.

"I'm sure we can rustle something up for the two of you." Eve smiled at the little girl in the stroller. "I'll be right back." She walked behind the counter and pulled back the Cling Wrap from the leftovers, then spooned a large serving onto a plate and a smaller one into a bowl.

"They're too late," Heather said over her shoulder from the sink. Eve was saved from dish duty today on account of her rib.

"It'll just go to waste anyway." Eve knew the leftovers could only be kept for a very short period of time due to health regulations. They were forced to throw out a ridiculous amount of food. It was hard to cook for a group that swelled and contracted, like an old wood drawer, with the seasons, although Eve had trouble figuring out what those seasons were. Certainly, the cold of winter brought in more people, but a rainy day could keep them away. She suspected the up-and-down numbers had more to do with social support money running out or rent coming due.

The drop-in centre had a different clientele than the food bank. Those people were often the working poor, unable to get by on the minimum wage they were paid. The drop-in was frequented by individuals who were often too broken to work, damaged either by illness or addiction. They were mostly men — the young mother was an exception. The only other women that came regularly were Cindy and Cherie. Cherie believed that the government had been breaking into her apartment and moving her cat figurines around. Cindy was a paranoid schizophrenic who wore a stovepipe hat with deely bobber flowers popping out of it — a touch of whimsy that was in stark contrast to her violent aggression. There had been a beautiful trans woman with haunting kohl-rimmed eyes, but Eve heard she'd gone back to rehab and it stuck.

"Here you go." Eve brought the food over to the mother and child. She put the plate on the table and set the bowl on the plastic moulded tray of the stroller. The toddler reached in and grabbed a fistful of beans with her hand, smearing most of it on her face to add to the sweet muckiness of her shiny red cheeks. Eve wetted a piece of paper towel behind the counter and handed it to the mother, who gently wiped her daughter's face with it.

"I try my best," she said to Eve, forcing her thin lips closed in a tough line.

"That's all any of us can do."

Not much older than Abbey, Eve thought. She instinctively put a hand on the young mom's shoulder. The girl pulled away, not used to kindness, or not trusting it — most likely both. When the child began to loudly protest the wet cloth, her mother threw it on the table with a discarded coffee cup. Then she meticulously began to separate the wieners from the beans on her own plate, exerting control over this one small part of her life.

Abbey used to insist Eve do the same, separate the contents of her meals. Throughout her childhood — even now, in fact — she didn't like the different types of food on her plate touching each other. It made her anxious, as if the entrée and the side were cozying up on the plate to conspire against her. She didn't even like to be touched much herself as she grew older. A stark contrast to that initial first year when Eve had to wear her in a baby sling 24-7 to keep her from howling. She and Richard had tried that business of "leaving them to cry." The book said if you did that the baby would get tired and fall asleep within ten minutes. That night, Abbey's hoarse screams had still echoed throughout the house an hour later. Eve had finally gone into the nursery to find her baby had cried until she vomited all over the crib sheets and herself.

Michael had been so much easier. He'd need the usual late-night feedings, of course, but Eve could just stagger into the nursery and take him to bed with her to feed as she lay on her side. He would always settle easily. One time, she'd woken up from a deep sleep and jumped up in alarm when she saw she'd rolled over and her bloated breast-feeding boob was threatening to smother him. The line between parental exhaustion and infanticide was a thin one.

The bell rang on the front door of the drop-in and Eve looked up, expecting another latecomer for Heather to complain about. But it was Mark, wearing his faded "you can talk to me" jeans and a pink golf shirt she'd bought him for his birthday. He was speaking into his outstretched phone, recording last-minute notes on a patient, or perhaps dictating a grocery list. He was an organized kind of guy. Eve went back behind the counter and acted like she hadn't seen him. But he pocketed the phone and walked up with a bright "Hiya," too publicly friendly to be ignored.

"Hi, Mark." Eve was clipped but civil. She didn't want Heather to know there was anything between them, professional or personal. Heather openly scoffed at Mark's talk therapy. *All those people amount to are paid friends,* she'd said, *when your real ones are sick of listening to you.* Mark was no longer Eve's therapist. But he had been more than a friend. And she was still paying for it.

"Hey, Doc Kramer." Mark looked over his shoulder and saw the twitching man waiting outside his office who had called to him. Mark wasn't a doctor, but his clients here often addressed him that way and he didn't correct them. He held up a couple of fingers to communicate the need of two minutes. The man continued to twitch. Mark counselled at the centre pro bono, being a friend to the disenfranchised for free. Normally, he worked out of a cozy room in one of the converted Victorian mansions downtown and charged a fortune.

When Heather went out back to the storeroom, Mark leaned in across the counter. His cologne smelled tart and heavy, like a musky fruit. It repelled and enticed Eve all at once.

"I'm sorry." Mark kept his voice just above a whisper.

Eve put on another pot of coffee. A puff of steam rose from the coffee maker and it lightly burned her nose. She didn't answer him or turn around.

"I shouldn't have just showed up at the house like that." Mark ran a hand through his wavy auburn hair. She should never have trusted that hair. Any man with curls after thirty-five had something to hide.

"No," Eve said, turning around to face him to show that she meant it. "You shouldn't have." She tried to channel the hitwoman character from her books in a bid to intimidate. But he wasn't going to make a scene here at the drop-in with everyone looking. Mark was nothing if not discreet.

"We need to talk."

"I've said everything there is to say, Mark."

"You can't be serious, Eve. I know you love Abbey, but Richard isn't worth it." He looked up in frustration, or to try and catch a glimpse of Eve's alleged seriousness in the air.

"Mark, you really have to —"

"He's cheating on you, you know," he hissed in a whisper, his eyes narrowing. It highlighted how unique his irises were, dark and of such a strange colour that Eve had never been able to put a name to it.

"How do you know that?" Eve whispered back. Had he been following Richard as well as her? And she *knew* he'd been following her. It was hard to tail a woman with eyes quite literally in the back of her head.

"Doc Kramer!"

The twitching man was getting more agitated. He started cursing across the table at a girl named Beth who wasn't there. Mark looked over his shoulder again, beamed a professionally whitened smile. He made a short friendly wave before turning back to Eve.

"Wait for me. We'll go for coffee. I know we can get past this."

But there was nothing to get past. Eve knew where she stood. She had responsibilities, duties no one could ever understand or know about, and none of them were to Mark. She knew a bad choice when she saw one, although it had not stopped her from making such choices before. Her choice to call on the Ragman eighteen years ago was proof of that.

When Mark was behind the closed office door with his client, she took off her apron and threw it in the soiled linen hamper.

"I'm leaving a bit early today," she told Heather.

"I get it," said Heather. "Your rib and all." She dismissed Eve with a wave of her rubber-gloved hand. She was back to washing dishes.

Eve bent down to get her sweater from under the counter. She fetched the leftover cigarette package from the pocket and dropped it discreetly on the table beside the impoverished mother. The girl covertly pulled the smokes from the table and hid them in her cracked vinyl purse. All the while, she kept her back to the stroller. Eve guessed she didn't want her daughter to see her weaknesses either.

On her way out, she noticed Cherie stood at the entry to the washroom, crying.

"What's wrong, Cherie?"

"The toilets are all on their sides and I need to pee."

Before Eve could say anything, Heather came up behind her and entered the women's washroom still wearing her rubber gloves. After banging on the cubicle walls a few times, she returned and put a wet hand on Cherie's bony shoulder.

"I've set them right now, child. It's okay to go in." Heather might be a stickler for the rules, but she was just as committed to compassion.

Cherie stopped crying and smiled.

"Who the fuck took my bike!" They all turned around as Cindy kicked a chair hard with one of her heavy army boots. It skittered across the floor, narrowly missing Harold and his Freddy Krueger nails. He turned his back on her in a dignified and hopelessly prissy manner. The springy flowers on Cindy's stovepipe hat bounced angrily back and forth. Cherie started crying again. Heather shook her head.

Only Eve noticed that Cindy's foot had never made contact with the chair. It was not rare to find this type of talent in places such as this, fitfully bestowed on minds with just enough cracks to let sorcery in. But Cindy held too much anger at humanity to channel her gifts in any meaningful way. Eve had once had the power to move and change things. Her abilities made so much stronger than Cindy's by the focus of a sound mind and body. She knew what it was to hold psychic and emotional energy in her hands, to knead and shape it into what she wanted. But that energy only came to her in fits and spurts now, if at all. She found herself jealous of Cindy and her loose-cannon magic, if only for her ability to act out against an unjust world.

The little doorbell jingled as Eve walked out into the blinding sunlight of the afternoon. She wouldn't need her sweater. As she heard Cherie's cries echo off the tiles of the washroom, she knew the only thing that separated her family from the patrons of the drop-in were the sturdy walls of her middle-class home. Those walls hid all the things that lay on their sides, impossible for any of them to set right.

EIGHT

Dad is *so* having an affair. I heard my parents arguing last night on the back deck, after I went to sleep. For fuck's sake, I bet the whole neighbourhood heard them. Not that I care what people think or anything. But Mom was bombed and acting like such a bitch. It's not surprising that Dad's cheating on her. I wonder who it is? Probably somebody at work, that's the only place he ever goes. He met Mom at work. She was some hotshot software rep and he was a client. Which is really high on the sleaze factor.

I wonder if they'll split. I mean, that's a possibility with these things, isn't it? Shannon Dempsey's father left her mom for a yoga instructor named Kino he met at the gym. He was taking that class for gross older men, *Yoga for Stiff Guys.* I've seen them through the glass when I go to work out, trying to do cobra with their saggy junk mashed into the mat. Kino is part Hawaiian and has all these cool tattoos all over her. She always smells like essential oils when she picks Shannon up at school from basketball practice. Shannon's mother decided to take up with the guy who delivered her filtered water after that. I think he went to school with Shannon's older brother. At least my mom isn't pathetic enough for that.

She's probably young and stuff, the other woman. I bet she'd make a lit stepmother, like Kino. The type that buys you and your friends booze to take to parties and knows where to shop. But my mom would probably insist I live with her, and Dad can barely afford one family, let alone two. What if they had a kid? Shit, you're always hearing about those dads with their new families who forget about their old ones like they never happened. The kid from the first family ends up begging for scraps, while the new kid gets his nursery outfitted from Nordstrom. There definitely wouldn't be enough money to send me away to school, maybe not even enough for a sucky local university. And med school? I'd graduate with so much fucking student loan debt I'd be a goddamn grandmother before I paid it off.

Being a doctor is all I've ever wanted, since I was a kid. I remember travelling in the ambulance with Mom to the hospital with Michael. She was totally out of it, my mom. The lights were on, but nobody was paying the electricity bill, if you know what I mean. The ER crew rushed around my brother when we got there, like there was something they could do, which there wasn't. Still, the nurse cut off his pyjama shirt and the doctor came in with her paddles. She put them on his skinny little-kid chest and yelled "CLEAR!" and everybody stood back. Michael's body jumped on the table like a fish flopping around in a boat. Mom didn't think I saw that, but I did. When I pulled back the hospital curtain from where I was hiding by the oxygen masks, Michael was on the table with the doctor hovering over him. She looked like an archangel, that doctor. Everyone else was struck dumb, waiting for her to conjure life where there was none. I knew then what I wanted more than anything in the world. I wanted the respect that doctor commanded when she yelled "Clear."

Sorry, diary. Had to answer a text from Selena. She wants me to come over and make posters for her stupid missing cat, Cuchulain. Honestly, what does she want from me? I already went over after school and helped her feed the kittens with an eyedropper. Can you believe they actually have baby formula for cats? Selena's mother got it from the vet. We had to boil water and mix it up. I don't think the kittens will survive anyway. I could feel the fluttering heartbeat of one of them when I squeezed too hard, trying to get him to stay still for the eyedropper. It'd probably be a blessing if the litter doesn't make it, since nobody wants to take any of the damn things home anyway.

I needed to talk to Selena about Dad and everything, but she was too caught up with Cuchulain and the kittens. Maybe I shouldn't tell her. It'd only make me look bad, spilling about my dysfunctional family. Her parents are so fucking perfect. She's always talking about her mom and her classy career travelling with the symphony, knowing it makes my mom look like a trash fire with her dumbass hitwoman novels.

I have to go to Dad's office for "Take Your Kid to Work Day" tomorrow, so maybe I can do some snooping around then, see if things are serious. I had wanted to stay home with Mom, so I could just watch Netflix all day, but she says she can't work when I'm home, even if I stay in my room. Like the mere presence of me crushes her damn creative process.

Zanax is tomorrow as well. Selena definitely won't be coming now. I bought a ticket at school today anyway. Screw her. I'm not afraid to do things myself. I am used to being the one on my own, doing what needs to be done whatever it takes, like the doctor with the paddles, I make the decisions.

And everybody else better just stand back.

NINE

When Richard got home that night, there was nobody to greet him. Except the dog, who looked up lazily from his basket with half-hearted acknowledgement before going back to sleep. Abbey had the door to her bedroom shut tight against him and Eve was in her writing room with the door locked. Richard had built her the space by gutting an oversized linen closet. He wanted her to have a room of her own, just like Virginia Woolf. He stood outside the door, afraid to disturb her, or maybe he was just a coward. He'd been avoiding Julia all day at the office as well, despite knowing he'd definitely have to end things with her now.

He went downstairs and grabbed a beer and a bag of cheese-filled pretzels to eat in lieu of dinner. Then he settled himself down on the back deck, moving a patio chair

How he came from that lazy summer afternoon staining his teeth orange with Jeremy Holloway in his mother's avocado kitchen to here, he didn't know. He still felt like a young man, although he'd be fifty in a few weeks. Sure, he didn't wake up with a hard-on every morning anymore, and his knee got at him if he walked the dog for too long. But inside, where it mattered, he still felt like the young man he'd been in his early twenties. The one who'd sucked back Northern Cream Porters with the other newly minted men after a day of clearing blasted rocks in the hot sun. He'd thought he'd had a lot on his mind back then, what with struggling to pay for school between long hours hunched over thick textbooks in the library. At home, he'd had to hide in a locked washroom to study, for fear his dad would catch him being "idle." His father had thought any man with a book in his hand needed it replaced with a tool so he could be put to work doing something useful.

But those worries seemed infinitesimal now. While he still felt twenty-one within himself, he knew his life was no longer that of a young man, despite his ability to keep up with his spirited mistress. He longed for the days where he thought getting a bad mark on a mid-term or being cuffed by his dad were the worst things that could happen to him. Richard had reached an age now where the loss of all he had built for himself was his greatest fear. His career, his comfortable lifestyle. If he were to lose those things, he knew it wouldn't matter how many wheelbarrows he filled, he'd never be able to clear the rubble and rebuild his life again. Besides, the worst thing that could happen already had. He washed these thoughts out his mouth with a swig of ice-cold beer, imported but unfortunately nowhere near as satisfying as that dark northern swill of his youth.

"How's it going?" A disembodied face popped up over the fence next to the willow tree and gave Richard a start. He choked and sputtered on the half-swallowed beer before he could manage a reply. It was his next-door neighbour, Bob Kettleman, a retired accountant who lived for perfecting his lawn, cutting the edges by the patio stones with a pair of scissors. Richard had heard him the other weekend in his backyard, spouting off into a cellphone about the limp morals of left-wing liars. If Kettleman were American, he wouldn't have just voted for Trump, he would have had him declared the new pope.

"Not too bad," Richard said, once he was able to talk again. "How's the lawn?"

"Oh, all right." Kettleman scratched his wiry beard with the tine of a leaf rake. "Got a touch of crabgrass I'm working on. Had to have the herbicide for it shipped from the States."

Richard could just imagine what banned, cancer-inducing chemical his neighbour was currently injecting into the earth.

"Looks like you could use some yourself." Kettleman indicated the more-weed-than-grass backyard on Richard's side of the fence. "Along with a pooper-scooper."

Richard looked at his lawn. Every four feet or so there was a small mound of dog crap, spread out like a feces minefield. He hadn't noticed it before. Richard was bad at noticing things.

"Well, you know how it is. I've been pretty busy at the office and all. Working on a new merger, lots of information infrastructure impacts." This was the only weapon Richard had to wield against his lawn scissor–armed neighbour. Kettleman no longer worked. And he wouldn't know what an information infrastructure impact was if it grew up next to his crabgrass. Retired guys could get sensitive about that, feeling emasculated with no job to swing around like a vocational dick.

"Sure." Kettleman laughed nervously. Richard's shot had hit the mark. "Well, if you need any help with those weeds."

"I'll be sure to ask," Richard told him, saluting the old man. They smiled and said nothing more, as menfolk do to signal a conversation was over. Kettleman's face disappeared back behind the fence.

Fuck the goddamn dog shit. Richard slammed the beer down on the glass patio table after a furious swig. But now that he had seen it, he couldn't unsee it, and if he didn't do something about the little turd mounds soon, he knew Eve would. When he pictured her bent over shovelling shit, wincing with her bad rib, it made him feel like a monster.

He abandoned his beer and went to the garage through the side gate, grabbing a shovel and one of the jumbo brown-paper bags they used for leaves. Before slipping on his work gloves, he removed his wedding ring and dropped it on the tool bench, as he did before beginning any sort of manual labour. Once in the backyard, he lifted the little shit piles from the grass like burned eggs off a frying pan and dumped them in the bag. His dad would be proud.

Look where your sissy education got you, son, still shovelling crap like the rest of us.

It all made him angry. So much made him angry these days, particularly Eve. It was not something he was proud of, this newfound habit of losing his temper. He tried not to dwell on it much, and when he did, he downplayed the incidents so he could better live with himself. After his outbursts, he was never sure what had set him off, but in the moment, his rage always seemed justified, rather than a reaction to his own insecurities. The sight of Eve busying herself with household chores on the weekend got him particularly irritated, causing him to feel lazy if he sat idle with his tea and a Sunday paper. They all seemed to be make-work projects anyway, like cleaning those damn garbage cans. *Who the hell cleaned a garbage can that scrupulously? Had she expected us to eat off of the fucking things?* And yet, he had felt terrible when she'd gotten hurt, wishing it had been his rib that got broken instead of hers.

He made his way with his shovel, methodically criss-crossing the lawn to the back of the property. Mapping out a grid as if he were searching for a lost child or a body. He was almost finished when he saw it, or rather when he saw the flies circling. He got up close enough to lift up the bendy bottom branches of the burning bush for a better look. The lump of brown-and-black fur was caked in dried blood, as if it had been in a gory mud bath. Richard tried using the shovel to pull the carcass toward him from under the bush, but the head came away. It rolled down the incline of the tiered garden. He had to jump out of the way to keep it from hitting his business casual loafers. The head looked up at him from where it had landed in the last pile of dog shit. Its lips were torn off to expose sharp, ghost-white teeth, giving it the illusion of having a perpetual grin.

The rest of the body parts lay in crudely carved chunks. Richard pulled the dismembered remains out from under the bush, piece by piece, with his work gloves, then loaded it all onto the shovel. He carried the animal around to the driveway and dropped it into the immaculate garbage can. The face seemed to float as it smiled up at him, looking through gouged-out pits where its eyes had been. A Cheshire Cat from a different kind of Wonderland.

Richard put the lid down on the can and walked away, banishing the image to the dark, inaccessible gardens of his mind.

TEN

Eve heard Richard outside in the backyard from upstairs in her writing room. She couldn't imagine what had inspired him to do yardwork on a weekday evening. He was probably feeling guilty, looking for physical labour to atone for his sins. His version of a hair shirt. Usually after six, Monday to Friday, he'd watch TV or surf the net while intermittently responding to work emails on his iPad. No one had time these days to focus on one thing at a time. This burst of repentant activity might mean the affair was serious, but she tried not to think about the implications of that. She should feel more upset about Richard's betrayal, but after the initial shock, she was finding herself strangely ambivalent. After all, they'd both been betraying each other for a while.

Normally, Eve didn't like to write with everyone at home, preferring the oasis of calm and tranquility afforded her while her daughter and husband were away at school and the office. Then nobody would come knocking on her door, unable to find their cellphone, wallet, favourite pants, Ninja smoothie maker, *insert here tireless list of items her family was responsible for owning and she was responsible for finding*. But it had been the same in Eve's own house growing up, this looking to the resident matriarch instead of looking for yourself. It was as if people thought a woman's womb developed a GPS with age and experience. It was true that Eve had an uncanny ability for locating things, a talent that her family didn't quite understand or appreciate. Unfortunately, it made them reliant on her gifts, atrophied any skills of sight they may have possessed on their own.

If she were honest with herself, it was not just the interruptions of her family that dammed her creative juices. She just couldn't clear enough mental space when she knew Richard and Abbey were hovering out there in the household ether. Couldn't relax enough into the alternate universe of her writing with her whole body still on alert. Her mind's eye roved the perimeter of the house when her daughter and husband were home, looking for threats, motivated by the fear of history repeating itself. Eve had tried to learn from her mistakes, but at times she still felt hopelessly apprenticed to them.

Luckily, the marketing work she needed to complete for her editor this evening was less creative and more game show–like.

Come up with thirty keywords that your readers might use in a search engine! Jessica had written in a follow-up email, complete with a smiley emoji and something that looked like a tube of lipstick. Eve couldn't be sure without putting on her up-close glasses. *Book*, *fiction*, and *crime* had been obvious and easy choices, but as she got closer to the mid-twenty mark, she was grasping at straws —*friendship, booze, casual sex.*

Mark had sent a couple of texts after she'd left the drop-in centre today. Enough to show he was annoyed, but not enough to be considered obsessive. He made a profession out of instructing people how to behave rationally. Although it all seemed a matter of outward appearances. You could be a junkie as long as you didn't act like one. Go home and cower in a corner and scream in the evening as long as you showed up at work every day and washed your hair.

Of course, as her therapist he had tried to get her to talk about those darker private moments, digging further and further into the open wound that was Michael's death. "You can't deal with the symptoms unless you find the underlying cause, Eve."

But the underlying cause was too much to bear.

In therapy, they never seemed to work on her panic attacks, which could be triggered by something as simple as buying peanut butter at a well-lit grocery store. Or the flip side of the anxiety coin, depression, where answering the phone seemed to take more energy than launching a full military offensive against Cuba. In those early days, Eve had felt naked and vulnerable, with the better part of her powers stripped away from her, unable to protect herself against the world or even her own emotions. A witch and a woman missing her skin. Mark didn't know the full extent of her loss. It was ironic that a man who prided himself on his ability to look into others to advise and counsel could really only scratch the surface of people and their problems. And because Mark didn't understand, he was convinced her salvation would come only by returning to the day of Michael's death. Mark didn't want to deal with her symptoms. He wanted her to go to their source. And in the name of progress, he had made her relive the worst day of her life over and over again.

Eve had been home that day from work and not happy about it, taking care of the two kids, both down simultaneously with chicken pox. Richard couldn't do it, so she had to, not because his job was any more important, he'd insisted, but because she was so much better at it. And so, Eve had been hoisted with her own petard of parental competence. They both knew the real reason was because she was the mother. Even with a master's degree and a fully developed sense of third-wave feminism, the guilt always seemed to be left firmly on her doorstep when it came to the children. When Eve was too busy to make a field trip or class play, it meant she was a failure. When Richard was too busy to get to the same things, it meant he was a success. This was the difference between men and women, mothers and fathers. Gloria Steinem be damned.

Eve had been upset about the unexpected intrusion into her harried workday. She should have just resigned herself to dabbing spots with calamine lotion and playing The Game of Life at the kitchen table. She could have allowed herself to become immersed in slotting a tiny pink peg in a car to represent herself as she snaked through the PAY DAY spaces and life-changing moments. Milestones shouting out, "GET MARRIED!" "BUY A HOUSE!" "TWINS!" until she'd reached the end of the game with the opportunity to retire at Millionaire Estates or its shadier counterpart, Countryside Acres. But she hadn't been able to let go of the day that should have been. A day with grown-ups in neutrally carpeted meeting rooms, filled with people who saw her as more than a pink peg. She should have been spending those last few wonderful moments with her son. Instead, she'd been on the phone trying to take a conference call, an important meeting she thought she couldn't miss. Michael had kept her up all night with a fever, but in the morning he'd been well and full of energy, bored and covered in itchy dots. He'd followed her to the second-floor loft where she'd gone to take her call, buzzing around her like a persistent fly.

"Look at me! Look at me!" he'd called out to her in a bid for her attention. But Eve had been trying so hard to listen to her boss, who'd been discussing a business requirements document she'd put together. She'd softly batted Michael away with one hand as she covered the receiver with the other.

"I am looking," she'd said distractedly. "I am."

But she hadn't been looking. Hadn't seen him climb up and perch himself on the railing of the second floor, holding on with the backs of his knees and fingers sticky with Children's Tylenol Liquid. When she had looked and seen, her reaction had been just a second too late. She'd watched helplessly as Michael's feet disappeared over the railing. He'd been wearing pull-on slippers with big plush faces of Thomas the Tank Engine. They'd grinned up at her as he fell backwards to the first floor, landing with a thud and a sickening crack. Everything Eve had understood to be true in her life had been swallowed up by the gaping maw of that sound and the sight of the empty railing. In shock, she'd stood there at first with the phone in her hand, not fully processing what had happened. She'd been frozen but shaking, like a computer screen before a virus annihilated its hard drive.

How many times would they go over that day in Mark's tastefully decorated office full of cushions and promises of healing? How many ways could they look at it to find the source of Eve's anguish when it was so damn obvious? But she'd always held back, not able to tell him everything that had happened. She often thought she'd begun sleeping with Mark just so he'd stop trying to peel back the sodden layers of her grief. He didn't realize those layers were necessary batting to keep her insulated from a truth no mother was meant to bear.

EVE HEARD RICHARD RATTLING THE garbage cans outside, and it jarred her out of her thoughts. After a few minutes, she quickly added the keywords *girl*, *bologna*, and *fuck* to make thirty. *That'll get me some hits from Google.* She copied and pasted the list into an email and sent it off to her editor before she lost her nerve.

Abbey was standing at the kitchen island looking out on the backyard when Eve came downstairs. She started at first when she saw her mother, as if she were an unexpected intruder, then forced a smile.

"How's the book going?" Abbey asked in a singsong voice that betrayed a hidden agenda. She set the kettle on the gas stove to make tea. Eve was a coffee fan, but her daughter was strictly an organic herbal girl, the more twigs and seeds the better.

"I was working on keywords for the marketing campaign," Eve said. "Have you got any for me?" Abbey hadn't read any of her mother's novels, but she knew the premise of them.

"Murder?" Abbey suggested, getting her Lucid Dream tea out of the cupboard. Eve had bought it for her from a store selling Indigenous-sourced goods when she was on a book tour. If you could call a few lonely book signings in struggling indie stores north of the city a tour.

"Got that one already."

"Mystery?" Abbey said. They were going through the motions here. Abbey knew her mother would have come up with these more obvious words. Regardless, it was just small talk before her daughter got around to asking for what she really wanted.

"Have that one too, I'm afraid." Eve opened the fridge door to fetch some cold water from the pitcher, but it had been left next to empty. She took it to the sink to fill it, then put it back in the fridge to chill. "What have you been up to?" Possible ulterior motives or not, she wanted to enjoy a pleasant conversation with her daughter for a change.

"I was texting with Selena. And getting some homework done. You know, the usual."

Eve wasn't quite sure what the usual was for her daughter or any of her friends. Everything seemed to happen in silos nowadays. Young people sat quietly as they sent out texts and posts of selfies on their phones with practised thumbs. It was a world of silent social connection. When Eve was young, her mother had tried to eavesdrop on her whispered phone conversations with Janet. Eve had kept her hand protectively cupped around the mouthpiece of the cordless until she learned to mute her conversations with spells. If a mother tried to listen through the bedroom door of their teenager nowadays, all she would hear was the feverish hush of technology.

"Actually," Abbey said, "I was hoping I could borrow the car tomorrow night."

Bingo.

"What for?"

"Zanax is going to be at our school. It's like a dance."

"Xanax? Like the prescription drug?" Eve asked. "What kind of a band is that?"

"It's Zanax, Mom, with a *Z*, and it's not a band, it's EDM. Jesus." Electronic dance music. Eve knew what that was. She quite liked the Chainsmokers.

"Is it like a rave or something?" Eve asked, concerned. She'd heard the stories of kids dancing to the mind-numbing beats, pumped full of Molly and ketamine. Abbey had never shown an interest in that sort of thing. She and Selena rarely even went to parties, too busy with their studies and extracurriculars.

"No, Mom. It's not a rave." Abbey dragged out the *o* in *Mom* in exasperation.

Maybe Abbey had developed new friends to go with her new interest. This opened up a whole other can of worms, stuffed with wriggling teens who Eve didn't know. Perhaps even a boy. Although Eve wasn't sure Abbey was interested in boys. Or girls for that matter. Perhaps she was interested in both? Physical attraction was so fluid these days. Who wouldn't choose both genders if they had the chance? Right away it doubled the pool of prospective partners. But a romantic association of any type had yet to surface in Abbey's life, despite her preternatural attractiveness.

"Who else is going?"

"I don't know who else is going." Abbey sighed. "Does it matter?"

Eve supposed it didn't. She was being an alarmist, but alarm seemed to be her default setting when it came to her daughter.

"Is Selena going?" Eve pressed.

"No," Abbey said, turning away. She fetched a mug down from the shelf and dropped a perforated tea strainer that was shaped like a silver acorn in it. It clattered against the hard ceramic sides of the cup. "She has to stay home with the kittens."

"How come?" This felt more like a conversation than what had come before. Less stilted and rehearsed. But by Abbey's reaction, Eve sensed she'd gone off script.

"Listen, it's a Friday, so it's not like I have to go to school in the morning. I don't know what your problem is."

"It's just —"

"Don't you trust me?" Abbey demanded, cutting Eve off. Her speech was tight, each word a trigger, because the question itself was loaded.

Eve knew from experience you couldn't trust a typical teenage girl any farther than you could throw her. Mostly because she used to be one. Maybe Selena's parents had forbidden her from going to Zanax with a *Z* because they knew more about EDM than Eve did. Maybe all the stories she'd heard about ketamine and Molly and young people's vital organs melting from the inside were true and she shouldn't let Abbey go either. Not that she was at all sure she could stop her.

"But you two usually do things together," Eve said. "I just wondered why she wasn't going."

"Because her cat's disappeared and her parents are away, and for fuck's sake what's with all the questions!" Abbey grabbed a much-too-big knife from the block beside the cutting board and a lemon from the fridge. She slammed the white door shut, causing all the glass bottles of sauces they never used to rattle against one another on the shelves.

"What do you mean? Has something happened to Cuchulain?"

Abbey ignored her, bringing the knife down hard on the kitchen counter to slice open the lemon, forgetting the cutting board. She appeared genuinely upset about the animal's disappearance and it surprised Eve. She'd always thought Abbey was jealous of Selena's pet and the time and attention it seemed to take away from their friendship.

Her daughter had never done well with animals. That was another reason Eve had said no to a kitten. Michael had kept a succession of white mice when he was in kindergarten that he'd play with for hours. The first one "fell" down the stairs while being carried in a pocket. The second one got caught under the gerbil wheel where he'd been crushed like a medieval torture victim. The final two appeared to have fought each other to the death. Eve had found them lying broken and bloody at the bottom of their cage, wood shavings stuck to the deep gashes in their white furry sides. In every case, Abbey had been close at hand.

The teakettle started a high-pitched scream, but Abbey didn't take it off the hob. She turned to face her mother with one hand on her hip and the other holding the butcher's knife. "Do you trust me or not?" she demanded.

The knife dripped cloudy lemon juice to the kitchen floor and the scent of its bitter freshness filled the room.

Eve didn't move, kept her own hands stuffed in the pockets of her jean shorts to hide their twitching. Abbey's irises were the steely grey of drill bits, untempered by the underlying blue that hid within. In a better mood, they could look like the inside of an oyster. But not now. Eve looked past her daughter's eyes and tried to enter her mind, though she knew she shouldn't. She caught a glimpse of sleek fur, a flash of something bright. But before she could even process the pitiful cries of the kittens, she was knocked back by the vivid image of Michael lying broken on the floor. Eve could see herself as well, holding his body, her mouth opened in the overemphasized O of an Edvard Munch painting. She dropped the connection between them before the wail from that mouth flooded her mind like a tsunami. The teakettle shrieked on the stove.

"Well, Mom." Abbey smiled, holding the knife closer. "Do you trust me, or not?"

"Yes." Eve leaned against the kitchen counter for support, looking away. "Of course, I trust you."

"Good." Abbey stepped behind her and threw the knife into the sink with a clatter. She switched the burner under the teakettle off, but it still took a few moments for the screaming to die down.

By the time Eve went out to the driveway to see what Richard was up to, he was gone. She was about to go back in the house when he came through the side gate from the backyard with a shovel and a tall brown leaf bag in his hands.

"Hi," he said, not expecting to see her there, wondering why she was.

"Hi," she said.

"I was picking up the dog crap," he said, possibly expecting praise. She expressed her thanks, but they both knew it wasn't the same thing.

Richard opened up the green bin beside her and started dumping the brown turds into it. Eve was still skittish from her confrontation with Abbey. When he banged the lid shut, it made her jump and protectively bring her hand to her right side. Eve looked over at the battleship-grey can reserved for refuse that wouldn't rot away into the earth, the one that had hurt her.

"I wouldn't look in the garbage can," Richard said, following her gaze.

"Why?"

"I found something, under the bushes. A wild animal must have got to it." He propped the filthy shovel up against the side of the house next to Eve's overgrown attempt at a herb garden. "It's not a pretty sight."

The sun was beginning to fade behind the trees, and Eve could see the long shadow of her husband cast across the driveway. The silence between them multiplied with all the things they chose to leave unsaid. She was accustomed to that silence, would normally feel no anxiety from it. But slowly she felt her adrenalin start to flow. One of her hands started to shake. She shoved it in the front pocket of her cut-off shorts and felt a familiar sickness well up inside her. It was an intense premonition, threatening to take over, to spill out of her like the rancid red wine of the night before.

"Are you okay?" Richard looked less concerned than wary. It wasn't like her to break the rules, to let him see up close that there was something wrong. "Listen, about last night. There's nothing to worry about. You have to believe me, Eve. I don't know what you —"

"I'm fine," Eve said, cutting him off. But she wasn't. There was a voice calling to her now, becoming louder. She needed to get rid of Richard so she could deal with what it had to say.

"Could you have a look at the shed door?" she asked, gritting her teeth against the voice inside her head. "It's come loose again."

"Okay," Richard said slowly, trying to get a sense of her real feelings. He waited for her to say something more, about the affair, about anything. When she didn't, he walked over to the garage and started rooting around through his tools. His whole body was relaxed now that he'd been given something constructive to do, something tangible that he could fix with his hands, something where no emotions were required. He still gave her a cautious look before he opened the latch on the gate and returned to the backyard.

Eve stared at the large grey garbage can with the hard plastic lid and rubbed at her side. She didn't want to open it, to return to the scene of the crime, but the cries had moved from her head to the can. She couldn't drown them out.

Look at me! Look at me! Just like Michael on the railing that day. But this was not the innocent call of a child for attention. It was a command.

She didn't want to look. Richard had told her not to. She shouldn't. She needn't. She should just walk away. But the portent became even louder, more insistent. It seemed impossible that Richard or even the rest of the neighbourhood wasn't hearing it.

Look at me! Look at me!

She held her hands over her ears trying to block it all out. The grey garbage can wavered and morphed in the air until she couldn't see it properly through tears. No longer the colour of a battleship, the can was now the colour of a dove. Dove grey, like the softer version of her daughter's eyes or the pearl finish of a child's much-too-small coffin.

Look at me, goddammit!

Those had been the last words Eve had heard when she'd reached in to clean the grime deep inside the garbage can. Before the push that sent her roughly against it, feet desperately trying to gain purchase on the asphalt driveway as the hairline crack in her rib spread.

She took her hands away from her ears and walked toward the source of the cries. They stopped only when she lifted the lid and looked down at the cat torn to pieces. Eve could see the ragged slashes across each one of Cuchulain's pink swollen teats.

Eve slammed the lid back down and hurried back to the house, feeling unable to trust anyone, even herself, anymore.

ELEVEN

So, today was "Take Your Kid to Work Day," which is easily the dumbest idea the school board has ever come up with. Every kid in their final year is supposed to spend the day at work with one of their parents or some other adult so the teachers can get a day off. As if they don't get enough holidays anyway.

When I got up, Dad was about to leave. He'd forgotten I was even coming. But that's him. Mom made a big deal about it, as if it was HER he had forgotten about. Anyway, she let me borrow her pencil skirt and blazer from when she used to go to work in an office. She was thinner back then, so it fit okay. I had to borrow a pair of "sensible pumps," as she put it, as well, but they were a half size too big and I had to stick a wad of toilet paper behind each heel when I went for a pee at break time.

I thought I'd spend the whole day with Dad, doing what he does, but mostly he goes to meetings and doesn't do anything. In the meetings, they all just sit around a big table and argue about stuff. It was so boring. So, at eleven o'clock, when he tried to make me go to another "round-table discussion," I asked him if I could just stay in his office and do some filing or something. He didn't seem too happy about that, but he was late for the roundtable. He asked an underling to put together some papers for me to put in alphabetical order or something else completely useless, but they never did, so I just closed the door and searched the internet for epic tattoo fails.

That's when SHE came to the door. She had honey-blond highlights and her hair was long and straightened, not cut into one of those professional bobs that most women have in order to be taken seriously. She had librarian glasses on, not the ones that you actually need to see, but the ones girls wear so you'll think they're smart when they're not.

But it wasn't what she looked like that tipped me off that she was Dad's squeeze. It was the way she opened the door. Quick, like she was planning to slip in with no one noticing. And no knock. No knock means you feel like you own the place.

Her name was Julia. She asked where my dad was. I told her he was in a meeting. Then she got this pissed-off look on her face and asked who I was. I think she actually thought I might be competition or something. Gross! Like I would go out with a guy as old as my dad. He's like practically retirement age. It's disgusting that someone as young as even her is fucking him. But when I told her I was his daughter, she got all sickly sweet, saying how she'd heard all about me, and how much she loved my blazer. Total suck-up. She even asked if I'd like to go to lunch sometime, already trying to win over "the daughter" to her side. Like it was important for us to be friends. I would never be friends with someone like her.

I saw the texts she sent my dad on the burner phone I found in his desk drawer. He'd locked it, but the keys weren't too hard to find. What a ho. I mean I'm okay with using sex to get what you want, but that bitch has no self-respect at all. I know her type with their duck-face selfies on Instagram. Drunken photos taken next to microblade-brow airheads just like themselves with "Besties forever!" written underneath. A person like that my dad will just chew up and spit out anyway.

When she closed the door, I watched her walk back to her desk through the window Dad has that looks out on his cubicle farm of employees. She looked back and gave me a sheepish smile before she disappeared behind the half-wall of her stall.

Anyway, it was a good thing she took off, because not long after that Mom showed. When I saw her coming, I tossed the phone back in the drawer and slammed it shut. I didn't even bother locking it, just stuffed the keys back in Dad's hiding place. I don't care if he knows that I know.

Mom had come up with this idea weeks ago, when I was pissed that she wouldn't let me stay home to watch her "work." She said we'd all go out together for lunch, one not-so-happy family. Jesus, maybe we should have invited

Julia and we could've all pretended to be fucking besties. My mom is so deluded. And get this, she knocked before she came in. That kind of says it all.

Dad was late getting out of his meeting. He'd probably forgotten about lunch too, so I went to get him. I had to stand outside the Algonquin meeting room for ten minutes before I finally caught his eye through the window to the hallway. All the meeting rooms at Dad's office are named after Indigenous tribes of the region. They have one of those plaques in the lobby that acknowledges we are all on land that belonged to the original peoples of Canada and to be respectful. As if admitting you stole shit from someone makes it okay. I think if you asked a kid living with no running water on one of those shitty reserves, he'd tell you he'd rather have the land back and you can stick the plaque and your respect up your ass.

Once Dad finally figured out that I was waiting for him, he came out and I went to the washroom to stuff more toilet paper down my sensible pumps and fix my makeup a little. By the time I came back to Dad's office, they were both in there waiting for me. We went for lunch at a Thai place. Neither Mom or Dad said much, so I had to do all the talking. Honestly, it's like I'm totally fucking responsible for both of them.

In the afternoon, the underling finally showed up with work for me to do, so I spent the next two hours stuffing envelopes with these huge stapled quarterly reports. There were like a thousand of them. How many trees does that kill? Hasn't anyone heard of the internet? They should just post that shit on a website, and if people are too backward to figure out how to use a computer to access it, they're going to be run over by the future anyway.

Anyway, I'm glad that day's over. What a shitshow. At least I have Zanax to look forward to. Mom finally let me have the car, but not before she interrogated me. I should be the one interrogating her. She and Dad haven't slept in the same room since that night I caught her smoking on the deck. But that's just another thing I'm supposed to ignore and not ask about, like that Julia slut trying to be my buddy today. She must really think my dad is going to leave my mom for her. Guess Mom isn't the only one that's deluded.

We dropped the new Funnel Head poem in Dylan Penske's locker yesterday after school, but we couldn't gauge his reaction today because of this "Take Your Kid to Work" bullshit. Selena got to go downtown with her parents to where the symphony practises, which I have to admit sounds even more boring than my day. She said she spent the time studying, trying to get an edge on me in Chemistry probably. I can't believe she even has her name in for the Thompson scholarship. I mean, it's not like she needs the money to go away to school like me. Her mother's family is loaded, made all their money with some cog in the 1860s that revolutionized electric engines. Who even knew they had electric engines in the 1860s? Her grandparents had a hundred grand set aside for her tuition when she was born for Christ's sake. Anyway, Selena says her dad is making her apply for it. But I don't know whether to believe her or not. The reality is, I don't know who to believe anymore. Seems to me that the only truth you can count on is that everybody lies.

Zanax is tonight. I got an old blond wig from the thrift store that I'm going to dye blue, and some body glitter. Also, some crazy sunglasses so I won't go into an epileptic fit from the strobe lights. Selena put up the missing cat posters for Cuchulain this morning before she went downtown with her parents. She scanned and blew up a picture of the cat that she took at Christmas. It's wearing a ridiculous red Santa hat with padded white antlers sticking out on either side. I mean, are you Santa or are you a reindeer for fuck's sake? But it was the only photo Selena had. I wonder who took care of the kittens while everyone was at work?

TWELVE

Andre Mueller is such an asshole.

Richard sat at his desk, trying to wrestle a spreadsheet into submission so he could validate his department going 150 percent over budget for the last system upgrade. Mueller was supposed to do it. But when Richard looked at the figures the scheming little German had put together, they didn't add up to anything except Richard getting his ass handed to him on a platter by the executive committee. Mueller had conveniently sent the spreadsheet out by email before he left for a week's vacation in Aruba. A perfect place to sit and wait out his co-worker's demise before returning to take full advantage of it.

Climbing the ladder in the corporate IT world could be brutal. You'd think all those computer geeks would be peaceful, sitting around crunching code while they discussed the newest *Star Wars* remake. But once you made it into upper management, half of them had virtual knives hidden in their pocket protectors ready to stab you in the back. Eve never seemed to have a problem with such things when she worked in the industry. Richard liked to think she was protected by the strength of her feminine wiles, but the reality was, she just seemed to have an uncanny sense of knowing who to trust.

It was strange seeing Eve in the office today, like being transported back in time. After Abbey had pulled him from his meeting, Richard had hurried back to his office to find his wife talking to one of the developers. She'd been dressed business casual, a simple white silk, button-down blouse and a pair of black dress pants that hugged the curve of her ass just enough to turn a guy on but not enough to be unprofessional. She'd leaned in to say something to the developer and Richard thought he caught him trying to get a look at the swell of her breasts where her blouse gaped a little. She had always been sexy, his wife. And not just on the surface. Once, when she'd gotten a promotion, she'd tried to seduce him on the oversized desk of her new office after hours. But he'd been too nervous of hidden cameras or late-night window washers to oblige. He wished now that he'd been less afraid, taken advantage of her wildness while he had the chance.

"You did remember about lunch?" she'd said, when he stood there staring blankly at her from just outside his office door. He'd still been mesmerized by his wife here at work, taken out of context. Eve looked so much like her old self. Years younger and hot as hell. It was as if she were an apparition from the past come to give him a second chance at sex on her desk blotter. Like an erotic ghost in a XXX-rated version of *A Christmas Carol*.

"Of course," he'd replied, although he hadn't remembered about lunch, or even "Take Your Kid to Work Day." He'd almost left Abbey behind at the house in the morning. She'd chased him down the driveway in her mother's chunky high heels.

That's when a sigh had come from a nearby cubicle, an expression Richard had elicited more than once in more intimate circumstances. He'd turned his head toward the sound, realizing that the only thing that separated his wife and his mistress at that moment was a flimsy padded cubicle wall. When he'd looked back at Eve, she was frowning, her brow furrowed. All the years that had passed came crashing down between them in a matter of seconds. The illusion of *before* was gone, and it was just the Eve of *after* that stood there. When they'd gone to lunch, it had been an exercise in restraint, keeping up appearances for Abbey. For the rest of the day, Richard could not quite get over the feeling that he had lost something.

He wished he could lose about 100K in overspending, he thought, banging away at the spreadsheet in the darkening office. He was so damn tired. He hadn't slept well. That cat had freaked him out. He'd thought he'd heard some animal prowling around the garage last night, trying to get at it, but when he went out to check, there wasn't anything there. He rubbed at his eyes before moving fifty thousand into Mueller's staffing costs. They'd think the conniving SOB couldn't manage his project team efficiently. The rest he distributed evenly across the Wellness budget allotted to each of his six reporting work clusters. Nobody knew what they were supposed to do with that money anyway, beyond at-desk neck massages that weirded people out and ice cream Fridays where the cones were always soggy. He'd validate the money by pretending to offer free morning yoga for stress, then schedule it at 6:00 a.m., when it would stress people out too much to attend.

His task completed, Richard rocked back in his padded leather office chair and brought the tips of his fingers together into a teepee alignment usually reserved for deep thinkers or criminal masterminds. Richard was neither. He was procrastinating. He didn't want to leave the office because he wasn't sure of where to go. Home or Julia? He collapsed the teepee and went to nervously twist at his wedding ring, but it wasn't there. He'd forgotten to put it back on after his yardwork last night.

Julia had left for the day by the time he got out of his last meeting at five. By then, Eve was long gone, and Abbey was packing up to go as well, expecting a lift from him. He'd sent her home alone in a taxi, saying he had to work late.

Richard was not sure how he felt about his daughter being in the office today. At first, he'd been ecstatic, showing her off to his colleagues, all bright and beautiful, and on the brink of adulthood. Abbey had his eyes, and it was as if he could look out from them and see the bright future she had ahead of her as if it were his own. Richard didn't often ponder his daughter, but when he did, he thought of her as an avatar of himself, standing on the edge of life's possibilities. But his vicarious pride had been pierced as soon as people started making comments about apples and trees. He knew they were talking about Eve rather than his fruit-bearing capabilities. His wife had been the flashy rising star before tragedy struck them. Richard had been the tried-and-true workhorse who eventually won the race. Everyone would always think of Abbey as Eve's shining chip and him as the less illustrious block. It might have been different if Michael had lived long enough, a son to favour the father, but he hadn't.

The more Richard saw his daughter as an inheritor of his wife's abilities, the more of a funk he found himself in. And the more he felt seduced by the message on the phone in his drawer. Julia wanted to meet him at one of their usual spots, a river gorge just north of the city where you could park hidden in the long brush grass. Richard had been clumsy at car sex at first, but he was getting the hang of it. And even with a gear shift stuck in his thigh, he'd felt like a champion thrusting into Julia's nubile young body in the bucket seats of his family-sized sedan. Not like a dwarf star outshone by his wife and daughter. Not a corporate lackey looking to hide his own incompetence. If Richard could see himself more clearly, he would know that he was neither of these things. But the loss of his son had left him with a highly developed sense of insecurity. A father emasculated by his inability to protect his one and only heir. He pounded his despair into the yielding flesh of his mistress or into extra hours at work rather than into self-realization. To admit he had failed in this one thing was to admit he was a failure at them all.

The burner phone buzzed in his locked right-hand drawer, shaking against the pens and paper clips inside. The droning vibration of the phone echoed off the empty office walls, amplifying its demand. Richard located his keys inside a box of staples he kept for a stapler he didn't possess. He turned the key in the lock, but the drawer wouldn't budge. He yanked on it repeatedly, cursing, the incessant trill of the phone like the sound of a fly caught in a camp lantern. He tried smacking one side of the desk and pulled on the indented door handle so hard it made the tips of his fingers raw. Nothing. Eventually, the phone went silent, and he sat back in his chair staring down the drawer in a misplaced bid to intimidate. As if to taunt him, the phone startled him with a punctuated hum, probably a voice mail alert.

Richard closed his eyes, took a deep breath, then refocused on the problem. Reaching forward, he turned the key the other way in the lock and pulled hard on the drawer. It came flying open and hit him in the knee. Another choice couple of curses were thrown out onto the still, recycled air of the empty office. The drawer must have been unlocked to begin with. He could have sworn it had been locked this morning. He rubbed at his knee and grabbed the offending phone out of the drawer and saw the notification for voice mail. But when he clicked on it, there was nothing but dead air. The missed call had been from a private number. There was also a recent text from Julia he hadn't seen yet.

He put the phone down, daring it to buzz and vibrate again. It sat mute on his desk next to a framed picture of Eve and Abbey. His daughter and wife smiled up at him, grass caught in their fanned-out hair. He had taken this picture himself. Eve and Abbey had been in the backyard, working on a botany experiment for Abbey's grade eleven environmental studies class. He remembered the two dozen earthenware pots with lima beans planted in them, each carefully positioned for a different allotment of sun. The variable in the experiment was light, and so the pots were placed in different locations to get the benefit of different amounts of exposure. Some were put in a blistering central location, where there was no shade any time of day, others in a dark corner where overgrown shrubs kept out the light even at the highest of noons. Richard had been assigned the role of photographer for the study, to record the progress of the fledgling plants. He had followed behind as Abbey and Eve moved from pot to pot with a tape measure from the sewing basket. Abbey would call out height in centimetres while Eve dutifully recorded the figures in a blue notebook.

His daughter had conducted the experiment with military precision, intent in getting perfect on the assignment that would count toward 20 percent of her grade. So serious they'd looked, like they were recording the details from the site of a genocide rather than the growth of beans. When Abbey had broken one of the less hearty plants trying to take its vitals, Richard had held his breath, bracing himself for the meltdown. Abbey had stared disbelievingly at the broken plant. Richard had fingered his camera strap. Eve had covered her mouth as if to cough. But she'd been laughing. Not unkindly, but laughing just the same. It had been so long since he'd heard Eve laugh.

And then, just as impossibly, his high-achieving daughter had drawn her tight lips into a wry grin and laughed along with her mother. The two of them had fallen into one another, chortling, tears bursting at the corners of their eyes. They'd collapsed on the lawn together, giggling as they threw tufts of dry grass at each other. Richard had stood there with his Nikon around his neck, flabbergasted. He'd raised the camera and captured them from above as they lay in the grass with their heads bowed together. It had made him so much happier than taking the pictures of the sad little plants, some of them banished to a scorching end as soon as they peeked out of the ground, others stunted, deprived of the warmth to coax them into the light.

Before this picture, he'd kept a stock family photo of all of them, including Michael, on his desk. It had been taken years ago at Sears, when it still existed. He'd kept the picture up long after the image stopped resembling any of them — except for his son, who would be eight years old forever. He still had that photo, stuck at the bottom of his underwear drawer, next to his old rugby socks from college and a silver dollar his mother gave him on his fifteenth birthday.

Looking at the photo of Eve and Abbey laughing with summer grass caught in their hair, the sun dogs winking at the camera, he couldn't remember why he'd felt so eclipsed by the women in his family earlier that day. In the picture, Eve and Abbey were beaming up at him with their natural smiles, bestowing their delight on him. And for that one magical moment, he'd been the one and only person on the receiving end of their radiance in the grass. Their spotlights had shone on him, and in that light, he had thrived.

THIRTEEN

"Why didn't you tell me?"

Janet stood on Eve's doorstep, holding a huge leather drawstring purse clutched under one arm and a lamp fashioned out of a baseball bat in the other. She wore a bright-orange minidress made almost entirely out of mismatched zippers. The dog jumped excitedly around her Doc Martens platform boots as Eve opened the front door.

"When have I ever had to tell you anything?" Eve said, letting her old friend in the house with a feigned sigh that caused a twinge of pain in her healing rib.

"I can't always be looking out for your signal." Janet stepped past Eve and dropped her bottomless purse onto the hall table. The drawstring fell open to reveal a funnel, a candy-red fishing lure shaped like a penis, and one lone googly eye that rolled out, coming to a precarious stop on the edge of the glass tabletop. It stared up at them, the pupil settled to the right, in a state of disembodied confusion. Janet stooped to check her reflection quickly in the mirror above the table, adjusted one of the zippers on her dress, and then handed Eve the bat lamp. She read the scripted red lettering down the side. *Louisville Slugger.*

"Here," Janet said. "This is for you."

Eve took the lamp and held it up appraisingly. It was fitted with a retro filament bulb screwed into the batting end, and a white Frisbee attached to the handle as a base. The shade was a clear plastic dome, a perfect miniature replica of the bubble umbrella Eve had owned as a child.

"I thought you were all about the intersection of technology and art," Eve said, forgetting her thank yous. The last gift Janet had created for her was a Monet-print felt hat decorated with the innards of a disembowelled flip phone. She only wore it on special occasions.

"I'm experimenting with sport as a sublimation for sex now." Janet spit on a finger and used it to smooth down a lock of hair that had been flattened on her forehead in a curlicue. The rest was teased six inches into the air in a gorgeous honey-brown Afro that only added to her considerable height. The unique colour of her hair came compliments of a great-grandfather from Finland who'd made a stop-off in Jamaica. Janet bent down and scratched the dog behind the ears with her long, tapered fingers.

Eve looked at the lamp, tried to figure out what was sexy about it.

"I don't get it."

"Come on, Evie." Janet lingered on both the *come* and the *on,* before dismissing the dog with a quick whisper in his floppy white ear. He walked down the hall and obediently lay down in his basket. She stood and turned to Eve with her hands on her hips. "The bat is obviously a phallic symbol. Duh."

Eve continued to stare at the lamp, perplexed. Impatient, Janet stood behind her and placed a warm hand in the middle of her back, mindful of the injury that she had sensed from over sixty miles away. Eve relaxed and allowed herself to cross the physical divide between them. In the mirror, Janet's deep-brown eyes were momentarily replaced by Eve's green hazel ones, gazing from above her own shoulder.

"Oh," Eve said, from Janet's lips, just before she returned to her proper body.

"You get it now, right?"

"Sure," Eve said. "I get it."

"The bubble umbrella represents young girls and the prevailing Lolita complex inherent in the patriarchy."

"I have no idea why I didn't get that from the start."

"Well, Eve. You've got your talents, but you've never understood about art."

Janet travelled down the tiled hallway and turned right into the kitchen. Eve heard the refrigerator door open. She placed the lamp next to Janet's purse on the hall table. The sharp barbed edges of the penis lure winked at her in the foyer light. She pulled the drawstrings closed and tried not to be drawn in by the stare of the googly eye.

Looking in the mirror, she saw dark circles on pale skin that underscored the budding claws of crow's feet.

Her once plump lips appeared partially deflated. All this seemed in deep contrast to the rich creamy brown skin and full sensuous mouth of her friend that the mirror had so recently reflected. Eve wasn't usually prone to vanity. But she had conjured a rare glamour at the office today when she'd visited Richard for lunch. She'd allowed herself to be seen as she was when on the cusp of her thirties, her flesh full of juice and unlined. She might have been bound by Janet's spell from enchanting her husband, but she could still pull an illusion from time to time as long as it wasn't aimed directly at him. She'd watched as Richard had stood there transfixed and it pleased her. Until he'd been distracted by that woman in the cubicle and Eve had realized who she was. She'd dropped the glamour all at once, with relief. It had taken a lot out of her to manage even this simplest of spells. The effort had been somewhere between faking an orgasm and pasting a smile on your face at a funeral.

"Just as I suspected," Janet said as Eve walked into the kitchen, leaving the mirror's reflections behind. Janet's compact, orange-zippered bum stuck out of the fridge above impossibly long slim legs. Janet could never keep weight on, no matter what she ate. That wasn't magic, just metabolism.

Janet stood and put her hands on her skinny hips. "Where are they?"

"Where are what?" Eve sat down at the kitchen table, wishing she hadn't given away her cigarettes to the girl at the drop-in.

"The ashes from last Beltane? I told you to keep them in the fridge." Traditionally, each May Day, a portion of the ashes were to be saved from the celebratory balefire of Beltane. You were supposed to sprinkle them into the four corners of your house throughout the year to chase away malignant spirits and misfortune, which usually amounted to the same thing. Janet insisted they lost their potency if you didn't keep them refrigerated.

"I used it all," Eve lied. The truth was, she hadn't celebrated Beltane this year, nor the year before that. When Janet invited her to spend it with her, she always found an excuse not to attend and light the ancient fire. She no longer trusted the cleansing passion of that May Day flame to wash away the coming year's bad luck and disaster. After your eight-year-old son fell to his death from a second-floor railing, your belief in amulets was sorely shaken.

"So, are you going to tell me what happened?" Janet had returned to rooting around in the fridge, this time looking for food rather than ashes. She was always hungry.

"I fell and broke my rib."

"I saw what happened," Janet said from behind the white insulated door. "And you didn't fall."

"Then why did you ask?"

Their ability to read one other was not entirely attributable to special gifts. All women who are close enough can see through each other's bullshit. But if you were a good friend, you usually didn't call one another on it. Janet was a good friend, but she was also a card-carrying protester of crap when she heard it. She knew Eve's fall hadn't been an accident, but Eve didn't believe she knew for sure who'd caused it. Seeking to avoid the subject, Eve decided to fake her out with a different confession.

"Richard is having an affair."

Janet stood up too quickly and bumped the back of her head on the roof of the fridge, crying out. In one hand she had a Tupperware with leftover squash ravioli in it and in the other a jar of Nutella. She dropped both on the kitchen table so she could rub the injury on her head with the heel of her hand.

"No shit!" she said, with a grimace. "I didn't think the boy had it in him."

"Is that some sort of comment on his manhood?"

"No, girl, it's just a comment on his lack of imagination." Janet opened up the cutlery drawer and rattled around inside until she found a small fork with a faded pink princess tiara etched on the white handle. It had been Abbey's when she was a baby, and Eve couldn't bring herself to throw it out. Janet always used it when she visited.

"So, tell me about it." Janet sat down with her princess fork and popped the top off the Tupperware. She speared a piece of ravioli and ate it without heating it up.

"I saw her at the office today. Her name's Julia." Eve picked at a blob of egg yolk stuck onto a red plastic placemat. "She's so young I think she still has her fucking milk teeth."

"Well, you didn't think he'd choose some old hag from Accounting with a harelip, did you? I mean that would just be insulting."

"I suppose so."

"So, what are you going to do about it?" Janet opened up the jar of Nutella and dipped a piece of ravioli deep into the contents. When she pulled it out, the rich chocolate-nut butter stuck to it like tar.

"That's disgusting, Janet." But Eve couldn't hold back her smile.

"What?" Janet said, popping the gooey monstrosity into her mouth. The Nutella clung to her lips while she chewed. After she swallowed, she licked it off with relish. "You didn't answer my question."

"What's that?" Eve said.

"What are you going to do about your husband's lazy cheating ass?"

"What the hell am I supposed to do about it?" Eve had found the burner phone in Richard's desk drawer when she'd gone to the office for lunch. He didn't even have a password on it, the overconfident prick. But even with the evidence of his affair burning in the palm of her hand, she couldn't find the wherewithal to confront him about it. She'd left the phone where she'd found it in his desk.

"Fight for him or fuck him," Janet said, getting up to go to the refrigerator again. "That's what you do about it." She took out a can of Coke and popped the tab, holding her mouth over the hole when it started to fizz. Janet was aware of Eve's past infidelity with Mark. It didn't matter. She was always going to side with her friend.

"It's not as simple as that."

"Yes, it is." Janet sat back down with the Coke, picked up the fork again to stab the last ravioli.

"There are other things to consider."

"You mean Abbey." Janet dropped the fork into the now empty Tupperware container. She stuck her long pointer finger into the Nutella and licked it off before putting the top back on the jar.

"Yes. I mean Abbey." Eve fidgeted again with the red placemat. She licked her own finger and tried to rub off some sticky jam before she stopped herself, realizing how unhygienic it was.

"You know you're all wrong about that."

Eve looked out the window across the back deck. She could see Bob Kettleman next door. His head moved back and forth along the fence like a duck in a shooting gallery as he mowed his lawn for the second time this week. The winged branches of their burning bush shuddered from the vibration every time he passed by.

"You've never understood about Abbey, Janet."

"I understand what it is to want a child, Eve." Janet narrowed her eyes at her friend. Eve could see where her long black eyelashes curled back, leaving mascara tracks above the lids.

"I know you do." Eve lowered her own makeup-free eyes. Janet didn't have the same fertility issues Eve had suffered from, but her lack of a partner had made her barren in her own way. They had talked about sperm banks and going ahead with a pregnancy on her own. Janet was well able to raise a child by herself. But somehow that final act of planned single parenthood smacked of concession for Janet. An admission that she would never find a woman to share her life with and was settling for a baby to replace one. Whether it was due to procrastination or stubbornness, Janet held out for the dream of a nuclear family even in her forties, with two eclectic mother electrons orbiting the stellar child she still dreamed she would create.

"You're not the first to be lured to the dark side," Janet said. "Remember what Nanny used to say. You got to be prepared for a little dark with the light."

"The witch that can't curse, can't cure," Eve quoted.

"Exactly."

"I didn't curse anyone."

"Maybe." Janet took another furious swig of the Coke. "But you crossed the line."

Eve *had* crossed the line, or to be more precise, the divide. There was deep chasm that ran between the natural ebb and flow of female magic and the charismatic power of the Ragman. Abbey had been the result of Eve's fateful decision to step into that abyss. Her greatest joy and greatest sorrow all rolled into one.

"I worry about her." Eve thought of the mutilated animal rotting outside in the garbage can and then quickly blocked out the image for fear of Janet picking it up. She hadn't had the heart to tell Sharon Patel that Cuchulain was never coming home, nor the courage to admit to Janet who she feared might be responsible. If Abbey had struck out at the cat out of jealousy, it wouldn't be the first time. There had been that girl in primary school, a third wheel who threatened to wedge herself between Abbey and her best friend. Richard and Eve were called in to meet with the principal. Abbey had punched the girl in the face, breaking one of her newly minted front teeth.

"You shouldn't worry." Janet pulled a toothpick out of a zippered pocket and picked at one of her straight white teeth. "I'm telling you, she's just like all girls that age. Like we were. Don't you remember?"

Eve realized there were similarities. She recalled a phase when her mother couldn't open her mouth to say "Good morning" without Eve rolling her eyes, certain of a hidden subtext. But she hadn't been like Abbey, had she?

"We weren't that bad as teenagers."

Janet drew in a heavy breath, threatening to inhale the toothpick. "Don't tell me you've forgotten Harold Jenkins and his accordion?"

Eve drew a faint memory of a hot June assembly, a young pimply boy playing through what seemed to be endless creaky stanzas of "Spanish Eyes." She and Janet had wanted to gouge out their own eyes rather than sit there and listen to it for one more agonizing minute.

"You found his accordion in the cloakroom after the assembly," Janet reminded her. "Poured your Orange Crush on it. Fried the fucking keyboard."

"That wasn't me," Eve objected, horrified. "That was you."

"No, my friend." Janet pointed the finger that was so recently covered in Nutella at Eve. "It was you."

It was her. However, Eve remembered a version of events where she'd only meant to make the keys sticky so that Harold's fingers would stick. She had convinced her young catty self that he would find it as funny as she did.

"I didn't realize it would leak down and ruin the entire instrument," Eve said, ashamed. "Or at least, I don't think I did."

"See what I mean," Janet said with a wry smile. She slipped the toothpick back in her pocket "We're all the same at that age. Our damn brains aren't fully formed. It's neurology. It's hormones. Who knows?"

"But Abbey, she can be so volatile," Eve said. "She smashed a glass on the deck a couple of nights ago." Eve recalled the fury in her daughter's eyes so quick to displace her earlier blip of vulnerability. "Sometimes I swear she's bipolar."

"Jesus, Eve, if we were all judged by how we acted at seventeen, we'd all be bipolar."

"But Abbey's different" — Eve lowered her voice — "because of the way she was made."

"She was made by you and that cheating asshole, Richard."

"You know what I'm talking about." Eve wanted to believe what Janet was saying. That the conjuring of the pregnancy had no effect on the creation of the child. That what was going on with Abbey was just kid stuff. Janet was the only one who knew about Abbey. As well as the truth about Michael. She never judged.

"People are so much more than the sum of their parts, Eve. Nature versus nurture and all that."

"You don't think anything is preordained?"

"In a world where both evil and good are so randomly distributed, how can it be?"

Janet reached out and put a still, gentle hand over top Eve's fidgeting one.

"Don't worry, honey. Nothing of the Ragman has touched Abbey. You know it's always the witch who pays the price for that anyway." Janet didn't mean to make pronouncements. She was only stating the facts as they both knew them. Just like all people, witches had to be on the lookout for the trickster within. And if you allowed yourself to be seduced by that inner fraud, you alone were left to accept responsibility for the consequences. Any witch who tried to hide from judgment behind the defence of "the devil made her do it" was deluded and a danger to herself and others. Much like those who ran with scissors or called old boyfriends after drinking too much tequila.

"Haven't I done that already?" She swallowed hard. "Paid the price?" She looked up at Janet, even sitting down she was strikingly tall.

"Maybe you have," Janet said, squeezing her hand. "But it's up to you if want to keep on paying it." Janet downed the last of the Coke and threw the empty can across the kitchen. It fell perfectly into the recycling bin, after the cupboard door flipped open briefly to let it in. Then she undid a zipper on her dress and pulled out a blue velvet bag. Eve couldn't imagine how she'd managed to conceal it in the form-fitting outfit. She hadn't seen the slightest bulge.

"Some Beltane fire ashes," she said, handing the bag to Eve. "Just in case the Ragman comes collecting."

Eve ran one thumb along the rich blue velvet, still warm from being worn so close to Janet's body. "Thank you," she said, and a tear fell at the kindness of her friend. She wiped at one eye with the back of her hand before placing the bag in her lap.

Janet reached out and gently lifted her chin to face her, smiling. "I love you, Eve," she said, then called Eve by her craft name. Every witch was given one when she joined the sisterhood. When spoken, Eve's sounded like a rustle or a breeze. The speaking of it brought a pleasing rush, one that made her feel more alive.

Janet released her chin and stood. "Now, get your power heels on. We're going on a road trip."

"Where?" asked Eve, alarmed. Abbey would be home soon with Richard from work.

"To do a little payback of our own."

"THIS IS NOT A GOOD idea, Janet."

The two women sat at the bar of the Delta hotel sipping cosmopolitans. Eve felt dowdy in her black tailored trousers and white blouse, still unwashed from her trip to see Richard and Abbey at the office. Meanwhile, Janet had opened a zipper on the right side of her dress to make an attractive thigh-high slit. She owned the attention of every man in the place, along with many of the women.

"This is where I divined she's going to be, and this is where we'll stay," Janet said, sipping on her drink.

"I am not questioning your divination skills," Eve said, taking a sip of her own. "I am questioning the wisdom of confronting my husband's mistress at the Delta while tanked on cosmos."

Despite Eve's protests, Janet had managed to convince her to go along with her scheme. When Richard called to say he would be working late and Abbey breezed in, took the car, and left saying something about hair dye, Eve had been left with no domestic excuses. To back out after that would only point to cowardice. Still, she had tried to beg off. But Janet had woven a healing spell around her rib that provided such relief she'd acquiesced, if only out of sheer gratitude.

"Whoa, honey, who said *we*? It's you who's going to talk to that little piece of candy floss, not me."

"Why are you here, then?"

"For the entertainment."

"What if Richard is with her?"

"I didn't see that," Janet said simply. But Eve wasn't sure. She wanted to call Richard and confirm he was truly at the office like he said, but she'd forgotten her cellphone at home along with her purse. Janet had rushed her out of the house, afraid Eve would lose her nerve. She could ask Janet to use her phone but didn't want to call into question Janet's divination skills again. Instead, she returned to her drink, and focused on the sugar-coated sweetness of the cocktail instead of the bitter reason she and Janet were there.

They moved from the bar to a booth and ordered dinner. Janet consumed an entire plate of fish and chips despite having her pasta and Nutella snack earlier. Eve picked at a soggy personal pizza where the feta fell off the limp crust every time she picked it up.

When Julia came into the bar, Janet was in the ladies' room. Eve was holding her fork suspended over a side salad when her husband's mistress noticed her in the corner. She watched Julia's beautiful face betray only a brief moment of surprise before she recovered, and then the little piece of candy floss strode across the room and walked right up to her.

"Well, hello, Eve, how are you?"

Eve felt a piece of feta get caught in her throat. She croaked a greeting. It sounded like a goat's hiccup.

"You probably don't remember me." Julia beamed as she held out one finely manicured hand with a Claddagh ring on the third finger. Eve had a similar piece of jewellery, bought in Ireland while travelling on a gap year. The two hands that made up the ring held a heart with a crown at the top. If you wore the ring with the heart side out, you were single. If you wore it facing in, you were taken. Eve didn't know where her gap year Claddagh ring was now or how she would wear it, but Julia wore hers with the heart facing in.

"You work with Richard," Eve finally managed to cough up, having dislodged the feta.

"Oh, I think you know I do more than work with him." Julia looked around the room. Eve assumed she wanted to see if anyone was close enough to listen.

"Excuse me?"

Julia ignored her. "You and I met at the Christmas party, you know, last year."

Eve tried to remember the Christmas party. All she recalled were stale canapés and a cash bar that everyone complained about. This was not working out the way she'd thought it would, or the way Janet had told her. Eve was meant to be the one in control, with Julia backing down in shame and guilty contrition. The little harlot wasn't playing by the rules. "Listen, I don't understand why you're …" Eve began, but Julia cut her off.

"Oh, I think you understand perfectly well," she said, flicking her long hair back as a portly businessman walked past. His body visually shuddered with desire at the sight of her. Julia turned back to Eve and leaned in close, smiling in a way that deserved flashbulbs. She smelled like a Juicy Couture store looked.

"Just stay out of my way, okay, bitch?"

Before Eve could say a word, Julia pivoted on her Jimmy Choo strappy stilettos and walked out of the bar. Eve sat with her soggy pizza and felt her face go crimson. Janet was still in the ladies' room. She had no one to bounce this woman's audacity off of, so she had to hold the hot ball of humiliation in her own hands. It burned her fingertips with shame.

The man who had shuddered earlier turned around from the bar holding two drinks. His face fell when he saw Eve sitting by herself. Eve had been made to pay for so much in her life, but she refused to be on the hook for the disappointment on a horny businessman's face. The glasses in his hands burst into shatters with her misplaced anger. The brightly coloured liquid of the cocktails fell to the ground at his feet, staining the Italian shoes his wife had bought him.

Eve stormed out the door and into the street, hard on the heels of a woman who was refusing to pay. She didn't notice the two crows that sat sentinel-like on the wrought-iron railing of a hotel room balcony above her. She didn't see anything but her own fury at those who did not suffer as she did for the sin of wanting something they weren't meant to have.

FOURTEEN

You won't believe it. Dylan Penske fucking killed himself! It's Saturday, and I just found out this morning when Selena called me first thing. I don't dare tell Mom. She'd freak. Selena heard about it from a girl who's a candy striper at the hospital where they took him. Not that there was anything they could do. He'd blown his head off with one of his dad's collector shotguns. He tried to hang himself first with a belt, but it didn't work. He still had the black belt around his neck when they wheeled him into emergency. His father brought the shotgun along in the ambulance. As if the doctors could pull the bloody buckshot out of his son's caved-in head and stuff it back into the gun. Selena was all upset, like we might have had something to do with it. But come on, if you are in the mindset to blow your brains out, a few Funnel Head poems aren't going to send you over the edge. And besides, they were funny. Probably the only bright spot in his day.

I didn't have time last night to write about Zanax. Then again, it wasn't that exciting. Sure, the light show was pretty awesome, and the beats were sick, but half the senior class was on Molly. They think that makes them cool, but really, all it makes them is boring. Although Max Tyson had some kind of MDMA meltdown. At first they thought he was dancing, writhing on the floor like a worm with his shirt off. But then blood started leaking out of his nose and somebody called a teacher. I guess he was okay, because I saw him later slam-dancing against a gymnastic horse tucked behind the stage in the gym. Only people on drugs find other people on drugs interesting. To the rest of us, they just look pathetic. It might have been better before everyone got so high, but I got there late. It took me a while to find the blue hair dye to colour my wig, among other things.

That wig was great though. Between that and the big red rhinestone sunglasses I wore, no one knew it was me. I could glide through the crowd totally anonymous in a skirt so short you could see the cheeks of my ass if I bent over. I got to behave any way I wanted, knowing it wouldn't stick to me like dogshit on a shoe later when everyone was back in school. I have too much invested in my future to end up like other people, with grainy phone camera footage haunting them for-fucking-ever on the web. But nobody knew it was me. Even Selena wouldn't have recognized me. So I didn't have to worry. When Max Tyson rubbed up against me on the dance floor, his shirt off, exposing his scrawny chest, I decided to shock him. I ground my pubic bone right back into his crotch, crushing his pitiful hard-on. Then I whispered something in his ear that he'd never forget and tweaked one of his peach-fuzzed nipples. I walked away then, off the dance floor, leaving him there to figure it out. This was all before his meltdown of course.

Before I left for the night, I flashed my own nipples at a girl who was on her way into the washroom. I'm still not sure why I did it. Maybe just to see what would happen. The other girl just stood there mesmerized, her hand still on the door, half in, half out of the washroom. I could hear the other girls inside, messing around at the mirrors, laughing, and exchanging makeup. So close to coming out to see my nipples as they hardened in the cold fluorescent light. The girl wasn't from our school. She had frizzy red hair and freckles. I don't even think she was a senior. *I don't want to get in trouble*, she said, still not taking her eyes off my breasts. I pulled my top back down and walked out the front doors of the school. Cowards interest me less than people who are high all the time.

I still can't believe it about Dylan Penske. I mean, what would drive a person to do something like that? Really. I remember when Evelyn Gerbert's pad fell out of her underwear in the hallway when everyone was walking between classes last year. She was wearing her XL kilt and I guess her underwear was loose or something and the adhesive on the pad wore out. Although for god's sake, who does that happen to? She just froze in the hallway, not moving, staring at the bloody pad with the defective blue sticky strips running up the back curled up on the linoleum floor. Even when people started kicking the pad around, laughing, calling her a pig, making jokes about rags, she couldn't take her eyes off the thing. I mean it was horrible, but it's not like any of us could have done anything for her. Someone said she stood there until halfway through third period. That's when a teacher found her. She was crying in the empty hallway, still staring at the bloody pad on the floor. All that, and Evelyn Gerbert didn't kill herself. Although I think I would have if I'd been her.

Besides, I have a theory about things. Everything that happens to you is something you have coming. It's karma. It's cause and effect. It's fate. The kids like Evelyn Gerbert and Dylan Penske, the ones who have all the bad shit happen to them, it can't all be an accident. It's too fucking consistent. Sorry to say, but Dylan Penske chose to be weak, and Evelyn Gerbert chose to be fat, and everything else kind of flows from there. Whereas people like me make different choices and excel. No matter how you look at it, everybody gets what they deserve. I know that sounds harsh, but it's true.

Speaking of excelling, I have right in front of me an envelope from McGill University's Scholarship and Student Aid department. My mom didn't get the mail yesterday. She was too busy with Auntie Janet, doing who knows what. She didn't even get home until well after me last night. And Janet wasn't with her. I heard her trying to tiptoe up the stairs, but the floorboards creak right outside my room. I knew it was her, holding her high heels in her hands, trying not to wake anyone. I also knew what she'd been up to, at least earlier in the night, but I'm going to hold onto that little piece of information until I need it. Until I find something I want to trade it for.

So, I didn't discover the envelope until this morning, after Selena called about Dylan Penske. I know it has the results of my application inside, but I don't want to open it until I have somebody to get it all on video so they can capture my expression when I read that I got the Thompson Scholarship. I can't ask Selena for obvious reasons, or my parents. They don't even know I've applied. Maybe when Auntie Janet gets back, she can do it. Mom said she might stay over for the weekend. Janet's cool. Not like my mother at all. I don't know how they ended up being such good friends. I'm not sure I can wait for Janet to show, though. Maybe I'll just prop my phone up and film it myself. That way I can do a few takes if I need to.

Selena keeps texting me to call her again. But I want to take care of this first. She probably just wants to moan about Dylan Penske some more anyway. Maybe I'll go get some fruit for breakfast first, then film me opening the letter. Mom's out, and Dad's downstairs watching rugby. He doesn't even know I'm awake. I can't wait to post it all on Instagram. I'll act totally worried and unsure, maybe add some embarrassed laughter before I open up the envelope. Then I'll start reading the letter and stop midway a couple of times, like I'm too scared to go on. It's good to dole out the suspense. Then people will watch as my expression changes from nervous concern to fucking ecstatic as I read the news out loud. A free ride scholarship from McGill, all four years! Tears. Then I'll cool it off, tone it down to my modesty smile, like I don't really deserve it. Like it was nothing. Like getting here was easy. Even though everyone knows that it wasn't. People get what they deserve, and I'm only getting what's coming to me.

Karma's a bitch that can be made, baby. And a person like me, I make my own.

FIFTEEN

Richard unmuted the television to hear the commentators as he sat up on the couch. There was a tricky play being disputed and he wanted to understand what was at stake. The announcers were a bunch of British boneheads with accents that got on his nerves. Listening to the quick-flying debate on the scrum between a former head coach and a knee-shattered ex-forward, both from Hackney, made him cringe. His mother used to watch *Coronation Street* every weekend from the kitchen at full volume, struggling to hear over the frying bacon and eggs of his father's breakfast. Richard would lie in bed, desperate to sleep in, only to be assaulted by the trumpeting glottal stops and raised vowels of East End Londoners at maximum decibel. A dropped *h* still made him want to mash a pillow over the back of his head and scream. But he loved rugby, ever since he got into playing it in university. It was a stretch for him to be voluntarily awake this early on a Saturday morning, even now as a grown man. But the games were all played overseas, and the time difference required him to set his alarm early if he wanted to watch the action live.

He hurled a few obscenities at the screen, disagreeing with the analysis as well as the legitimacy of the forward's parentage. Then he lay back down on the couch and gagged the announcers with the mute button again, discarding the remote on the floor. The players moved back and forth on the screen in silent undulating waves.

Clasping his hands behind his head, he closed his eyes for a second to savour the quiet. Abbey was sleeping in, undisturbed like he wished he could have been at her age. She had got in late last night from that concert or whatever it was they had at the school. Richard had been the first one home, coming in just before midnight. He'd wanted to ask Eve what Abbey's curfew was, but his wife didn't return home until some time after his daughter. He'd feigned sleep in their king size bed so she would think he'd been home since after work. Eve's friend Janet was supposed to stay over, so he was saved from another night in the guest bedroom. Richard was glad to be back in Eve's bed. And not just because the one in the extra room screwed with his back.

When he had got up this morning, he'd seen through the open door that the folded guest towels lay undisturbed on the bed. Janet hadn't slept there. The two of them must have had quite the evening with Eve getting home so late and Janet still out on the prowl. Richard had always found Janet a little too wild for his tastes. Oh, he'd fantasized about her a few times. But after he'd guiltily masturbated to the image of those long legs in thigh-high boots, his dick would always hurt him, as if he'd tugged on it too hard. This alone had made him distrustful of her.

He was glad Janet had made an appearance though. Eve could do with some girl time. Richard was worried about her after the way she'd reacted to the dead cat. He'd been watching from around the corner of the house when Eve opened up the garbage can against his advice. Her behaviour seemed erratic, to say the least. But then again, Eve always had far too much empathy for animals. When Michael's last pet mouse died, she'd held the little broken body in her lap and stroked the white matted fur with real tears in her eyes. For god's sake, it was only a rodent.

Despite her late night, Eve had woken up before him this morning to go to her mother's, a weekly pilgrimage she made every Saturday. She wasn't due to be home until the afternoon. He wished they'd had a chance to talk, a rarity for him. But he wanted to catch her when Abbey wasn't around to eavesdrop. Also, he was afraid.

He'd lost his wedding ring. Eve was bound to notice eventually. She'd had it made specially for him, had it inscribed on the outside with runic characters she claimed would bring the marriage luck. On the inside she had etched a simple "To Richard" and the date. He'd loved that ring, but always had a hard time wearing it. His dad had brought him up to believe any man who wore jewellery on his hands was just asking to have his finger ripped off, either by the machinery of a good honest living or the shame of being a pansy. That's why he'd taken it off before doing the yard-work and left it on the tool bench. But when he'd looked for it this morning, he couldn't find it. Eve was going to kill him, particularly with everything that was going on.

There was a loud knock on the front door. Annoyed, Richard managed to sit up partway and twist around on the couch to get a look through the sheer curtains. Even though he only had a partial view, he recognized the fringed tufts of Sanjay Patel's balding pate. Indian guys don't usually lose their thick black hair so early, but Patel was a special case. He'd told Richard that the trait was passed down through his maternal Irish grandfather, balding by twenty-five and fully grey by thirty. The latter had happened overnight in the 1970s, his granddad had insisted, when an IRA bomb went off in a mailbox less than a minute after he'd dropped a Christmas card to his sister in it. He uprooted the whole family to Canada after that, only to find Quebec separatists blowing up mailboxes there as well. Sanjay's mother told him that right up until her father's death at eighty-nine years of age, he still refused to open his own mail.

"Hey, Sanjay," Richard said after he opened the door. Patel stood on the front stoop, running one hand through what was left of his hair. In his other hand, he held a cylinder of rolled up papers. Richard hoped to hell he hadn't come to invite him and Eve to one of his concerts. Richard liked a bit of Vivaldi's *Four Seasons* when he was in the mood, but for the most part, he found classical music a good excuse for a nap.

"Hi, Richard," Sanjay said. His voice seemed to boom after the stillness of Richard's muted morning. Worried they'd wake Abbey, Richard stepped outside, leaving the front door open a crack. Sanjay was a decent guy. But he wanted to make this encounter brief so he could get back to the rugby game. The cool cement of the front steps leaked through the socks he had on. The late spring morning sun hadn't reached the front of the house yet. Sanjay stuck his free hand into a pocket to warm it, but Richard wasn't about to let him come in out of the cold. This was a tactic he'd learned from his business dealings. You had to create an atmosphere of slight discomfort for everyone involved so people wouldn't linger over banalities — just say whatever they had to say and then get the hell on their way.

"I guess you've heard about Cuchulain?" Sanjay said. It took a moment for Richard to remember that this was their cat. He'd never seen the animal himself. At the few parties they'd attended at Sanjay and Sharon's, it had always been outside roaming the neighbourhood. How did a person even call for a pet with that many syllables in its name?

"What happened to Cuchulain?" Richard's words were casual, but as soon as they'd left his mouth, he realized the connection. He remembered the Cheshire grin festering with sprouting maggots in the garbage can. He'd thrown a shiny white kitchen bag on top of its squirmy smile before rolling the can to the curb for pickup.

"She's gone missing." Sanjay peeled back a photocopied poster from his cylinder roll. Richard saw the picture that dominated the page, a black-and-beige tabby wearing a kitty-sized Santa hat. The branch of a Christmas tree photobombed the picture, along with a hand that was trying to keep the hat in place.

"Shit, Sanjay. That's a shame," Richard said, and meant it. He'd lost a dog to a Pepperidge Farm bakery truck when he was thirteen. He'd never walked or fed the fat corgi his entire childhood, but when his father had lifted the lifeless bundle in an old towel onto the front lawn, Richard had cried hard enough to get a cuff from the old man to shut him up. Jeremy Holloway and he had buried the animal in a ravine that ran behind the house. When he went back a week later to put down flowers, something had dug the dog up and dragged it away. Richard hadn't stuck around to see where it had gone.

"I wondered if you'd seen her, you know, around?" Sanjay held the poster out. Richard took it like he was being handed the corpse of his long dead dog.

"Sorry, man. I'm afraid I haven't." Richard couldn't tell the guy he'd thrown his cat out with the kitchen scraps. It would be like *Porgie the Corgi* all over again. He went to give the poster back, but Patel wouldn't take it.

"Maybe you can keep the poster, ask around," Sanjay said. "Selena's a mess over it. She just had kittens, you know."

At first Richard thought Sanjay meant his daughter, but then he put it all together. He nodded as if he knew all along about the reproductive escapades of the Patel family's pet. He was not good at keeping up on other people's news. Eve was the one responsible for updating him on who was putting an addition on their house or planning a second honeymoon to France. But their conversation had dwindled over the last five years, consisting mostly of the bare bones of a slightly shared life. What time Abbey had to be picked up for basketball or whether the roof needed to be repaired. Eve had been the one in the marriage who kept an eye on the world of others for him. With her keeping him in the loop, he was at the ready when they found themselves in social situations, asking after someone's latest basement renovation project or an aging mother's health. But these days, he just stood there dumb, nodding in the right places when people spoke to him. As a result, he was not overly surprised when Sanjay mentioned yet another thing he didn't know about.

"It's such a good thing she found out about the Thompson scholarship today. My Selena. Just before I left the house." Sanjay beamed, despite holding a cylinder full of dead cat posters. "It took her mind off Cuchulain. She got it, you know. The scholarship."

Richard was nodding, knowing nothing, when he heard the crash from the kitchen. A hollow bang and then a revolving rattle sounded before whatever was dropped settled on the floor. He looked quickly through the crack in the door, then returned to face Patel.

"Sounds like the dog is kicking his bowl around again. I guess I forgot to feed him," Richard said, acting sheepish. He knew it probably wasn't the dog, but it felt like a solid enough excuse to get rid of Sanjay and get him back to his game. He held up the poster. "I'll make sure to keep a look out for the cat."

Sanjay shook his hand and thanked him, then walked away down the steps. Richard slipped back in the front door and shut it. He dropped the poster on the hall table, knocking a lone googly eye to the floor. The mirror shimmered slightly with an image he wouldn't have recognized as himself, a man standing in the dark street last night, wiping the snot from his nose, ashamed of what he'd done. But he didn't notice his reflection. Men weren't quick to recognize magic. And when they did, it was only in the most rudimentary of ways. They felt it when they attended the birth of a child or lost themselves in a woman's eyes, but it often frightened them, inspiring suspicion as often as wonder. Some had the gift to see, but it was rare. Bypassing the poster, the mirror, and the googly eye, Richard went to the kitchen to figure out if it was indeed the dog's bowl that had caused all the racket.

Abbey stood with her back to the sink. A metal bowl with cut-up fruit Eve had prepared for snacking was spilled out on the floor. His daughter's face was bright red, like she'd been holding her breath.

"Are you okay, Abbey?" He looked down at the chunks of pineapple and orange cantaloupe. A deeply purple grape had rolled across the floor to rest by a kitchen chair.

Abbey didn't answer him. He wondered if this was some sort of hormonal thing with teenage girls he wasn't aware of. Something to do with periods or boys. Or maybe she was having a seizure. Richard had been a lifeguard as a young man and had enough first aid training to know they didn't always fall to ground or jerk about. But Abbey was completely controlled when she finally spoke, and the only jerk appeared to be him.

"I met that lady — Julia," she spat at him from across the kitchen. "At your work."

Now it was Richard's turn not to breathe. He thought about the unlocked drawer in his office. The booty phone in plain sight with no password on it, because who wanted to take the time to enter a fucking password when a woman was texting you a picture of her panties.

Abbey sidestepped the mess on the floor, squashing the grape into the granite tile. She stood beside her father, facing the opposite way. Fat hot tears threatened to squeeze out the corners of her cool grey eyes.

What had he done? To Eve. To Abbey. To his family. Were a few sweaty grunts on top of a woman who was not his wife worth all of this? He'd been weak, seeking refuge from the pain Eve and he shared in what he'd believed to be pleasure. Now he knew it was just a mistake he got used to making. But that was all over now. He'd rectified that mistake on Friday night, for good this time. Now, all he needed to do was make it up to his family.

"Abbey," he began, reaching to wipe the tears away, like when she was little and skinned a knee. But she stepped away to face him, an angry woman betrayed, not a hurt little girl at all.

"I met her," Abbey said, allowing one furious tear to fall, before she donned a forced and inappropriate smile. It chilled Richard worse than the cold pavement had on the front porch with Sanjay.

"Oh, Abbey ..."

"She was a fraud, *just like you.*" Abbey enunciated each word with that tight-mouthed grin. Then her face fell, the mirthless smile gone, and she was a little girl again, running back up the stairs to her bedroom, her ponytail swishing behind her like a metronome.

ABBEY DIDN'T COME DOWNSTAIRS UNTIL dinnertime, and then she only picked up her meal and returned to her room. She'd given the excuse of a Netflix binge, the new season of *13 Reasons Why* was out. But Richard knew better. By then he had cleaned up the fruit and dumped it in the green bin. Eve was home from visiting her mother, but Janet was still missing. Richard had never gotten to see the end of the rugby game.

"Abbey has a basketball game tomorrow at four. She's playing forward for the first time," Eve said, as she cleared the dishes from the table set for two. "You remembered, didn't you?"

Richard stood and took the plates from her cautiously, mindful of her rib.

"Of course," he said. Even though both of them knew he hadn't. He started to scrape the leftover food from the dishes into the garbage under the sink by mistake.

"That should probably go in the green bin," Eve reminded him.

Richard paused mid-scrape, looking into the plastic kitchen bag hung on the back of the cupboard door. Within it, the black-and-white poster of Cuchulain lay in jagged torn shreds among shards of broken glass. He hesitated a moment, considering, then dumped the rest of the food scraps in on top. Then he loaded the plates in the dishwasher next to the metal bowl that had held the spilled fruit. Sometimes it was too late to change a mistake.

But when it came to his family, Richard decided he was ready to try.

SIXTEEN

The buzzer blasted from the big clock on the wall, making Eve jump even though she knew it was coming. It was half-time. The team mascot danced onto the court with his oversized head and stuffed bodysuit. He was supposed to be a gladiator and wore a bronze helmet and a short pleated centurion battle skirt. There was something obscene about a warrior with bare hairy legs bumping and grinding at a girls' basketball game, even if he was made out of rubber. Eve and Richard sat high up in the gymnasium bleachers, directly under the electronic scoreboard. So close that whenever the timer went off it felt like a personal assault.

Eve closed her eyes and breathed out the anxiety heightened by the buzzer. She'd enjoyed the first half of the game, but it had been a stressful trip to get there. Abbey had insisted they stop to pick up a supply of her favourite kombucha drink from the health food store. It made them late. They only just managed to drop the girls off in time, arriving at the entrance five minutes before game time. The two friends had clambered out of the SUV in their high-top basketball shoes, clutching the bottles of overpriced green tea as they ran for the door. Eve hoped the coach hadn't bawled them out.

"Do you want anything?" Richard stood up from the hard bench and stretched. He had been trying very hard to be nice to her these last couple of days, and it made her slightly uncomfortable. Like there was another shoe left to drop, and he was softening her up for the impact.

"No, that's okay."

Richard stepped up to the top bleacher, walking along it like a balance beam to the aisle before jumping down to the floor to make his way to the washrooms. He was in good shape, despite never going to the gym or otherwise fighting to maintain his physique. Men his age could be like that, while women had to sweat in core strengthening classes just to keep their middle-aged muffin tops at bay.

Mark went to the gym regularly. He was the type of man who seemed to do everything right. Had his snow tires on in September. Replaced the batteries in his smoke alarms each spring. His habits were like the well-worn words of a spell, repeated over and over to conjure a perfect life. It had attracted Eve at first, until she realized his magic was a superficial one, like that of most people who tried to find salvation in the strength of a to-do list.

Eve turned her attention to the home team players' bench. Abbey was readjusting her ponytail, trying to put back a few errant strands that had come loose during play. She wound the elasticized band around her hair so many times Eve was afraid it would snap. The team mascot took his gladiator head off to drink from a water bottle. She noticed his real face was blotchy and had pimples.

Abbey had kept up a brave front, congratulating her friend on her scholarship with hugs and warm smiles when Selena came to the house before the game. But Eve was privy to the hitched sobs in her daughter's bedroom the night before. When she'd knocked, Abbey told her to go away. Eve didn't understand then what she'd been upset about, but she knew enough to back off when her daughter adopted a certain tone. Sharing pain with your mother could sometimes open the floodgates too wide. Many young girls, as well as full-grown women, preferred to handle their hurt outside a mother's long reach, where the dam of emotion could be better maintained.

Had Eve known about the scholarship, she might have made excuses to Sharon Patel when she called this morning looking for a ride to the game for her daughter. She wouldn't ask, Sharon had said, but there was an emergency rehearsal Sanjay had scheduled. They were a mess for their upcoming performance of *The Firebird* at Roy Thomson Hall in Toronto. But Eve liked Selena, even liked Sharon on a good day, so she'd agreed. It was only then that Sharon told her about the Thompson scholarship. How proud they were of Selena. What a close race it had been between the girls. Sharon really hoped Abbey wasn't taking it too hard. Eve had looked through the door to the kitchen and seen Abbey sitting alone at the breakfast table, a bowl of untouched Honey Nut Cheerios in front of her. Her eyes were red-rimmed and demoralized. For once, her daughter looked like all the fight had gone out of her. Eve had retreated back to the hall with her hand cupped over the receiver so Abbey wouldn't hear her congratulations.

Eve adjusted herself on the unforgiving wood of the bleacher. There was no back support for her rib, so she placed her purse behind her as a makeshift cushion and tried to lean against the side railing. She kept the cellphone inside the bag pressed against her lower back. It was set to vibrate, so as not to disturb the play. Usually, she would just turn the damn thing off, but Janet still hadn't shown, and she didn't want to miss it if she called. She'd sent a text Friday night, asking where Eve had gone after leaving her with the bill. But Eve hadn't responded until much later, which had probably pissed her off. Her friend could have discovered where Eve was through other means, but she respected her privacy and did not invoke that talent unless it was absolutely necessary. Eve no longer had the ability to divine Janet's whereabouts, but she could sense she was okay. They retained that much of a psychic bond. It wasn't unlike her to go missing like this, to be drawn in by a shiny thing or person and then disappear for a few days. This was a characteristic of those with an artistic temperament, the tendency toward distraction. Still, Eve hoped Janet would call soon. She needed to hear her voice. Although Eve wasn't sure she was prepared to share what happened after she rushed out of the Delta after Julia. A decision that had led to other much worse ones.

Play resumed, and Eve concentrated on the game again. Richard returned to cheer loudly beside her. His booming voice competed with the air horn that blasted from the opposing team's block of fans. Across the aisle, a mother waved a gigantic foam fist with the pointer finger in a permanent Number 1 position. Another woman consulted a laminated list of team players' names with corresponding jersey numbers. The coach had distributed them so each girl could receive personalized encouragement even if you didn't know who they were. *Go Ashley! Good pass, Shannon! Better luck next time, Cassie!* A man in the front row rang a cow bell held tightly in his fist. It was all part of the carnival madness of parents who cheered their children on to vanquish someone else's progeny. The Gladiator mascot replaced his head. He raised a rubber shield and sword from the sidelines in military support.

The girls ran up and down the shiny wood floor of the high-school gym, sweat glistening on their foreheads. Abbey's eyes were no longer red from crying, but focused and defiant as she guarded a girl much bigger than her. Abbey had never been one of the taller ones, having had her major growth spurt only just this year. But what she lacked in reach, she made up for with tenacity. In every game, she had to keep a delicate balance between the number of personal fouls she racked up and the points that playing rough could net her. The one time Eve's mother had come to watch Abbey play, she'd been shocked to see what looked like her granddaughter tripping another player to get control of the ball.

"There's always been something wrong with that girl," her mother had said.

Eve had wanted to talk to her mother about that comment when she visited her yesterday. About what kind of wrongness she might have seen in Abbey. Or about the horrible run-in with Julia. Or even about her affair with Mark. But instead, she'd kept busy tidying and dusting her childhood home as she usually did, avoiding such conversations.

"Don't move anything," her mother had warned from her chair in the living room.

"I won't, Mom." Her mother didn't want her to touch any of the yellowed pieces of paper, curled at the edges, that were left all around the house. Each held the same fading shaky blue script. They were notes written by Eve's father, who'd been gone for years, but her mother refused to throw them out. Instead, they were left in situ throughout her home. *Buy cat litter*, read the one on the dining room table. *Oil change for car*, reminded another resting on the toilet tank. Eve had picked up each one carefully and cleaned underneath, before placing them back down exactly as she'd found them. Eve's father had suffered a massive stroke that rendered him speechless shortly before he died. They'd stood at his death bed, as he smacked his lips together discordantly, unable to communicate the things he may have needed to say. Eve's mother had always felt cheated of the possible profoundness of her husband's last words, so she refused to let go of the mundane ones he'd inadvertently left behind.

Eve wished she could have talked to her mother about her granddaughter. But those words seemed to curl up inside of her like the yellowed papers. She didn't want to worry her mother, or disappoint her, she wasn't sure which. Perhaps she should write down the truth in a note and leave it among her father's, to be swallowed up in banal requests, where it wouldn't hurt either of them to hear it.

Her mother might have agreed with Janet and told her all girls were like Abbey when they were young. But Eve still found this hard to believe. She remembered her and Janet playing Slapjack behind Nanny's farmhouse as teenagers, long summer afternoons spent laughing with the smell of hay and manure in the air. Abbey didn't seem to possess that amount of carefree joy in her day-to-day life. Her daughter had a more regimented approach when it came to happiness, convinced it came from following the rules. When Michael sat on the railing that day, he was breaking them. Eve had been busy on the phone. She hadn't seen Abbey walk out of her bedroom, her pink fleece blanket with the red hearts on it drawn around her, a discarded book on the floor. She hadn't seen until it was too late. Eve had dropped the phone reaching out to try and pull her back, but only managed to grasp the soft nap of the pink blanket, pulling it off in her hands, as Abbey pushed Michael over the edge.

"Look at me." Michael had smiled gleefully from the railing in his pyjamas. And Abbey had stepped toward him.

"You shouldn't be doing that."

And then he was gone.

Only Janet knew. And she insisted it was an accident. That Abbey was only a child herself. That it wasn't the Ragman forcing her daughter's hand, speaking those cold warning words. Just a kid who didn't know any better, who'd wanted to stop her brother from doing something dangerous. But Eve had been there. Eve had seen the truth.

There was always something wrong with that girl.

The sound of the crowd in the bleachers roared up, surrounding Eve in a wave of the present. Richard was up on his feet, cheering. The only daughter he could see was the one who'd made a perfect shot on a rebound to tie up the score with seconds left in the third quarter. The shock of the buzzer sounded again, knocking Eve out of the memory she tried every day to forget.

"Did you see that?" Richard said. "That was fucking amazing!"

Abbey glowed as her teammates held her up, carrying her to the sidelines. They grabbed drinks from the cooler the coach kept behind the bench and Abbey popped the top off one of her kombuchas. She leaned her head back so far to drink it that her ponytail touched her spine. Then she whipped her head back up and wiped at the sweat and the drink that clung to her lips, breaking into a bright laugh. She fell in with rest of the girls in black-and-yellow Gladiator jerseys, a part of them. At home there was a picture on the fridge of Abbey and Selena in their uniforms, arms around one another, grinning. Underneath, Richard had written in block letters *Glad Girls!* with a thick black Sharpie.

Eve understood she needed to see Abbey like this. As Richard saw her. As the world saw her. Not as that twelve-year-old in a pink blanket who'd made a horrible mistake. For surely it hadn't been intentional. Janet was right. Only Eve could be made to pay the price for the sins of Abbey's conception. Her daughter was just a normal teenage girl, full of all the venom and vigour that supported that precarious bundle of budding hormones. She was no different from her peers, angry outbursts and all. Eve dealt with the horror of what happened to Michael with a sadness that insulated her from the world, but maybe Abbey used fury as her protective armour. A far healthier approach when Eve thought about it. However Abbey managed, Eve hoped her daughter didn't remember the role she'd played in her brother's death. She had been young, and youth had a way of forgetting. Abbey never said anything about it. And with the exception of Janet, neither had Eve.

"I'm sorry," Richard said. He was sitting down in his seat again, so close to Eve that their knees touched together. Eve turned to look at the man who have given her daughter the colour of her eyes.

"For what," she said. There was so much to be sorry about, for both of them.

"I'm sorry about what's happened," he said. "To us." He could be talking about the affair. He could be talking about Michael. He could be talking about the falling away that any two people could experience over time in a marriage, where life's rough edges eroded the shaky foundations two people who fall in love always stand on.

"I want to make things better." Richard fidgeted with the laminated card of team players' names and numbers in his hands. Eve didn't know he had one. Maybe he got it from the lady with the Number 1 finger.

The players returned to the court, and the clock behind Richard and Eve started up again as the final quarter began. Richard dropped the laminated card on the bench next to him and took Eve's hand in both of his. His touch felt warm and familiar, and she relaxed a little.

The referee's whistle sounded and both of them looked up. The opposing team had gone for a basket and the ball was stuck between the backboard and the hoop. It happened sometimes. The coach went to get a broom to knock the ball down. Eve's phone vibrated at the small of her back. Apologizing, she released Richard's hands and went to grab it out of her purse, not bothering to look at the call display.

"Hello?" She couldn't hear in the noisy gym. "Is that you, Janet?" Eve took the same route as Richard had at half-time to get down out of the stands. By the time she reached the floor, the referee had the ball down and Abbey was in position to take a rare jump ball. Abbey glanced quickly at her mother before turning her attention back to the ref and her opponent. Eve stood just outside the open gym doors so Abbey could see she was still watching. The referee blew his whistle and threw up the ball as Eve dug her finger into one ear so she could listen better with the other. Abbey missed the ball and the girl from the other team dribbled it swiftly down the court.

"Janet?" she whispered into the phone. "Janet, is that you?"

"Eve?" It was her mother. "Are you out?"

"Yes, Mom." Eve tried to keep her eye on Abbey as she moved to block one of the forwards from taking a shot. The other girl moved frantically left and right looking for someone to throw the ball to. But Abbey bobbed and weaved and met her every move, like a black-and-yellow hornet. "I'm at Abbey's basketball game."

"I just wanted to tell you there's a bad storm coming. I saw it in my email." Eve had set up weather alerts to her mother's iPad from Environment Canada. By clicking on the link provided, she could keep track of every potential weather disaster in her vicinity. The tornado warnings that never produced tornadoes, the travel advisories that predicted black ice. It was a favourite pastime of her mother's, to contact Eve with the latest threatening meteorological prediction to make sure she was aware of it.

The girl on the other team with the ball moved to go around Abbey. Abbey stepped in front of her, and the girl stumbled and lost control. The ball bounced out of bounds. Eve bit on one ragged fingernail, waiting to see if her daughter would get called for interference. But the referee must have decided it was an honest mistake. He retrieved the ball and handed it to Abbey. She walked to the sidelines. The referee blew his whistle. Abbey madly looked for a teammate to receive the ball. She usually passed to Selena, but she was still on the bench. The Gladiator mascot sat beside her. Eve could see his eyes through the wire mesh in his centurion smile.

"It could be bad for driving. You better make sure you get home before it gets dark." It was one o'clock in the afternoon and they were ten minutes from their house.

"Listen, Mom, can I call you back?" Abbey was running to the opposite end of the court now, her team having kept possession of the ball. The coach tapped Selena on the shoulder, and she stood up at the ready. Taking one last swig from her bottle of kombucha, she ran out onto the court to relieve Abbey, who'd just been passed the ball from a teammate. It didn't seem fair, but the score was so close. They needed a basket, and Selena was taller and more refined with her jump shot.

But Selena didn't make it to relieve Abbey. She stopped and took to one knee on the mid-court line, like one of those football players protesting the American national anthem. Her fingers clawed and groped at her throat as if to pull off invisible hands that sought to strangle her. The guard up against Abbey saw her and got distracted. Abbey popped around her and made a perfect shot off the back of the net. The woman with the laminated card screamed as blood spurted from Selena's mouth in choking waves. It spilled out onto the varnished gym floor, making a glossy puddle.

"Eve, are you still there?" her mother called from someplace far away. Eve had dropped the phone to her side without hanging up. Her mother's faint voice reached up like a desperate cry from another dimension.

The coach rushed onto the court followed by the gladiator. He tripped trying to reach Selena in his cumbersome bodysuit, falling on his sword. Tiny sparkles twinkled in the shiny pool of red expanding on the floor in front of Selena. People might have thought it was a trick of the bright white fluorescent lights overhead. But Eve knew what it was.

Shards of vicious broken glass.

SEVENTEEN

Selena is in the hospital.

I was having the game of my life when all of a sudden everyone started screaming. I turned around and there she was in the middle of the court, spitting up blood! She'd swallowed glass from a drink I'd given her. I can tell Mom's all upset because she thinks it could have been me that got hurt, but I would have noticed if there was glass in my drink. I'm observant that way. I don't know how Selena missed it. Dad had bought the kombucha on the way to the game and I'd made sure he got one for Selena. Her mother never buys her healthy stuff like that. Sharon says kombucha's just a fad. Like Tamagotchis or something. Anyway, Selena'd been drinking it just before the coach tagged her to replace me. Which was really stupid because I was totally killing it with a triple threat. If they had replaced me, I wouldn't have made that basket to break the tie. I wonder if they'll count it. I mean, I understand they had to call the game and all, but that doesn't mean everybody's hard work has to be for nothing. They should at least let the score stand. We actually have a chance of making the provincials this year.

Anyway, they took everyone's drinks away after that, including our water bottles. They even fished the plastic throwaway ones that are murdering the environment out of the trash. The cops all had latex gloves on. It was like an episode of *CSI*. That was after the ambulance took Selena away. I didn't get to see much of her before that, when she started coughing up the blood. The coach and half the gym were on her in like two seconds. Ashley Stravinsky's dad is a doctor and they let him through the crowd to try and help. Although I don't know how much he could have done. I looked up online what you're supposed to do if you swallow a sharp object, and you can't really do anything. Except try not to lose your shit until they get you to the hospital. I wanted to get through the people, to get to Selena. I *am* her best friend. But my mom held me back, grabbing onto my arm, pulling me into her. As if I couldn't handle it. I'm going to be a doctor myself, for Christ's sake. If she thinks I'm going to freak out over a little blood, she's nuts. I know I was crying and stuff, but that was completely understandable.

Of course, Mom hadn't even been watching the game. She was on the fucking phone. Couldn't even disconnect for a one-hour basketball game. But that's typical of her. She never pays attention to me. It's like I don't exist, except when she's pissed at me for something. I mean, I was dying yesterday when I found out about the Thompson scholarship, and where was she? Over at Grandma's house cleaning. Grandma got a ton of money after Grandpa died. She can afford a goddamn cleaning lady. But my mom wants to look like a good daughter, doing it herself. I think she just wants an excuse not to have to talk to Grandma when she's visiting. Mom's always getting upset at her over nothing. Their relationship is so messed up.

I hadn't even opened the envelope from McGill when that dumbass Mr. Patel had to go blabbing to Dad about it at the front door. Selena's dad must have known I was up for the award too. He was just pretending he'd come about their stupid cat so he could brag about his brilliant daughter beating me out. Dad didn't even get it. He congratulated him and came into the kitchen like nothing had happened. As if my life hadn't just been completely destroyed. Dad doesn't usually make me angry. Not like Mom. But the way he stood there, so clueless, looking a total blank — it drove me crazy. I wanted to reach out and mash his face into the kitchen counter until it actually held an expression. Instead, I hit him with what I knew about Julia. That got a reaction. That whole situation is completely crazy. I can't even picture the two of them doing it together. It's disgusting. Partly because he's my dad and partly because he's so goddamn old.

Anyway, I haven't told either of my parents about the scholarship. They wouldn't understand. They're too busy with their own meltdown of a marriage to give a shit about what's happening with me or give a damn about my happiness. Parents talk about wanting their kids to be happy, but they don't want us to be. Not really. Unless it's their brand of happiness, full of the outdated baggage they carry around packed with all the things they wanted but didn't get. As if their kids are somehow responsible for living out a better version of their screwed-up lives instead of our own. Parents don't realize that all their kids really need to be happy is for them to let us do whatever the hell we want, instead of what they want for us.

Dad's at the hospital right now with Selena. I wonder if she's in the same one as they brought Dylan Penske to when he shot himself. He could be in the morgue right now while she's in emergency. Although he's probably at the funeral home by now. They don't let dead bodies sit around for long. Mom and Dad sent me to this summer camp at the university for girls in the sciences when I was in junior high. They let us work with the arms of real cadavers to see how the nerves worked. The lady who brought the arms said they move the bodies along pretty quickly at the hospital. They've got bed shortages as it is.

Dad had to go with Selena to the hospital because her parents weren't there and she needed a guardian. The coach would have gone, but he had to stay and talk to the cops. I had to talk to the cops too, along with the rest of the team. Although I had to stay the longest because it was my kombucha. Mom kept hovering over my shoulder while the detective asked me questions, interrupting every few seconds as if I was some kind of moron who couldn't speak for myself. She's here with me at the house right now, trying to be supportive and shit. Like when she knocked on my door last night after it happened, all worried and empathetic looking. I hate that look. I mean, I know Selena's going to be okay. Mom doesn't have to be so upset. Like I said, I read about it all on WebMD. They just have to expand Selena's esophagus with a balloon and pull out the glass. She'll be fine. I did read that damage to the soft tissue can be tricky though. It all depends on where the shards got lodged. If some made it all the way to her stomach, it could be a while before Selena comes back to school. She's got to maintain a certain average for the rest of the year, or they won't let her keep the scholarship. That would be impossible to do from a hospital bed. Which would be really shitty, but if she's not well she probably shouldn't be going all the way to Montreal for school anyway. There are decent universities here. A couple of them aren't even that bad. I wouldn't go to any of them, but Selena has always been a bit of a homebody. It would probably be better for her. She'd be happier. And unlike parents, as her best friend, I actually want her to be happy.

Anyway, I hope she's okay. When they took her away in the ambulance, she looked so small, bundled up in a blanket and tied down on the stretcher. They must have given her something to sedate her because she wasn't twitching anymore. Mom says I can't go to the hospital until tomorrow at the earliest. But that's okay, because when Dad comes home he can tell me how Selena's doing and when she'll be coming home. Because if it's going to be a long time, she'll have to forfeit the scholarship. That may sound harsh, but it's just the truth. You've got to live in the real world. But at least Selena will know that the scholarship will be going to me. I was the runner-up. So it won't be so bad. If you are going to lose something, it's better if it's to a friend. And I'm Selena's best friend.

I know she would want me to be happy.

EIGHTEEN

"Health card number please." One of the nurses who helped to wheel Selena through the emergency room doors badgered Richard with questions he couldn't answer. She had a fine spray of Selena's blood on the sleeve of her blue scrubs.

"I'm sorry, I don't know her health card number." A violent hammering started up on the glass behind Richard's chair. Shaken already, he turned to see a woman wearing a black stovepipe hat that sprouted flowers. They were purple and red and shaped like daisies. She shouted from the waiting area, brandishing a bicycle pump in her hand. The glass muffled her demands.

"Date of birth?" asked the nurse, not looking up from her computer.

Richard tore himself away from the wildly shaking flowers of the stovepipe hat. He thought hard to recall Selena's last birthday. It had been cold out and Abbey couldn't drive yet. She and Selena had asked him to take them to the movie theatre. They were going to see that superhero movie all the kids were crazy about, the one where the hero was a bit of a fuck-up. Anti-heroes were in, he supposed. The girls had worn jackets. Was it early winter or late spring?

"I'm sorry," Richard apologized again. "She's not my daughter."

He was ashamed by the degree of comfort he drew from those words. It could have been Abbey on that stretcher, rushed down the corridor with attendants hollering vital signs. It could have been Abbey's blood on the nurse's blue scrubs. It was just an accident of fate that Selena drank from the bottle full of glass and not his own daughter. This parallel possibility floored him. Having lost one child already to random circumstance, he couldn't fathom a world cruel enough to see him faced with losing another.

Richard's first reaction when Selena had fallen to her knees on the court was to selfishly search the gym for his own child. Scanning the court, he'd located Abbey underneath the opposing team's basket, holding the ball she'd just sent whistling through it. Everyone had been rushing onto the floor, but he couldn't take his eyes off of Abbey. She tilted her head from side to side as if she were working out a kink in her neck, then dribbled the ball twice, sharply, on the floorboards. It looked like impatience, but

Richard knew she'd just been in shock. He'd gone to race down the bleachers, but people were up by then and blocking his way. Eve had gotten to their daughter first. She held Abbey in her arms while she cried, the basketball discarded and rolling around at the sidelines. When Richard finally reached them, he'd wanted to hold them both. But he stood back instead, too fearful of rejection.

To think that his own daughter might have drunk from that bottle. That she might have been taken from him before he had a chance to rewrite the story she had in her head of what kind of man he was. Before he could prove to her that Julia was gone from their lives forever and that he would never lie to her or her mother again. At least, not about the things that were important.

The woman with the stovepipe hat thudded on the Plexiglas window with her bicycle pump in a slow rhythmic beat. Richard clutched his hands in his lap, nervously wringing them.

"If she's not your daughter, what relationship do you have with the patient?" the nurse asked, one eyebrow raised. Richard didn't like the implication of that arch. Or maybe he was just sensitive, having recently and repeatedly bedded a woman who was only a few years older than Selena. They were important years, he'd convinced himself. Like dog years, he had weighed them differently. But under the nurse's accusing gaze, he found it hard to hide from the brutal honesty of the math.

"She's a friend of my daughter's." Richard puffed himself up in the chair. "I was attending their basketball game with my wife." He emphasized the "wife" part. He wanted to confirm to the nurse his ability to have a relationship with a fully grown adult. The nurse still eyed him suspiciously.

Richard wished the nurse would ask him about what had happened, not about these other trivial bureaucratic details. It surprised him, this desire to spill his guts to a stranger. But he needed to unload the image of Selena, catatonic and leaking blood out of her pale red mouth in the ambulance. To re-gift the experience to someone else, like a hideous, unwanted Christmas present. Those colourless lips, as if they had just kissed dry ice, reminded him of Michael's when they'd taken Richard to see his son for the very last time.

"Then what's your daughter's birthday?" the nurse asked with a sigh, fingers poised above the keyboard. One of them had a tatty Band-Aid on the tip. The glass behind Richard continued to reverberate with the stovepipe hat woman's steady beat.

Richard had to think hard again. He eventually came up with a month and a number that was, give or take a few days, the date of Abbey's birth. The nurse dutifully entered the information into Selena's file.

"Is she going to be okay?" Richard asked, after he'd answered the rest of her questions as best he could. He'd found Selena's address and phone number by pulling up Sanjay Patel's details from the contacts in his phone. Luckily, Richard didn't need to call him. The coach had done that. Richard remembered when the hospital had tried to reach him about Michael. His phone had been set to silent in a meeting. It was only when a teary-eyed receptionist broke into the room that he'd looked down to see the fifteen missed calls.

"The doctors are taking care of her," the nurse said. Richard wanted to ask her more questions, so she could give him more reassuring answers. But she'd gotten up from her desk to stare down the woman in the stovepipe hat through the glass. The woman stopped her banging and stared back with the angry flowers jiggling back and forth. As they glared at each other, a thick binder of hospital procedures fell from a bookshelf behind the nurse's desk. It landed with a crash to the floor. Neither woman looked away from their standoff through the glass. The stovepipe hat woman finally admitted defeat, turning abruptly away as the bendy flowers bobbed and weaved above her head. She sat down on a plastic chair opposite, crossing her legs. Rainbow-striped leggings popped out of a tattered pair of knee-length short pants Richard's mother would have called culottes. On her feet she wore a pair of well-scuffed army boots that looked like she did a lot of kicking with them.

The nurse returned to her desk, smoothed her hair down at the crown where a couple of witchy grey hairs had popped up.

"I'll take you to the inner waiting area now." She popped a sheet of paper from the printer onto a clipboard, then tucked it under her arm. "Follow me." The nurse stepped around the heavy hospital binder, leaving it on the floor where it had fallen. Then she opened the door next to the window and they entered the chaos of the outer waiting room. Richard fell in behind her. An old woman with salt-and-pepper hair smiled sweetly from a plastic chair. The lady with the stovepipe hat waved her bicycle pump at him like a thunder stick. He gave both of them a wide berth.

The big double doors through which Selena had so recently travelled opened when another nurse buzzed them through. They swished behind them and closed, sealing him in like he was in a vacuum jar or a coffin.

The nurse dropped the clipboard in an overflowing in-basket. Richard heard an old man moaning from behind a curtain. A young woman softly sobbed in Spanish as she rocked back and forth in a chair.

"Take a seat. It's quieter here," the nurse told Richard before she left to go back through the double doors.

Richard sat down in a chair not far from the Spanish girl. A large television set with closed captions was bolted in the corner of the waiting area with the volume turned off. It was set to a news station where a constant ticker tape of headlines ran under the video feed of silent announcers. The closed captions overwrote the ticker tape words, so that all the letters became unintelligible.

Richard had not sat here after being called from work about Michael. They had a special room in the hospital for parents with dead children. It was windowless and had an overstuffed love seat that took up the width of one end. The doctor had sat at a small desk with nothing on it, not even a stethoscope or a pen. The desk served only as a prop. It was designed to lend the doctor a degree of professionalism and authority, so when they communicated the news there would no demands for a second opinion. The finality of death could not be disputed when it was told to you from behind the official dispatch of a desk.

Richard pulled out his phone and found Sanjay Patel's details still open in his contacts. He thought about calling him but decided against it. Sanjay would only bombard him with questions worse than the nurse had. None of which he felt he could answer. Richard attempted to calculate distance and speed in order to determine the Patels' estimated time of arrival. He felt trapped with the heavy responsibility of standing in as a parent for another man's child. Eve had volunteered him to accompany Selena. It had only seemed right, since they'd been the ones to drive her to the game. But his empathy was overloaded by the scorching similarity of the situation with the one in his own past, and he longed to pass Selena over to her parents like a hot potato. He pictured Sanjay driving back from Toronto on the highway, his graceful conductor hands white-knuckled on the steering wheel. He'd reach over from time to time to touch his wife in the passenger seat and murmur reassurances. Sanjay had always been a better father and husband than Richard was, searching for lost pets, sharing his passion for music with his wife. Richard bet he picked up the call about Selena on the first ring, no teary-eyed receptionist had been required to fetch him.

Richard swiped Sanjay's details from the screen and looked up at the TV. A meteorologist with a brightly coloured turban was soundlessly predicting rain. Richard returned to his phone to call up rugby scores on the internet and text. He was on a call with Eve, checking in on her and Abbey, when the double doors flew open. Sanjay and Sharon Patel rushed through, followed by the blue-scrubbed nurse. They huddled into one another like two people on the deck of a ship about to go down. Richard told Eve he had to go and pocketed the phone in the front of his chinos. He realized, looking down, that they had a fine spray of blood on them too, just like the nurse's scrubs.

Sanjay released his wife and walked up to Richard, enveloping his body in a crushing bear hug. His balding head rested uncomfortably on Richard's Adam's apple. He hadn't realized Sanjay was so much shorter than he was. When he finally released Richard, Sharon rushed up to take her husband's arm, pulling him away like a jealous lover.

"What happened?" she demanded, her voice breaking with each syllable.

"I don't know," Richard said. The images he'd wanted so keenly to unload to the nurse were not fit to share with the Patels. They would have enough frightening footage ahead of them. "It all happened so quickly."

"They said she ingested something," Sharon snapped. "Something in a drink?"

It was the coach who'd spotted the tiny pieces of glass in the bloody mess Selena had coughed up. The team mascot, the one in the crazy gladiator getup, picked up Selena's drink and saw the remaining shards winking at the bottom of the bottle. The same bottle Richard had paid for at the health food store before the game.

"Yes. There was something in her drink," Richard admitted. Sharon held him with a direct gaze that unsettled him. He didn't know what to do with his hands. He finally settled for hooking his thumbs in the front pockets of his chinos, spanning the fingers to cover up the blood.

"It was glass," Sharon spat, pulling away from her husband to get closer to Richard. "Glass in my baby's stomach! Glass!" She shouted in Richard's face, so close she sent a speck of saliva onto his chin. "From the drink your daughter gave her! I never buy her those drinks, I never ..."

Sanjay took her arm, pulling her gently back to him. Sharon fought him at first, casting her eyes wildly around the hospital's inner waiting room. She reminded Richard of a parade horse he'd seen on Canada Day, after a rotten kid threw a firecracker in front of his prancing hooves. Sanjay pulled her closer.

"You don't understand," Sharon wailed, before she collapsed into his small frame, weeping.

"I'm sorry," Sanjay said. "This has all been ..." He couldn't finish the thought. He brought his lips tightly together in a bid to gain control as he held Sharon, absorbing his wife's tears while not allowing his own.

Richard scrunched his hands into fists in his pockets, trying to maintain his own emotions. He sought a quick exit, an excuse to leave. Anything to no longer be forced to witness the Patels at this moment, with all pretenses laid bare. Their raw humanity hanging out like dangling exposed nerves for all to see. The Patels held something so precious and gut-wrenching that it made Richard want to run out of the hospital screaming. Something Richard and Eve had never been allowed. Hope.

When the woman with the stovepipe hat burst through the double doors, the distraction came as a relief. Everyone turned to face the commotion, including the Patels. The woman bellowed nonsense warnings. *Elorac! Salguad!* Two burly security officers tackled her before she had a chance to get far. She screamed and kicked wildly as they dragged her away, arms bent behind her back.

Richard watched as a clear plastic bag of garbage fell to the floor, along with its moulded stainless-steel stand. It came from behind the drapes of one of the examination rooms, appearing suddenly with a clatter. The woman must have kicked it through the curtain. Although she hadn't looked like she was close enough for that. The stand clattered when it hit the speckled white tile, a jarring sound that made the Spanish girl, still bent over in her chair, jump. Latex gloves pulled inside out and blood-soaked gauze mixed with shrivelled black-and-white bits of paper from a shredder spilled out onto the floor. The stovepipe hat came off the woman's head as she fought with the orderlies. It rolled across the floor, coming to rest with its colourful flowers bouncing back and forth on coiled springs. Richard stepped over the garbage and picked the hat up. Without thinking, Richard placed it back on her head, where it sat askew over one of her eyes.

The woman was no longer screaming, reduced by his small kindness to a threatening growl. The two orderlies continued to hold her arms tightly from behind. Richard thought how much it must hurt, to be restrained like that. The woman couldn't help her actions, her brain was simply misfiring and broken, sending her shattered signals. He wanted to say something to the orderlies, but before he could, she kicked him hard and square in the knee.

"Look at me!" she screamed and spat as the orderlies dragged her away and out through the double doors. They banged against the wall of the outer waiting room like shutters left unsecured in a storm. Richard sat down on the nearest chair and ran the palm of his hand back and forth over his knee, trying to rub the sharp imprint of her boot sole away.

The spilled trash remained on the floor. A nurse pushed a wheelchair through it. The black-and-white shredded paper clung to the skinny tires of the chair before becoming dislodged as she wheeled her patient through a single door marked *Staff Only*. It reminded Richard of the torn pieces of missing cat poster he'd seen in the garbage last night, lying among the remnants of the glass Abbey had shattered in her anger at her mother.

"I don't buy Selena those drinks!" Sharon Patel called out from behind him. Her husband shushed her.

Richard turned and faced the Patels. The pain in his knee was subsiding and he stopped rubbing it. Sanjay held his wife close as he locked eyes with Richard over her shoulder, searching for solace, or solidarity, or answers to questions he might have. Richard nodded back at him with a weary man's acknowledgement, knowing that this was the only answer he had to give.

NINETEEN

Eve wanted to get Abbey out of the gym right away, but she refused to leave until Selena was loaded into the ambulance. After letting Eve hold her at first, Abbey had pulled away to go sit with the rest of her team. They hung on to each other like young girls do when confronted with the unfamiliar face of tragedy. The police arrived with the other first responders and insisted on an interview with each student accompanied by a guardian. Eve sat in the bleachers with the other parents, feeling as if they would never be allowed to leave. They were prisoners in the high-school gym, locked in with Selena's hardening pool of vomit and blood that no one could clean up because it was evidence.

Eve climbed down the bleachers to go to the washroom. Richard's text vibrated in her pocket when she was drying her hands with the ineffectual wall dryer. She pulled out the phone with eager wet hands, hoping again it might be Janet.

How are things? The text above this was from last week, sent to Richard by Eve with no reply. It simply stated *Buy milk*. Eve leaned against the cinderblock wall of the girls' washroom and sent a text back.

OK. How is Selena?

She waited. The cold concrete of the wall seeped in through her thin T-shirt.

The same, Richard wrote back. Eve didn't know if that was bad or good. She shivered, thinking of Selena grasping at her throat. The shy girl who had come for her first sleep-over with a teddy bear in her hands, and then one day she was at the door with car keys instead, picking up Abbey. Eve wondered where the time had gone. She worried about Selena, but she worried about Abbey more, about what she might have done. It was impossible to think about Selena's fate without considering the larger ramifications for her own daughter.

How is Abbey? This was really what Richard's first question was about. Both of them were worried about Abbey, just for different reasons.

Waiting to talk to police, Eve thumb typed. Then added, *We're still at the school.*

She moved away from the frigid wall to stand in front of the washroom mirror. Eve concentrated her gaze and focused on the back side of the glass, where only trained eyes could see. The scene in the gym was reflected back at her in a silent pantomime. A forensics team dusted the coach's cooler for fingerprints. The parents sat huddled dejectedly in the bleachers like overgrown kids kept in for detention. A uniformed police officer soundlessly called a name and Ashley Stravinsky and her doctor father stood up to follow her. It was not Eve and Abbey's turn yet. Eve returned to her phone and hovered her thumbs over the screen for a moment and then thought better of her response. Written words were the worst ghosts — they could come back to haunt. She decided to call Richard instead. He answered on the first ring.

"Hey," he said.

"Hey," she said back.

"How are you holding up?" Eve looked in the mirror that no longer contained the scene in the gym. It reflected her ashen face and a row of unoccupied toilet cubicles. A couple of white cholesterol deposits had sprouted up under her eyes, visible in the harsh lighting, like the fine bubbles of milia you see on a baby's nose.

"Okay," she told her husband. The standard answer for those who were anything but okay. She wanted to get these niceties of conversation out of the way, to get to the real reason for her call. The question she couldn't ask using permanent words typed by text. But Richard had a different agenda.

"Listen, Eve, about what we were talking about earlier. I really want to —"

"Did they ask about where the glass came from?" Eve whispered sharply, interrupting him. Her hushed tones echoed off the empty bathroom walls. There was no response from Richard initially. She shouldn't have cut him off. But their relationship was the last thing she wanted to talk about now. They had a situation on their hands much greater than the sum of the two of them. Richard was silent for so long that she moved closer to the bathroom window, wondering if the connection had been lost.

"The glass came from the bottle, Eve. It must have been some sort of manufacturing error." *That's so like him*, Eve thought. Richard believed you could boil down almost every piece of evil in the world to a poorly developed process.

But Eve had also considered a manufacturing error. Her mother had told her she'd once found a mouse's tail at the bottom of a milk jug. That had been in the '70s, before anyone figured out you could make a fortune suing over that sort of thing. The only compensation her mother had received when she went back to the store to complain was a free jug of milk.

"It was just a terrible accident." This was exactly what he'd said about Michael. He was wrong then, and Eve was terrified he was wrong now.

"I've got to go," he said, whispering himself now. "The Patels are here." He hung up. Although it was hard to tell. The receiver made no sound up against Eve's ear, not like when she was young and the flatline of the dial tone confirmed the other person was truly gone. She listened for a little longer to make sure the line was indeed dead. When she looked up at the mirror, she saw a hazy image of Sharon Patel glaring at her from the emergency waiting room.

Putting the phone in her pocket, Eve turned away from the mirror and leaned back, suddenly thankful of the frigid washroom walls, far away from the hospital and the heat of Sharon Patel's accusing eyes.

"FULL NAME, PLEASE." THE UNIFORMED police officer ushered Eve and Abbey from the gym into the girls' change room. The police had set up a makeshift interview space there using a pupil's desk commandeered from a nearby classroom. The seat was attached and did not leave enough room for the hefty spare tire of the detective that sat in it. He'd positioned himself at the far end of the change rooms across from a bank of toilets. His belly squeezed up tightly against the lip of the desk. Eve was afraid if he tried to stand up the whole piece of furniture would go with him, tied around his middle like a bizarre swim toy.

"Please, Officer," Eve said to their uniformed escort, ignoring the hefty detective. "Could we possibly interview my daughter at another time? She's been very upset. And we —"

"Abbey Knight," Abbey said, cutting her off. "K-N-I-G-H-T." She recited the letters with staccato precision, like she had in the seventh-grade spelling bee, where, ironically, she'd been up against Selena for first place.

The detective stuck in the desk motioned for them to come closer. They sat down on one of the long wooden change benches. The uniformed police officer checked off their names on her clipboard and then went to stand at the entranceway to the gym. Far enough away to give a semblance of privacy but close enough to corroborate everything being said.

The detective took his time, flipping through the many files he had laid out on the laminated desk. A student had doodled a small, red-inked penis in one corner of the desk. As if he'd caught Eve looking at it, the detective covered the drawing over with a thick manila file. Eve tried to read him but found that she couldn't. Some people were closed books, their pages dark and tightly stuck together as if they'd had a pot of coffee spilled on them and it dried that way.

It was somehow indecent that this much paperwork could have been generated from misfortune in such a short time. But Eve knew the shuffling of documents was only a delaying tactic, designed for effect. A ploy so that she and Abbey could stew in their own juices long enough to be tenderized for robust confessions. She had gone through a similar experience when they'd grilled her about Michael. And it was a grilling, no matter how much the soft-spoken liaison officer had tried to reassure her that it was all procedure, standard for when a child was injured in somebody's care. They hadn't let her be present for Abbey's interview that time, but she had been allowed to watch through the one-way glass. Her daughter hadn't cracked then, and Eve doubted she would now.

"Abbey Knight," the detective said, looking up as if he'd only just noticed them sitting on the bench. "You were the one with the ..." he consulted his files again, "canbucha," he said, squinting at the paperwork.

"Detective, as I said to the officer earlier, my daughter has been through a lot. Couldn't we just —"

"Kombucha," Abbey corrected him. "K-O-M ..."

The rest of the interview went pretty much the same way, Eve interjecting with her fears and her daughter coldly spelling them away.

When they got home, Abbey went straight to her room and shut the door. She was angry because Eve wouldn't let her go to the hospital to see Selena.

"Why can't I go?" she had cried out in the car.

"It's just not a good time, honey." Eve had wondered if there would ever be a good time to visit a friend you'd just tried to kill with a fermented tea drink.

"You don't care about me!" Abbey had said, with real tears. "You don't care about me at all."

But Eve did care. She was just worried she had to admit that she really didn't know if Abbey had been involved in what happened to Selena. She'd tried to look inside her daughter's mind for clues, but each time Abbey threw up that terrifying image of Eve holding Michael at the end. Eve only had her fears and her intuition to go on. A combination that had a successful psychic divining rate of only a little above the 50 percent mark. But on the off chance she was right, she needed to protect Abbey, like she'd protected her before. If Abbey carried the seed of the Ragman within her, it was Eve's fault for sowing it.

Eve had tried to talk to her daughter in the car on the way home. Conversations with Abbey were often easier in a moving vehicle, mother and daughter side by side, speaking to the road instead of each other. Abbey had explained to her mother about esophageal tears and surgical techniques. They had both remarked on how pedantic the police had been. *Everyone knew it was just a technique, and who did they think they were kidding?* It had been a "skimming the surface" conversation with no deep dives into the pool. Neither of them had speculated on how the glass had gotten in the bottle of kombucha or mentioned the Thompson scholarship. Then Abbey had asked about visiting Selena, and when Eve had said no, she'd become inconsolable, crying and begging. When it became obvious that Eve wasn't going to give in, she'd crossed her arms in front of her loose basketball jersey and refused to speak, staring out the side window of the car for the rest of the trip.

Eve sat at the kitchen table now, gnawing at a jagged fingernail. Through the window to the backyard, she watched the willow tree's branches sweep back and forth in the increasing wind. The afternoon sky was the colour of slate. There was a storm coming, just as her mother and Environment Canada had foretold. Upstairs, Abbey remained behind her closed bedroom door, silent except for the swoosh and ding of text messages sent and delivered.

Eve felt powerless, sitting at the kitchen table. She wanted to search Abbey's room for any incriminating evidence but that would have to wait. In the meantime, she removed all the bottled drinks from the refrigerator and poured their contents down the drain with a strainer placed in the sink. None of them netted her anything except some pulpy bits she had to dig out of the mesh with a BBQ skewer. Afterward, she crawled on her hands and knees on the deck, looking for any trace of the wineglass Abbey had broken the night they'd argued about Eve smoking. Except for an empty beer bottle Richard had left under one of the patio chairs, there was nothing. The stained wood boards of the deck were swept clean. She also checked the outdoor garbage can. The cat was gone. Only a mound of cut-up fruit sat at the bottom of the can, the sharp smell of decay catching Eve's nose before she put the lid back on. If Abbey was responsible for the cat as well as Selena, it meant she was escalating. It would all get harder and harder to control.

Eve took her phone from the table and sent a text to Janet again. She had been attempting to send less conventional messages since Selena was hurt, but she was afraid those missives were getting waylaid by the storm. Janet might have taken on another form. This, too, would interfere with Eve's limited abilities to contact her. Janet often liked to make a transformation when the weather was threatening. She said she felt closer to the natural wonder of the elements when she shapeshifted into an animal. She'd run through the forest as a lone grey wolf, able to detect the ozone of the lightning with her heightened sense of smell. Other times, she'd burrow into the ground as a slug and let the rainwater feed her indistinct edges. Eve had never been a fan of transformations. The feel of her skin peeling off and growing fur or scales was too intense. Instead, she'd inhabit the body of an animal with her consciousness in order to run alongside her friend when a storm raged. Eve knew what it was to look through yellow eyes, to own the wild freedom of pure instinct and drive. Upon returning to her human shell, she'd find herself exhilarated and feeling slightly guilty, as if she'd just gone down on Mother Nature.

Eve ripped off the last piece of fingernail she'd been worrying. It tore off just past the quick and made the tip sting where the fraction of a nail bed lay exposed. An old man who came to the drop-in had told her his father used to punish him by burning his fingernails down to the quick if he lied. Perhaps Eve was trying to enact the same penalty on a smaller scale. Strangely, it was not the man that wore the pointed Freddy Krueger fake nails who'd told her this story. Sometimes, easy explanations were the wrong ones.

The doorbell chimed, startling both Eve and the flock of black crows that had taken shelter in the willow tree outside. She looked around for the dog who should have been barking, then remembered he wasn't there. Pauline Henderson had bugged her for weeks for a "puppy playdate" with her shih tzu, Mitzi, who she'd said had attachment issues. They'd dropped the dog off on the way to the game but hadn't picked him up yet. Sucking on her sore finger, Eve hurried to the door before properly considering who might be there.

"I came as soon as I heard." Mark stood on the stoop, his moisture-wicking nylon jacket was pulled up around his ears. The first smattering of rain had flattened a couple of his curls on the walk over. He scoffed at the idea of buying a car since he could easily stroll to work — saving both the environment as well as parking fees.

"What are you doing here?" Eve hoped Abbey hadn't heard the bell, that she still had her earbuds in. Eve stepped outside, closing the door behind her. The wind whistled through her thin T-shirt, bringing goosebumps to her arms. She scanned up and down the street. No one was out with the impending weather. Still, she couldn't take the chance.

"In here," she said, leading him down the steps. She brought him to the side entrance of the garage, let him in, then shut the door. It slammed hard in the frame with the help of the wind that continued to build with the storm.

The smell of motor oil and grass enveloped them in the unlit garage. Eve didn't bother to turn the light on. She could see better than most in the dark. It gave her an advantage when she wanted one.

"Eve." Mark moved closer, but she raised her hands in front of her and he stopped, respecting her space. For now.

"How did you find out?" Eve asked him. She wondered if he'd been following her again.

"A colleague at the school contacted me about it," he said.

"Bad news travels fast in the therapist world."

"Oh, Eve, come on, don't be like that." He went to come closer, but she held her hands up again.

"Don't."

"But I thought ..." Mark's voice dropped lower, adopting a sultry tone. "After Friday night ..." He continued moving toward her, more slowly this time. She slipped behind the wheelbarrow with the busted handle. Richard hadn't gotten around to fixing it yet. In a pinch, she could shove it toward Mark and impale his leg with the sharp, splintered end.

"Friday night was a mistake, Mark." Eve had shown up close to midnight at his apartment, dishevelled and breathless, not knowing where else to go after what happened. He'd laid her down on his soft and sensible Ikea bed and made her feel blissful and sexy, kissing her on her breasts and then her belly. Moving his way down to where he could make love to her with his mouth, so he wouldn't hurt her rib with full-on sex. But he *had* hurt her rib. Just not on Friday night.

"You're not still angry at me, are you, Evie?" She cringed. Eve didn't want the intimacy of nicknames with this man, despite the intimacies she'd afforded him in the past. On Friday night, she'd sought out the comfort of the one person she should have been the most afraid of, returning to him like a faithful pet. Eve remembered a line from a despicable fable she'd read once in the deep reaches of the library: *The woman, the dog, and the walnut tree. The more you beat them the better they'll be.*

It had begun with a stinging slap just the once when she challenged him in an argument. He had been full of remorse and apologies, and Eve had forgiven him. But then he'd started giving her nasty pinches on the arm when it suited him, or a rough shove up against the wall followed by sex she hadn't been in the mood for. But every time Eve tried to end things, Mark would find a way to wedge himself back into her life and her bed. It hadn't been until that day in the coffee shop, where she'd purposely met him so he wouldn't make a scene, that she'd told him it was over and meant it. Eve had used her love for Richard as the reason, rather than the abuse, which would only have given Mark a platform for more promises and apologies. But the truth was, she did love Richard, her imperfect, mortal mate, despite it all. For over two decades they had shared a life of late-night dreams whispered in bed together, of first mortgages and first steps. Of fucking and fighting and finding each other again, however tenuously. They had shared the joy of the coming of children and the grief when one had been torn away from them. Love like that tied them together more powerfully than the greatest of binding spells. She had told Mark she couldn't leave her family, particularly Abbey, for him, but he'd refused to hear her. He wanted Eve all to himself.

"I told you I was sorry, Eve," Mark tried to placate her in the dark. "I don't know what came over me. It was an accident."

But it hadn't been an accident. Eve had felt Mark's anger rise over her like a sick red tide just before the vicious push that broke her rib. He'd showed up at the house the day after the coffee shop, still refusing to accept her decision. She'd been outside working on household chores, energized by the firmness of her resolve. But Mark had followed her around, pleading his case as she went about her spring-cleaning tasks, washing windows and putting up screens. Eve had felt falsely secure in the open space and with her newfound assertiveness, believing him to be no danger. Even a woman with second sight could be blind sometimes. And Mark was like the police detective at the school gym, she could never see into him.

"Look at me!" he'd shouted from behind her. "Look at me, goddammit!" Just like Michael had called to her, and yet not the same at all. She had reached into the garbage can with her soapy wet sponge, scrubbing hard, sure that he would leave if she gave him the cold shoulder for long enough. The push had come savage and strong, and when her torso hit the lip of the can it had forced all the breath out of her lungs. She'd fallen to the ground, her mouth open as she desperately tried to draw air. The flaming pain in her lower rib had blossomed like the perennials she'd weeded earlier that day. When Mark had leaned over her, blocking out the warmth of the springtime sun, she'd instinctively pulled herself into the fetal position, preparing for the next blow. It came in the form of words instead of fists.

"I said *look at me*, bitch." He'd walked away then, leaving her to writhe on the driveway in the dazzling sunshine.

Back in the shadowy garage, Mark moved closer to the wheelbarrow.

"Eve, I know we can work this out."

"There is nothing to work out. It's over." Eve punched the automatic garage door opener on the wall with her fist. The aluminum door moved slowly along the tracks, opening the two of them up to the outside world. Wind whipped in from below the bottom of the rising frame, blowing leaves from last fall onto the cement floor. Mark looked down as a faded red maple leaf blew across the toe of his hiking boot. Eve had been so drawn to this man who'd listened to her pain and allowed her to speak of Michael without reproach. He'd never told her to stop being sad or to move on. But as the garage door lifted, Eve realized he'd worked to keep her grief fresh and raw for his own purposes, so she would remain dependent on him.

The garage door was fully open now. Mark looked almost angelic in the weak light that broke through the steel-grey clouds, his unruly curls surrounding his head like a halo. For a moment, Eve found herself mesmerized by the childlike quality he radiated, a boy-man of sorts. But then a quick flash of sheet lightning illuminated his eyes, hungry with anticipation, hunting for opportunities. The sudden transformation sullied the childlike quality he'd held moments before, exposing his true nature. He was a wolf masquerading as a lamb. A transformation she should have seen much, much earlier.

"You've got to trust me, Eve," Mark said. "God knows, you can't trust yourself."

A curtain of rain began to fall behind him like a theatre backdrop. She moved toward the open mouth of the garage door. The rain bounced up from the driveway and pierced the back of her thin T-shirt like needles. "I have to go. My daughter needs me." She turned and ran out into the storm.

Mark shouted after her. The heavy rain drowned him out and soaked her in the short distance from the driveway to the front door. Eve couldn't make out all that he said, but the winds carried the ill will of threats.

Once inside, she watched, shivering at the living room window in her wet clothes until she saw Mark leave. He dashed out of the garage with his hood pulled up. Once Eve was sure he wasn't coming back, she went outside and pushed the remote button again, bending down just in time to scoot under the garage door as it rattled to the ground.

Walking inside the house, her socks squished in her shoes. She went up to her bedroom. Bursts of lightning cast shadows as she stripped down to her bra and underwear. She pulled out the laundry basket from the closet and tossed in her wet clothes, adding some others from the hamper in the bathroom to make a full wash. Her rib caught her when she picked up the basket, but not as badly as before. It was healing after all. As she dropped the basket on the tiled floor of the main floor laundry, a burst of thunder shook the house.

Buried in the dirty laundry from the hamper she found her favourite blouse, the buttercup-yellow one with the V-neck Mark said showcased the roundness of her breasts. The same one that Abbey, with breasts of her own she sought to showcase, was forever borrowing. A deep red stain covered the front where it had dried into a stiff crust. Eve stood in the laundry half naked and stared at it. It looked like blood. Eve couldn't remember when she'd last worn it.

She carried the stained blouse downstairs to the basement rec room and cast it into the airtight stove in the corner, adding some dry wood and kindling that had been stacked next to it. Lightning crackled in the well window above her as she struck a long match and threw it in. She closed and locked into place the windowed door, and the kindling caught fire weakly. Eve focused every bit of anxious energy she felt on the flickering flame until it burst into a ball of brilliant orange.

As Eve stood in the dark of the basement rec room, shivering in her panties and bra, the storm rocked the willow tree in the backyard, ripping leaves from its hangdog branches. Abbey was upstairs in the kitchen, fixing a snack from the refrigerator before going back to her room again to communicate behind closed doors. The shadow of the flames flickered against Eve's chilled skin, so recently warmed by the touch of the wrong man's hands. She'd never told Mark about what Abbey had done to Michael, not as her therapist, or as her lover. But she'd told him about the mice. The ones she believed Abbey had hurt. Mark had reassured her that lots of children pulled the wings off of butterflies and didn't grow up to be serial killers. But she had felt him catalogue the confession for future reference.

Eve opened the door of the stove and threw another log on the fire, pulling a blanket from the couch around her bare shoulders.

It would be a long time before she felt warm again.

TWENTY

They had an assembly for Dylan Penske today at school. It was also for Selena, but she didn't get as much airtime because she isn't dead. Dad says they got the glass out of her, but he doesn't know how long she'll be in the hospital. I wanted to go see her after school today, but he said they're only allowing family to visit right now. I've tried texting, but she's not answering. Her phone's probably dead and she doesn't have her charger with her.

That therapist my mom sees was at school today as well. He was wearing one of those pathetic white sticker name tags. *Hello, my name is MARK.* They had a whole team of touchy-feely professionals with name tags on to help us "process our grief." They sat in a row of chairs on the stage of the auditorium dressed as if they were in a Michael Cera look-alike contest. Even the women. It's supposed to make them seem more accessible.

The head of Guidance stood at the podium in front of them and led us through a series of prayers and requests for intercession. We are allowed to do that because we go to a Catholic school. Other schools can only have moments of silence, so they don't offend the atheists. I don't know whether I believe in God, but when people get so fucking fanatic about believing there isn't one, it starts to look a whole lot like organized religion.

He came to the house yesterday too, *Hello, my name is MARK.* It's just like Mom to call her therapist for help. As if something bad had happened to her and not me. It was the same when Michael died. This focus on her. She'd stayed in her room, alternating between sleeping and crying after the funeral. If I came in, she'd grab me and pull me to her, getting snot in my hair, using me like a full-sized hankie in her sweaty bedsheets.

When she finally got out of bed, she took me for therapy with a weird little gnome woman whose feet didn't touch the carpet when she sat in her desk chair. She had toys in her office, puppets and dolls, as if I was a little kid who needed to point out the nasty bits some pedophile had made me touch. Mom insisted on staying with me whenever I went to see her, to make sure I didn't say anything. She didn't want me to tell the gnome lady that it was *her* fault Michael went over the railing.

I'd been reaching out to get him down. Mom was too busy on the phone, and I knew he shouldn't be up there. Then I thought I'd give him a scare, just so he wouldn't do it again, so I went to push him a little. But Mom reached out to grab me and I accidentally knocked him a bit. It was an involuntary reaction, like when the doctor hits you on the knee with a hammer. I learned all about reflexes at that summer camp with the cadaver arms. Anyway, that's why it's Mom's fault. She made me promise not to tell the gnome lady how Michael really fell, and I didn't. She probably thinks I've forgotten what happened after all these years, but I remember. I only came out of my room that day because my brother was making such a racket. I'd been reading my book and it was just getting to the good part where Voldemort comes.

I can tell Mom's still worried that I'll tell people what she did. She hovers around me like the worst helicopter parent. Everywhere I go, I can hear her blades circling nearby. It's hard to carry a frightening truth around inside of you. Especially when that truth is about your own mother.

Max Tyson got up on stage to say something about Dylan. He talked about all the fun times they'd had in elementary school, hiking up toboggan hills in their snowsuits and playing house league hockey. Those would be the only memories Max would have about Dylan, given he'd avoided him like a goddamn disease since they hit high school and Max got super popular. The only time I saw Max even notice Dylan in the last four years was at a party I was at in tenth grade. Max had taken a beer cap and stuck it to his forehead with sweat, the sharp ridged side facing out. He'd head-butted Dylan with it when he came out of the kitchen talking to Shannon Dempsey, who he was sort of dating at the time. That's before her dad left her mom for the yoga instructor. Shannon had tried to help Dylan wipe the blood off, but she knew he'd been marked. They broke up the next day. I don't think he went out with anybody else after that.

Two more people came up on stage to talk about Dylan, a guidance counsellor and Shannon Dempsey herself. She kept talking about what a great guy Dylan was and how much she'd miss him. She never mentioned the beer cap, or how she dropped him like a social-pariah rock after that. Everyone was pretending like they knew Dylan so well. But if that were true, they'd have known he was about to blow his head off with a shotgun, now, wouldn't they? Although I don't know if anyone could have seen that coming. I certainly didn't. Selena and I wouldn't have sent the poems if we had. But like I said, you can't blame us for that. It was just a joke. It wasn't our fault the guy was messed up.

I heard his art teacher might have been close to him. There was talk that she was making a showcase of some of the work he'd done in her class. But the school had put a stop to it. You could tell why. I'd seen some of his stuff when they put it on display in one of the windowed boxes in the hallway. He made these dark face masks out of plaster of Paris. They had huge white eyes shot through with bumpy red veins. Crazy wet tongues stuck out of them through the yellowed molars he'd embedded in their mouths. Each had a different twisted expression. They looked like those Greek drama faces, except there was more than just comedy and tragedy. I'd heard he'd used his own baby teeth for the project. His mom had saved them. Like I said before, the guy was really messed up.

Once the Dylan show was done, Ashley Stravinsky gave an update on Selena. I suppose they chose her because her dad was the doctor who treated Selena at the scene. You'd think they'd have asked me. But I guess I don't have enough credibility as *only* her best friend. My dad's not a doctor. Or my mom for that matter. Ashley didn't have anything new to say anyway. Just that Selena was stable, and we should all pray for her, which we already had.

The principal, Mrs. Anderson, came out on the stage at the end of everything. She made a speech about sticking together and the importance of communication. She told us her door was always open. *We're here for you*, she kept saying, and those dumb therapists, including Mom's, kept nodding over and over like a bunch of hipster bobbleheads. The principal actually had tears in her eyes. What a performance. I doubt she even knew Dylan Penske. Although she does know Selena. She'd made a big deal when she awarded her the Good Citizenship Award at our last assembly. As if citizenship counted for anything these days, except maybe in an election where half the people vote for the wrong people anyway.

It's all bullshit, all this hand-holding and open doors. Their doors are only open for the good citizens, the ones without any dirty secrets. No principal or teacher wants to hear about the darker stuff. It might tarnish a school's reputation, like those football players last year from that stuck up private academy. They'd raped a cheerleader after a homecoming game while everyone looked on and cheered. That shit was trending online for a week before anyone called the cops. The school knew about it but did nothing. We're here for you, *my ass.*

As we filed out of the auditorium, the therapists on stage started talking among themselves, all except for *Hello, my name is MARK.* I caught him checking me out when I turned around to tell Alana Byles that I wanted to skip Chemistry and I needed her notes. Bastard didn't even turn away when I stared right back at him up on the stage. The fucking pervert. Like I said, this stupid Catholic school-girl kilt is nothing but a freak magnet. But no one wants to know about that either.

The truth is, no one wants to hear you speak aloud about any of the dark stuff. Not the gnome lady, not the principal, and definitely not my mom.

She's got enough dark stuff of her own.

TWENTY-ONE

Richard ended up staying at the hospital a whole lot longer than he'd expected. The police showed up soon after the Patels, looking to speak to the man who'd travelled with Selena in the ambulance. He'd almost made it out the fire exit door when the nurse in the blue scrubs outed him, pointing with her tatty Band-Aid finger. The two detectives interviewed him in the same room where he'd been told the news about Michael. Five years hadn't changed the surroundings or the ineffectual desk, although the walls had been painted — a calming aquamarine blue. The police asked him where he'd bought the health food drinks, and why he'd been driving Selena to the basketball game. They wanted to know how long he'd known her, and where he worked. Afterward, the two of them went out in the hall and left Richard to sit alone in the aquamarine, like a fish they weren't finished reeling in yet. When they finally returned, the senior detective told him he could go, but not to leave town, just like in the movies.

Richard hadn't left town, but he did go to work the next day. Monday morning, he sat at his desk, trying to deal with the fallout of a scathing email from Mueller. He guessed they must have had Wi-Fi at the airport. The German had taken extreme offence to Richard's attempt to offload half the overspent budget on him. There had been escalations. On Sunday afternoon, when he'd been busy with Selena, the Patels, and the police, the forwards and replies had copulated and multiplied in his inbox like a teeming mass of virtual rabbits. He'd had to drop everything to deal with the fiasco, cancelling all of his meetings. He'd even closed and locked his open door. Scanning the numbers of the dreaded spreadsheet again and again, he tried to find a way to make things add up the way he wanted. But the lined rows and columns mocked him with their cold formulas, refusing to bend to his wishes. His foremost wish being that he wouldn't come off looking like an incompetent asshole.

Richard leaned back in his chair and rubbed the back of his neck, stiff from spending the morning bent over his laptop. Looking out the interior window of his office, he could see that the coat hook over the wall of Julia's cubicle was empty. She always hung her blazer over that hook when she was in the office, donning it only if a client came in and she needed to look more professional.

But there were no clients in the office, so the missing jacket meant there was also no Julia. She was usually in early, at least an hour before Richard arrived. He'd always had a problem with arriving late, often running an electric razor over his chin while he parked the car in the company lot at ten after nine. Sometimes Julia would take a couple of hours off in the morning to hit the doctor or the dentist. But it was almost noon and there was still no sign of her. Richard opened up the drawer on the right side of his desk and verified again that the damning burner phone was gone. He had just returned to the abhorrent spreadsheet when his legitimate cellphone rang with a call.

"Richard, this is Devon." The chief information officer didn't need to announce himself. Richard could see his boss's name on the call display. Nobody used the landline anymore, even for internal calls. Richard's office phone sat under a pile of hanging folders next to his abandoned desktop computer. He peeked around the dusty hardware to look across the floor at Devon's corner office only to find his boss looking directly back at him. He hoped Devon hadn't seen him cringe before he picked up the call. He leaned back in his desk chair, exaggerating a relaxed posture for effect.

"Hi, Devon, how are things?" Richard knew how things were. They were not good. The board of directors had seen the spreadsheet. They were worried about how their shareholders' investments were being managed. Devon, in turn, was worried about his bonus, already spent on a shiny new Mercedes to go with the shiny new girlfriend he'd met at Bar None. Devon was smart enough to have a degree from MIT and young enough to still be paying off the student loans from it. Like a lot of high-achieving young men, he had decided to overcompensate for his age by behaving like a grumpy old man.

"I'd like to talk to you, Richard. In my office." Richard swore he could hear an adolescent voice crack beneath the gruff request.

"Sure, Devon." Richard clicked on the spreadsheet tabs, hoping something would jump out of the tumbling figures and save him. "How about three o'clock? I was just crunching the numbers on this budget, and I should be able to give you an update by —"

"Now, Richard." Devon hung up the phone. Richard knew this because he could see him from across the floor, glaring at him through his open door.

"LISTEN, DEVON. I DON'T APPRECIATE being called in like a schoolboy here. I said I'd get the budget worked out for the end of the day and you need to trust me on that." Richard stood in Devon's office with the door closed. But the horizontal blinds on the window to the rest of the floor had been left open. Richard's call to the mat was on public display, clear for all his co-workers to see.

Devon sat behind his executive-sized desk with a deep frown. This was his usual facial expression, only varied on occasion with the wide, offended eyes of annoyance. "It's not about the budget, Richard. Take a seat."

Richard plunked down in the visitor's chair. It had been artfully designed so that it sat lower to the ground than the one that housed the shorter man behind the desk. Devon was well under Richard's six feet.

"Then what is this about, Devon?"

"It's about Julia McCabe."

Richard felt the wind go out of his righteous indignation sails. But he was an experienced enough seaman not to let his rigging hang out.

"What about her?" he said, narrowing his eyes, attempting to betray nothing, especially himself.

"Word is you're banging her." Straight to the point, fucking Devon. Richard felt his sails go completely slack.

"Who the hell told you that?"

"Does it goddamn matter, Richard? Are you screwing your project coordinator, or not?"

Richard held his hands in tight fists, wishing he could reach across the desk and pummel Devon's perpetually cranky face. The guy wasn't even thirty. What did he know about pain and death and family and the lure of a tantalizing pink tongue that wanted to lick the cream out of your middle-aged churro.

"I think we should have Human Resources in here, if we're going to discuss this any further." Richard was calling Devon's bluff but hoped he didn't take him up on it. Marjorie Howard, their assigned HR contact, was three years past retirement. Her HR degree had been issued when men still kept full bars behind their desks and referred to the secretary who stocked them as "girl." She looked like Richard's aunt Shirley, and he had no desire to discuss Julia and her churro-licking capabilities with her in the room. Luckily, Devon ignored his request, as well as his protestations.

"Julia's not in the office, Richard. She didn't call in either. Word is the two of you might have had a bust-up."

What the fuck, thought Richard. *Who the hell knew about that?* He was shocked by how much the office busybodies seemed to know about his personal life. He and Julia had been so careful, meeting only in secluded spots where they wouldn't be seen. Had someone been following them? Were they there Friday night? The idea made his balls sweat uncomfortably in his boxers. He had more than one secret to hide. He decided to come clean on the affair, hoping the rest of his dirty laundry would remain off the line.

"We did have a thing, but it's over. I don't know where she is." Closing his eyes, he leaned his forehead into his hand, rubbing at the lines that had started to develop there. "It's been a rough weekend, Devon." He paused. "My daughter. My daughter's friend …"

He saw Selena so clearly on the blank canvas of his closed eyelids, bent over with the vomit and the blood pooling in front of her. He rubbed his forehead some more, hoping to massage the image away. But it was replaced by Abbey standing beside him in the kitchen with the spoiled fruit on the floor, her eyes holding back the tears he'd put there. In his memory, the kitchen walls were painted a gut-wrenching aquamarine. Sitting in Devon's office, a single tear leaked out of the corner of his eye. He whisked the wetness away with one hand, as Devon got up from his desk. Opening his eyes again, Richard straightened up in the diminutive chair, getting a hold of himself and the situation. Devon walked behind him and pulled the horizontal blinds down.

"Richard." Devon had dropped the old-man edge from his voice. This might have been how he spoke before graduating MIT, when he was just a geeky brainiac playing Dungeons & Dragons in his dorm room with friends. "I heard about what happened yesterday at your daughter's basketball game. The police called here. Hell of a thing, Richard."

"The police called you?" Richard felt the comforting warmth of anger bloom inside him again, replacing his sadness. First, people were following him to rat about his affair, and now the police were hounding him. It wasn't enough that the cops made him feel like a goddamn criminal for buying Selena and Abbey a couple of drinks. Now they were invading his workplace. Was nothing bloody sacred?

"Yes, Richard. They called." Devon returned to his chair behind the desk. "They said you took the girl to the hospital. That your own kid could have been involved."

"She was not involved." Richard raised himself to his full height in the visitor's chair. "She just gave her friend one of her fucking drinks, Devon."

Devon tilted his head, evaluating. It was only then that Richard realized he'd shouted as well as sworn at his boss. The blinds might keep out prying eyes, but the walls of these offices were one step above particleboard. The rest of the floor would have heard his outburst. More fodder for the office gossip mill. Now they'd be saying he couldn't control his temper *or* his libido.

"I meant that your daughter could have been a victim as well, Richard." Devon's speech was even and controlled, making Richard's blow-up seem all the more inappropriate.

"Yes," Richard said, "I understand that." He wasn't shouting anymore, but he was still pissed off. Bust his balls about the budget, fine, but he didn't need his personal life raked over the coals. Devon should back the hell off and let him do his job. He was horrified to think he'd actually cried in front of this overeducated little twat.

"Richard." The grumpy old man voice had returned. "I want you to take a couple of days off." Devon shifted his focus to the screen of his laptop. It had recently pinged with an incoming message. He began to type as if Richard had already left. Richard stared at him in disbelief.

"Are you shitting me?"

"No," Devon said, still typing. "You've got a lot going on." He looked up from the keyboard. "It's not a request, Richard."

"What about the budget figures?" Richard couldn't believe Devon was benching him. Jesus. He'd made a mistake with Julia, he knew that. But he'd rectified it. It wasn't like these things never happened at the office. He bet Devon had even dipped his own pen in the company inkwell once or twice. The guy always seemed a little too chummy with Jessica in Accounting.

"I'll take care of the budget," Devon said, dismissing Richard with a swishing hand gesture, as if the budget could be swept away, perhaps under a carpet. "You can take the rest of today off as well. Come back on Thursday. Maybe even Friday." Devon returned to his laptop. Richard sat fuming in the visitor's chair, listening to the click-clack of his boss's keyboard, feeling like a rube.

"Fine," Richard said, fed up. He got up to leave. His hand was on the door handle when Devon spoke to him from behind his desk.

"So, you sure you don't know where Julia is?"

Richard paused with his hand on the doorknob. He could feel the round metal go sweaty in his palm.

"No." He kept his face turned away. "I don't."

Richard opened the door and stepped out into bright fluorescent light. He strode across to his office, his gaze focused straight ahead so he wouldn't have to see his co-workers watching him. Powering down his laptop, he packed it into a leather case with his cellphone and office keys and walked swiftly toward the exit for the stairwell.

As he passed, he saw Julia's coat hook hanging over the cubicle wall, still empty.

TWENTY-TWO

Eve was searching Abbey's room when she got the call Monday morning.

"Where the heck have you been?"

"You know me, sweet Eve." Janet gave a tired yawn, even though it was almost eleven o'clock. "I like to follow my nose, see where it leads me."

Eve picked up a book from Abbey's clear glass work desk. *Sense and Sensibility.* She held open the front and back cover, shaking out the pages over the bed. A receipt from the school library fell out. Eve picked it up from where it had landed on her daughter's puffy turquoise duvet as she cradled the cellphone to one ear. According to the faded slip, the book was two years overdue.

"And where has your nose led you since Friday night?" Eve grabbed another book and repeated the same procedure.

"Into the bed of a highly accommodating trapeze artist with a penthouse overlooking the river."

"I didn't think circus performers made that kind of money."

"They don't," Janet said. "She's house-sitting for a friend."

"In between circus gigs?"

"Yes." Janet sighed and yawned again.

Eve didn't make a habit of invading her daughter's privacy, despite her occasional peek into her thoughts. She felt like a burglar, robbing her daughter of her right to personal space. Eve could still recall her own horror as a teenager when she'd discovered her mother had snooped in her room. It hadn't been much of a covert operation. Her mother had used a red pen to correct Eve's grammar in her diary, unable to resist the lurid sin of poor verb conjugation. But despite this memory, Eve found herself declaring household martial law today. Her daughter's civil rights were being revoked, at least until Eve could convince herself that she'd had nothing to do with what happened to Selena at the basketball game.

"It's Monday. You've been gone for two whole days." Eve wasn't going to let Janet off the hook after she'd left her dangling all weekend. She picked up the books she'd discarded on the bed and carefully put each one back on the desk exactly as she'd found them. Abbey watched for that sort of thing. Eve had gone into her bedroom once to retrieve a sweater she'd borrowed and been caught out later when Abbey returned home. Her daughter had forced a slip of paper into the doorjamb and it had fallen to the floor when Eve entered, a primitive but effective form of perimeter surveillance. The resulting meltdown after Abbey discovered the breach in security had left Eve shaken for days.

"I know it's Monday, Eve. But you left me at the Delta all alone with the bill and a plate of shit pizza." Eve heard the crinkle of a wrapper and then Janet chewing on gum through the phone, a habit she'd developed since quitting smoking a few years back. "Where the hell did you go anyway?"

Eve sat down heavily on Abbey's bed. She ran her hand along the lingering imprint of her daughter's sleeping body left behind in the sheets, registering a residual warmth. Abbey had left hours ago for school. Any remaining heat Eve sensed was an emotional rather than a physical remnant.

"I just went home," Eve lied. She didn't tell Janet about what had happened with Julia, or that she'd gone to Mark's later on. There were misdeeds a woman couldn't own up to, even to her best friend. Before Janet could get a clairvoyant whiff of her deceit, Eve switched to another subject.

"Something's happened."

Eve told Janet about Selena, about the Thompson scholarship, and about the Patels' dead cat. She even told her about the broken glass she'd found in the kitchen garbage early this morning mixed up with the shredded poster. It could all be unrelated, but just on the off chance, Eve had driven north of the city and disposed of the garbage over a cliff at the Elora Gorge.

"Holy crap, Eve." Janet had always had a way with summations.

"Holy crap is right." Eve stood up from the bed and opened Abbey's closet, careful to check if there were any small slips of paper wedged into the doorjamb first.

Janet covered the receiver before uttering a few muffled words to the trapeze artist. Eve got a picture of a tanned nubile body hanging upside down from an expensive chandelier. She could see dyed red hair that almost touched the floor hanging below a flash of long-limbed leopard leggings. But her friend was too far away for Eve's mind's eye to reach. This image was more intuition, paired with a touch of whimsy and a knowledge of Janet's favoured type.

A partially suppressed giggle filtered through the phone, soon joined by the buttery richness of Janet's own laugh. But when she came back on the line, her tone was less than playful.

"Eve, are you seriously telling me you think Abbey might have had something to do with hurting Selena? I mean, *seriously*?"

"You know there have been incidents in the past," Eve said, rifling through the pockets of one of Abbey's jackets in the closet. "This wouldn't be the first time she's acted out."

"Jesus, Eve. I told you before, that was just kid stuff."

"You don't know her like I do." *Does anyone really know a daughter like her mother?* Although Eve would have said her own mother didn't truly know or understand her, despite being privy to the angst of her teenage diary. This was an interesting paradox, one that Eve refused to fully contemplate as she crouched down to dig her fingers into the toes of Abbey's athletic shoes. Bending made her rib slip, forcing her to sit down on her daughter's bedroom floor and catch her breath as she held her side.

"Maybe I don't know her as well as you do. But I know she's not stupid." Janet clicked her gum on the other end of the line. "Certainly not stupid enough to leave glass around after she used it to shred the insides of her rival."

Eve was forced to consider the logic of that as she sat on the fluffy white faux-fur rug she'd bought Abbey from Urban Outfitters. Abbey might be many things, but Janet was right, she was definitely not dumb. Even if her actions were being manipulated by the Ragman, she'd be clever enough to clean up the evidence. She wouldn't leave it in a kitchen garbage bag, or for that matter, in the toes of her shoes. Eve took the hand that had been gripping her side and brought it up to her head.

"I'm worried about her, Janet."

"I know, honey. And I'm sorry I haven't been around. It must have been terrible what happened to Selena."

Eve nodded, knowing Janet could feel her affirmation even if she couldn't hear it.

"It was awful, Janet. It was so awful. That poor girl." She bit back tears, so hard that later she'd find a tooth mark on her lower lip.

"It could have just as easily been Abbey who got hurt," Janet said. "I think that's what's really at play here, Eve. You'd rather think Abbey was responsible for this than believe it was something random that narrowly missed your own daughter."

There was a truth in that, Eve realized. It was one degree less terrifying to believe your daughter was a sociopath than to ponder the terror of random circumstances. Ones that could have put Abbey instead of Selena in the hospital with a belly full of glass. Abbey, with the blood streaming down her Glad Girl uniform, packed into an ambulance with tubes hanging out of her limp arm.

"Maybe."

"No maybe about it." Janet popped her gum for emphasis.

Eve lay back on the furry rug. Through the window of Abbey's bedroom she could see the top of the willow tree bend and sway gently, devoid of foreboding black crows. The sky was a brilliant blue, with only a few spun-sugar clouds drifting slowly by. A calm after the storm of yesterday, though Eve still felt anxious with the memory of the thunder and Mark.

"I just can't help thinking there's something wrong here, Janet." Eve looked away from the blueness of the sky, lowered her voice to a harsh whisper, even though no one was in the house to listen. "I can feel him, he's close."

Janet lowered her own voice and whispered back, "You sure about that?" Gone was her earlier lightheartedness and reassurance that all would be well. Janet might dismiss a mother's overactive imagination when it came to her daughter, but she wouldn't dismiss a witch's intuition when it came to the Ragman.

"I think so." Eve played with the fuzzy threads of the rug. "Shit, Janet, I don't know anymore. You know I lost most of my powers."

"You didn't lose them, girl, you just misplaced them." Janet paused, then went on. "If you're thinking there's something wrong, then you need to get out your book. See what there is to see."

Every witch had their own book of spells called a *grimoire*, each one as unique as fingerprints. The words needed for incantations were dependent on the one who spoke them, each a variation on a common theme, but still distinct, like a sense of style. A witch developed her own variant brand of spell casting over time, using trial and error, recording her experiences in the pages of her grimoire by hand. Eve had tried typing her spells into the computer once, but every time she went back to get them, they'd vanished from the hard drive.

"I can't divine anymore, Janet. You know that." Divining truths wasn't easy magic, and Eve wasn't even sure where her grimoire was anymore. When they'd moved, she'd packed it into one of the many unmarked boxes that now filled the attic. Boxes that held Michael's white Cubby bear, and some of his clothes — the little slugger baseball onesie Richard had bought when Eve was pregnant, the Thomas the Tank Engine slippers the funeral home had given her before dressing her son in a stiff three-piece suit.

"Nobody knows what they can do until they try, Eve."

"Could you come over? To help?" Eve hadn't attempted any real magic in years. Extracting people's thoughts and exercising her mind's eye were more reflexes than sorcery. She couldn't manipulate anything of consequence with them, couldn't see past the shallow realm of her immediate surroundings to divine the answers to deeper questions. Janet had always been convinced that Eve could coax her witchery back, lure it like one would a pet budgie accidentally escaped from its cage. But Janet hadn't been there, hadn't felt the cosmic tear Eve had when Michael was ripped away from her. The resulting wound was too brutally ragged to be mended. You couldn't replace a heart after it had been torn out of you.

"You know I'd be there if I could, baby," Janet said. "But I've got a flight to catch this afternoon. I have that meeting with the Hellerman Gallery in New York. My agent thinks I've got a shot at a show there in July. But if you really need me …"

"No, you go. I understand." Eve knew how critical this meeting was for Janet. If she got her work shown at the Hellerman, it could make her career, notwithstanding her recent interest in baseball bat lamps. Eve was probably overreacting about everything anyway.

"Listen, Eve, both you and I know that if you're the one feeling the Ragman, then it's you he's come to see. I wouldn't be able to tap into that circle of fate even if I tried. Only you can do that."

Eve agreed. Like an alcoholic who could only become sober by admitting they had a problem, a woman with a demon on her back had to use her own hand to grab him by the tail and pull him off.

"I'll come see you on Thursday when I get back from New York." Eve heard a singsong voice call to her friend in the background. She could sense Janet's smile through the phone, even though it wasn't directed at her.

"Get out your book, honey," Janet told her again. "You'll probably find there's nothing to what you're feeling. You're spooked by what happened to Selena. Worrying about your own girl. Love and fear, they don't only cloud a witch's judgment."

"I hope you're right." Eve stood up from the floor of Abbey's room, checking the branches of the willow tree for crows.

"I'm always right." Janet laughed, and this time Eve knew her beaming smile was meant only for her.

After saying goodbye to Janet, Eve pocketed the cell-phone in the front pocket of her jeans. She looked down at the remaining shoes in Abbey's closet, the ones she hadn't checked the toes of yet, and decided to leave them. She was being paranoid. The shards in the kitchen garbage were from the night Abbey threw her glass at the deck railing and had nothing to do with Selena. The Patels' cat had met up with some urban coyote. She'd panicked when she'd found the red-stained shirt in the laundry. But it was probably just thrown up Shiraz from the night she went to book club. She didn't remember wearing it that night, but she'd been pretty out of it. Still, she couldn't seem to overcome her sense that something was wrong. She needed to be sure.

Eve went to close the closet door, but before she did the sunlight picked up the sparkle of a pink glitter strongbox resting on the top shelf. Eve and Richard had given the box to Abbey one long-ago Christmas. It had a tiny silver padlock shaped like a heart, meant to protect a child's treasures and innocent secrets. Now that Abbey was older, there were so many areas in her life that Eve and Richard were locked away from. The flimsy heart lock struck Eve as ironic. She finished closing the door to the closet, leaving the locked box and the rest of Abbey's shoes intact. If the

Ragman had come to exact his price, Eve wasn't going to find him in her daughter's closet. She'd have to look farther afield than that.

Eve walked out of Abbey's room, careful to replace the tiny piece of paper in the doorjamb before she left. She stood in the hall for a full minute before she grabbed the rope hanging from the ceiling above her. When she pulled, the stairs for the attic came down, unfolding with a squeal of noisy hinges. Careful of her rib, she mounted the steps into the darkness to go searching for her long-neglected grimoire.

SITTING ON THE FLOOR, PROPPED up by cushions against the rec room couch in the basement, Eve stared down at the black leather-bound book on the coffee table. It had been a gift from Nanny, who'd walked the three miles into town to purchase it that first summer solstice Eve and Janet had spent with her at her farm. The old woman, surprisingly adept with her gnarled arthritic hands, had whittled a wooden stamp to personalize her present. Carefully dripping hot red wax onto the black leather cover, she'd then used the stamp to make an imprint before it solidified. Eve ran her fingers over the indented letters in the cardinal-red wax. *EVE*.

She opened the book and found the first incantation she'd ever written down. It was a binding spell against lice. Janet and Eve had worked on the spell together, using an ancient incantation to ward off the plague as a base and then improvising. Eve had been particularly proud of the adaptation she'd made, expanding it to include the banishment of the nit's eggs.

As she leafed through the pages of her grimoire, she followed her maturation, not only as a witch but as a woman. The book began with the basic spells of an adolescent girl's wants and needs, then slowly evolved into the more complex manipulations of matter and time that belonged to adult women. Occasionally, she had to brush away a lost piece of psychic energy that formed as a cloud over the text. The uninitiated often mistook these manifestations for spirits of the dead, but from Eve's experience, they were only adrift fragments of intense emotion looking for a human host. Eve didn't think the dead could manifest in any sort of tangible manner — at least not in a way where you could connect or speak with them. From what Eve had observed, when a person died their soul became a thread in a greater spiritual tapestry, part of a larger collective. She didn't think you could contact one soul in particular, any more than you could speak to one single cell at the tip of a person's finger.

The directions for divination were in the last pages of the grimoire, a more advanced incantation written down the year Nanny passed away from pancreatic cancer. The disease had been swift and ruthless, crushing the bent frame of the poor woman until she seemed to fold in upon herself, like a shrunken piece of origami. But her deep-brown eyes still held the fire of life as Janet and Eve sat vigil beside her at the hospital. They'd leaned in as she fought to whisper the last of her knowledge, intent on passing on a lifetime of wisdom between feeble sucks of crushed ice.

Divination could be tricky. It peeled back the layers of the natural order to reveal what was hidden underneath. Its reach was far greater than the mind's eye. But when you pulled back those layers, you risked releasing what lived in the shadows of them. To divine was to navigate the murky waters of an unknown world, like an explorer from the Middle Ages, when cartographers still drew sea serpents to mark unexplored regions. *Here there be monsters*. She sprinkled some of the Beltane ashes Janet had given her in all four corners of the room and sat back down.

Eve ran her finger down the page. The words she had written were in a lexicon only she and Janet understood, a cross between pig Latin and high-school French. Nanny wrote her grimoire in an ancient Jamaican patois that had been taught to her by her own mother, the seventh daughter of a long line of cunning folk. She'd refused to teach its linguistic mysteries to Eve or Janet, no matter how much they begged, taking the secret with her to her grave. Janet had plugged a few lines from Nanny's grimoire into Google Translate once, but its language banks had not recognized a word of it.

There was only one ingredient to collect for the divination spell, the carefully harvested branches of a burning bush. This was the real reason Eve had transplanted the shrub from their other house. Even with her abilities diminished, she wouldn't have dreamed of leaving that kind of power behind.

Though she knew the meaning of the words in the book, her comprehension proved slow going. Spell casting was a language she'd once been fluent in, but she'd not spoken it in years. Eve sighed and closed her eyes, wishing Janet was with her. Eve didn't believe she had the ability to pull off a divination on her own. Her confidence as well as her skills were rusty. She wanted to go back to bed and pull the covers over her head with enough T3s to wipe out her memories — of Selena coughing up blood, of Mark's abuse, of that smug smirk on Julia McCabe's face at the Delta. But that wouldn't help anyone, least of all Abbey.

She stood up from the rec room floor and climbed the stairs from the basement to the kitchen. Opening the junk drawer beside the fridge, she sifted through old takeout fliers and discarded balls of string to find the pruning sheers. The rain had stopped in the night, but fat drops still hung heavy on the willow tree. She walked barefoot through the wet grass toward the burning bush. Its leaves quivered in the light breeze left behind by the storm.

When her cell went off, it was the vibration against her hip that startled her more than the pithy little sound it made to announce the call. She fumbled in the pocket of her jeans and pulled the phone out, concerned it might be Abbey or news about Selena. In the bright sunshine, she couldn't read the screen to see who was calling.

"Hi, Eve. How are you?" Eve thought it was her mother at first. Their voices were so similar. But it was Pauline Henderson, the one with the anxious shih tzu.

"Jesus, I'm sorry, Pauline." Eve sat down on a tree stump and put down her shears. "I forgot all about the dog." With everything that had happened yesterday, they'd never picked up the animal from his puppy playdate. Eve hadn't even called the woman to explain why. Although she was sure Pauline had heard about Selena by now.

"Don't worry about it. I totally understand." Eve heard a dog barking in the background. "He can stay here for as long as you like. It's horrible what happened to Selena. Just horrible."

"It is."

Pauline waited on the other end of the line, saying nothing in response. She wanted Eve to "spill the tea," as Abbey would say, about what had happened to Selena. She knew Eve and Richard had been at the game. But Eve wasn't one to gossip, especially about something so heart-breaking. The tea was too scalding for that. When Pauline realized Eve wouldn't be volunteering up any juicy tidbits, she divulged some of her own.

"They sent grief counsellors to the school today. All the kids know what happened. My son texted me about it this morning. They had an assembly. And it wasn't just about Selena. You'll never believe this, but —"

"Grief counsellors?" Eve stood up from where she was sitting on the stump. Mark hadn't counselled at the school before, but he'd mentioned a colleague there who'd contacted him about Selena's accident. They might have asked him to help out. Mark could be in a closed room right now with her daughter, deceiving her with his soothing voice, touching her on the shoulder with a practised hand. The thought of Mark being so close to Abbey brought little beads of sweat up on Eve's arms. She shivered in the warm sun.

"Is there something wrong, Eve?"

"Nothing's wrong." Eve started walking toward the house. "I'm sorry, Pauline, I just remembered I have to be somewhere. I'll pick up the dog as soon as I can. Thanks for taking care of him." She hung up and stepped back into the kitchen. Fetching the grimoire, she stored it in a dresser drawer of the master bedroom underneath some faded lingerie she never wore anymore.

As Eve grabbed the car keys from the kitchen counter, she saw something glinting in the sunlight among the blades of shiny wet grass. The pruning sheers. She went outside to retrieve them. Distracted as she was, she didn't register the quivering leaves of the burning bush, or the flies that buzzed around its base, feasting on a scrap of bloody flesh and torn fur.

ABBEY WAS SURPRISED TO FIND her mother waiting in the car outside All Saints High School when classes let out later that afternoon.

She opened up the car door and leaned across the passenger seat.

"What are you doing here, Mom?"

"I was in the area and thought I'd save you the bus trip home," Eve lied. She'd been waiting at the curb outside the main doors of the school for over an hour now.

Abbey eyed her suspiciously. "Okay," she said, drawing the word out and adding a lilt, which denoted a question that would be thought but not asked. She slung her backpack onto the seat and unzipped one of the outer pockets, searching for something inside. Eve held her hands on the steering wheel and checked the rear-view mirror, getting ready to pull out. Cars filed out one by one from the school parking lot. Young people sauntered by, all dressed the same. They spilled out of the main doors and down the wide stone stairs. Some students got into cars, some made their way to the bus stop or down the street to walk home. Many gathered in clumps on the grass or the sidewalk, chatting and laughing in the June sunshine.

Mark stood to one side of the stone steps in a patch of shade. He appeared as he always did in public, hands in the pockets of his jeans, wavy red hair tousled slightly by the breeze. But then he raised his head, and he and Eve locked eyes in the mirror. She shuddered. Mark looked out at her from a set of deep black hollows in his face. His eyes held no pupils or irises, only the blank one-track glare of a predator.

"C'mon, Abbey." Eve gripped the steering wheel tighter. She couldn't tear her gaze from the sight in the rear-view mirror.

"I have to find my earbuds, Mom." Abbey rifled through the rest of her backpack. "Shit, maybe I left them in my locker."

Mark stepped out of the shadow of the stairs and started toward the car. The young people ebbed and flowed around him, like a school of fish darting around the steady progress of a shark.

"Oh, wait," Abbey said, pulling a pair of white earbuds from the bottom of her bag. "Here they are!" She plugged one end of the white wire into the bottom of her phone. Eve wouldn't buy her the more expensive Bluetooth ones.

"Get in the car, Abbey." Eve kept her voice even, but insistent. The shark was on the grass now. In a few seconds he'd be in striking distance.

"Okay, Mom." Abbey picked the backpack up and threw it roughly into the back seat. "I was only trying to —"

"I said get in the FUCKING car!" Abbey dropped into the passenger seat and closed the door, fearful of her mother's outburst or embarrassed by it. Eve could no longer see Mark in the rear-view. Turning to look out the side window, she spotted him on the sidewalk in her blind spot. He was so close he could have shut the door for Abbey himself.

Eve pulled away from the curb before Abbey could get her seat belt fastened, tires squealing. The dispersing students glanced up briefly then returned back to their conversations when they realized she was just a parent and subsequently of no interest to them.

"Jesus, Mom, what the hell is wrong with you?"

"Nothing," Eve said, accelerating down the street. "Nothing is wrong." She wasn't sure if what she'd seen was a sign or a trick, but she knew either one was a warning to be heeded.

Abbey rolled her eyes before putting in her earbuds. Then she lay back in the passenger seat and relaxed, humming to music her mother couldn't hear.

TWENTY-THREE

It was Dylan Penske's funeral today. A bunch of us skipped school and went. It was held in this creepy windowless room in a funeral home that was kind of like a small chapel but mostly like one of those carpeted conference rooms they have at the library that you can rent cheap. I didn't tell my mom I was going. She would have wanted to come as well, even though she didn't know him. She'll get one of those phone calls from the school with the automated voice, telling her I missed first and second period, but I really don't give a shit. She's been acting so weird lately, even weirder than normal. Like how she was waiting for me after school yesterday in the car. I hope she isn't going to get all overprotective after what happened to Selena. As if she hadn't been clocking my every movement before this. I thought she was following me that Friday night before

Zanax when she turned up at the Delta. I saw her there with Julia. I was in the parking lot, sitting in the car. But she didn't see me.

My mom never trusts me, and she'll use Selena's accident as an excuse to pry into my life even more now. What happened to Selena was crazy. Something like that is never going to happen to me. My mom has no reason to be so freaked out.

Dylan's casket wasn't open. Which was good because I am really not into that sort of thing. My dad said he went to an Irish wake once and they had this old guy sitting right out there in his coffin in the living room. The dead man's daughter-in-law almost spilled a drink on his corpse. But she'd been a bit tipsy.

The funeral home smelled like stale bread and dust. Like a church basement but with less disinfectant. When I went looking for the washroom, I saw the door to where they prepare the bodies. It actually had a sign. *Embalming Room*. I guess it's so no one walks in by mistake and sees them draining the blood out of their loved one into that well in the floor. They have to remove the blood to keep the body from stinking. I learned that at science camp too. They fill the veins and arteries up with chemicals and dye afterward to make the person look rosy and alive for the family. Which doesn't make sense to me, because why the fuck would you want to bury a person who looked alive? I wonder what Dylan Penske looks like or whether they even went to the trouble of using rosy dye. When your kid blows half his head off with a shotgun, it doesn't seem to me that you'd be much bothered with appearances.

I haven't been to a funeral since Michael's. It wasn't held at the same funeral home, but that one was just as gross. I hadn't wanted to go, but my mom made me. She said it was important for "closure." Such fucking bullshit. I knew my brother was dead. That he wasn't going to pop up somewhere in the living room alive as if he'd been playing goddamn hide-and-seek. I saw his body on the floor that day, his blank eyes staring up before Mom closed them. That empty stare was all the closure I needed. Where Michael was hiding, no one would ever find him. I didn't need to put on a black dress with scratchy tights to sit in a room full of sobbing adults to seal the lid on that.

Dylan's eulogy was done by some cousin, I think — definitely a relative. He had the telltale funnel-shaped head, but he was older than Dylan. His face was more fleshed out, making the chin stronger, the forehead less Cro-Magnon. He was actually kind of hot. I wonder whether that's what Dylan would have looked like if he'd lived to be a man.

After the funeral, all the girls huddled in groups of three or four and cried like they'd never known anyone who'd died before. Which I realize they probably hadn't. But they didn't need to make such a big fucking spectacle of themselves. The boys just put their hands on each other's shoulders a lot and shook their heads. There was a fair bit of vaping, a habit even more stupid than smoking. Honestly, all the kids at my school are uncouth assholes.

I saw Stephanie Roberts sobbing her face off in the parking lot. She has those really badly done eyelash extensions and they clumped together when she cried, like a wet feather boa stuck onto her eyelids. Stephanie is such a two-faced bitch. She would never have gone near a guy like Dylan Penske when he was alive. Of course, there was that time last year when she started talking to Matthew Crenshaw in French class. Nobody talks to Matthew Crenshaw. For one thing, his stutter makes two-way conversation a chore, plus his clothes smell of French fries. He works part-time at McDonald's in the back where he doesn't have to deal with the public. But Stephanie batted her feather eyes at him and asked him to explain conjugation to her in class. She waited patiently while he stammered out the verbs. *J-J-Je vais. T-T-Tu vas.* Honestly, it was painful to watch. I had to dig a fingernail into my bare thigh under my kilt just to keep from screaming. Stephanie must have done this bit for a whole week, smiling wide with a mouth full of veneers as Matthew tortured the French language. Then one day when he walked in and said hello to her, she acted like she didn't hear him. Each day, he tried to strike up a conversation with her, forcing out the words like chunky soup stuck in a pipe. Stephanie just acted completely confused, shrugging her shoulders to the rest of the class, like she couldn't understand why the hell he would be talking to her. It took him a week before he stopped stammering out hello, a few more before he gave up smiling in her direction every time she turned around to work on conjugating verbs with someone else.

We learned about this in our advanced science class, in the neurology section. It's called "extinction." You give a rat a food pellet every time he pushes a lever in his cage and then one day you just stop giving him pellets. It takes a long time for that rat to stop pushing on the lever. He'll push it until his little pink rat paws go bloody, our teacher said, especially if every hundred pushes, you fool him and actually give him a food pellet.

It's sort of brilliant what Stephanie Roberts did. I think she must have taken the same science class. Because a couple of times during the semester she behaved like she had before with Matthew, asking him questions, flipping her long honey-blond hair, and laughing like he was the most amusing fucking guy on the planet. But the next day she'd be back to being the ice queen again. Movies and books always show mean girls doing such over-the-top acts of cruelty, like pouring pig's blood on a prom dress or calling a guy a loser to his face. They don't realize that the whole point of being a mean girl is the quiet subtlety of it.

I wanted to talk to Selena about Stephanie Roberts's eyelashes, and about what Dylan Penske would look like if he'd grown up instead of shooting himself. But I can't. She's *still* in the hospital and I'm *still* not allowed to see her. I think her mom has taken her cellphone or something, because she's not responding to any of my texts. I even tried to phone her, but it went straight to voice mail. My mom said to leave a message, but nobody leaves messages anymore. People can see that you called. What's the point?

I'm afraid Selena's mad at me about the kombucha, or maybe she's mad that I might be given the scholarship if she can't get better in time to take final exams. I want to say I'm sorry I ever bought that dumb drink. And I'm really sorry she got hurt. I'm even sorry about her goddamn cat. I want to tell her that I don't even care about the Thompson scholarship anymore. She can have it. My parents will probably not even let me accept it, because after this glass thing my mom is never going to let me out of her sight again to go away to university or anywhere else. Everything is so fucked up.

I just want things to be like they were before. When Selena and I were laughing in her bedroom, sitting on the floor eating microwave popcorn, making up crap poetry to put in Dylan Penske's locker. Back when Dylan was still alive and not a boy who we wanted to get back at for having a boner. A boy who'll never grow up now to have a chin. I don't know what I'm going to do if Selena doesn't come back to school. I'll be alone with all the assholes, with no one to compete with but Ashley Stravinsky, who gets decent enough grades but is so clueless she thought Elon Musk was a rapper. My parents don't give a damn about me, and what's worse, when I finally found the washroom at the funeral home, I looked in the mirror and I had a huge throbbing pimple on my forehead. I always get one just before my period. Now I won't be able to go swimming at Stephanie Roberts's pool party on the weekend. She invited me after the funeral, and I've got a new bikini and everything, but tampons never work for me.

My life completely sucks.

TWENTY-FOUR

Tuesday morning, Richard woke up early and left the house before either Eve or Abbey was awake. He should have been used to deceit by now, but he couldn't bring himself to face the two of them at the breakfast table and pretend he had an office to go to. At least it was only for a few days. That was unless this business with Julia and the budget numbers didn't put him out of a job on a more permanent basis. He felt like an impostor donning his pressed khakis and slinging his laptop bag over his shoulder. But he couldn't stay at the house. That would require explanations, ones he was not prepared for and would have found too uncomfortable to make.

"Large coffee with milk and sugar," he told the barista behind the counter, a heavy-set, blue-rinsed woman wearing a kid's uniform. She was probably one of those retirees whose pension investments had been fucked over by the downturn. A lot of seniors were forced into menial jobs so they had enough scraps to feed the wolf at the door.

"Dark roast or medium?" she asked mechanically, eyes focused on the till.

"Dark."

"Steamed milk or regular?"

"Regular."

She grabbed a cup from a stack marked *Tall* and lifted up a black Sharpie. "Name?"

Richard couldn't remember when ordering a coffee had become such an interrogation. But he felt for the old woman. It wasn't fair that she was forced to pull espresso shots and learn latte art when she should have been doting on spoiled grandchildren and catching up on her soaps. He decided to try and make her laugh, something that usually endeared men to women, old and young alike.

"Hey, remember the days when you could get a hot beverage and still remain anonymous?" he said, chuckling. But it came out all wrong. She considered him with rheumy eyes, gave him no laugh, not even a smile. Although her upper lip twitched a little, revealing pink lipstick she had stuck on one tooth.

"I don't make the rules, buddy."

"I know," he said. "I was just making a joke."

The woman looked back at the coffee cup and sighed. "Name?"

"Richard," he told her, aware that the lineup had grown exponentially behind him. She scribbled on the coffee cup with the Sharpie, handing it off to a skinny kid down the line, who filled it with hot black liquid.

"Next," she called out, watery eyes back on the till. Only when he picked up his coffee at the end of the counter did he notice she'd written *Dick* on it.

Richard located a table away from the window that looked out on the street. He didn't want anyone to see him here. Although it was early and he could still be a guy catching up on emails over a cup of java before work. He took out his laptop and typed in the Wi-Fi password the skinny kid gave him when he'd handed over Richard's coffee with a smirk. The password was *Coffee.* Their originality was only surpassed by their lack of internet security in this place.

He checked on his emails, reading each one although he couldn't respond to any of them. To do so would, technically, be seen as working, even if he wasn't at the office. More than once, he found his itchy finger poised above the left clicker of the mouse, the screen arrow hovering dangerously over the reply button. The situation gave him the sensation of being gagged, even if his enforced silence was only a virtual one.

But in the coffee shop, he noticed that most communication was virtual. The only words spoken seemed to be at the cash register. Once served, everybody sat glued to their phones or their laptops, "talking" to people who weren't there, ignoring the people who were. Richard remembered when coffee shops had been lively, a place to gather with friends in between classes during his university days. There'd be half a dozen of them huddled together, their lettered jackets slung over chairs as they discussed the profs they needed to impress and the girls they wished they could.

Grant Saunders had been his best friend back then and had served as best man at his wedding. But the two of them had been reduced over the years to sending an annual Christmas card or the occasional LinkedIn message. That was pretty much the case when it came to all of his old friends. Richard wasn't sure how he'd lost touch with all of them, except that it had been a gradual process. These days, his socializing consisted mostly of work events — team-building exercises where the camaraderie was forced like toothpaste through a corporate tube. He supposed Julia had been a friend of a sort, but that was all over now.

Richard closed his work email and tried to focus on other things. He looked up some rugby scores, then viewed some trailers of movies he might see in the afternoon. But he kept getting drawn back to the siren song of his inbox. Work had always been his drug of choice, flooding his brain with soothing data that insulated him from deeper thoughts. About Julia. About his family. About Selena and the hospital, and the monotone voice of Sanjay Patel when Richard called him this morning for an update. Selena was stable but in serious condition. Patel hadn't offered up much more beyond that. And Richard hadn't pressed him.

Richard used work in this way, as a barrier against open wounds. Like the cone they put on dogs to keep them from licking and chewing an incision, work was Richard's Elizabethan collar. It shielded him from the compulsion to pick at painful scabs.

That was the problem with Eve, Richard thought. She didn't have enough work to distract her. There was her writing, but that wasn't the same as having a nine-to-five job, where you couldn't go back to bed in the middle of the day or have a breakdown at your desk without witnesses. He wondered whether it had been a good idea, Eve leaving her job in the tech sector. It had seemed like the right choice at the time. Better for Abbey. Better for Eve. That's what they'd said, what he'd said. Now he questioned his motivations. Eve and he had worked for different companies, but as their software rep she'd made regular trips to his office. They'd never had a problem with working together in the past. But when Eve finally went back to work after Michael's death, Richard found himself dodging her when she came for client visits. He didn't blame Eve for what happened to their son, but it was difficult to see her face without remembering the disaster they both had in common. Work had been his only refuge from that constant reminder. He'd been secretly relieved when she'd quit not long after. It was hard when your love and grief were rolled up into one.

He realized that over the years he'd sought more opportunities to look away from his wife and the tragedy they shared. It was easier that way. He'd thought if he kept up a strong facade that it would comfort her, but it had only driven a wedge between them. And then it seemed too late to change his approach. He'd found his own way to cope. But he couldn't tell her about it.

His face reddened as he remembered parking his car Friday night on the far side of town. He'd checked the street for anyone who might recognize him before he went slinking onto the sagging porch of the dilapidated Victorian by the train tracks. He and Eve had driven past the old house years before, during happier times. They'd laughed at the *Psychic by Appointment* sign, with a phone number burning in neon underneath. *If she were really psychic, shouldn't she know to call you*? he'd joked. But Richard no longer laughed about such things.

Michael had been dead six months the first time Richard had worked up the nerve to climb the rickety steps past that neon sign to ring the bell. When the woman answered the door, he hadn't known what to say. Much as Eve and he had joked, he'd hoped she might already sense his needs. But he'd discovered that wasn't how it worked.

"What do ya want?" she'd asked, hand on one hip in the doorway. The smell of old nicotine and cat litter had wafted out from the dark hallway behind her.

Richard had stood frozen on the front porch, partly from the temperature. It had been February and minus twenty-five degrees Celsius with the windchill.

"My son died," he'd said. And to his humiliation, tears had begun to flow. One or two crystallized on his eyelashes before he could blink them away.

"Come inside, before you catch your death," the woman Richard would come to know as Collette had said. He'd stepped into the warmth of the house, and she'd closed the door behind him.

And so had begun a dependency that now shamed Richard more than his affair. More than his perceived failings as a father and as a husband. Because this addiction showcased how much of a sham his illusion of strength really was. He was a house of cards held together with silence and denial, until the stress became too much and he ultimately toppled and fell apart. When that happened, he could not talk to his wife about it, or to his co-workers, or even to a best friend if he'd had one anymore. When that happened, there was only one person in whom he could confide, and that was the little boy who'd fallen off the railing onto the hard, unforgiving floor.

The woman with the laughable neon sign was the only one who could help him with that. Because Collette wasn't just a psychic. She was also a medium.

TWENTY-FIVE

As Eve walked into the drop-in centre, the bell made a little jingling sound above the door. The handful of people who sat at the Arborite tables didn't look up, too weighed down by circumstances to lift their heads. Only Heather standing behind the counter in a faded yellow apron acknowledged her.

"Hey, what are you doing here? I thought you only volunteered on Thursdays."

"I think I might have left my sweater behind last time," Eve said, approaching the counter. She darted a quick glance to the room where Mark conducted his counselling sessions. The door was closed. She needed to see him. She'd tried his regular office, the one housed in a rambling old mansion converted for professional use, earlier. They had no receptionist there, only a whiteboard in the shared waiting room with columns marked *In* and *Out* on it. A black magnetic disk, affixed next to his name, was in the column marked *Out*. He couldn't still be at home so late in the morning, being a creature of habit with a firm work ethic. She'd decided to try the drop-in, hoping to catch him in between clients. If that didn't work, she'd have to wait for him at his apartment. But that was a last resort. She was wary of confronting him on home turf.

Mark had crossed a line when he'd come so close to Abbey and the car. It didn't matter if what she'd seen in his eyes was real or imagined. She didn't want him anywhere near her daughter. She'd threaten him with professional misconduct if she had to, make public their affair no matter what the consequences. He could do whatever he wanted to her, but Abbey was off-limits.

As soon as Abbey left for school this morning, Eve put on her sneakers and walked the few blocks to downtown. She hadn't tried divining Mark's whereabouts. There wasn't time for that. The best way to find him would be through the old-fashioned process of elimination.

"I didn't see any sweater," Heather said, wiping the counter with a dingy grey cloth. They washed the kitchen linens every night at the drop-in, but much like the clientele, everything came back looking tired.

"I'll have a look in the Lost and Found just in case." Eve moved behind the counter and bent down to remove a large cardboard box they kept in the cupboard underneath. Pretending to look for her fictitious sweater, she sorted through the discarded water bottles and old mittens left behind from the winter months, never letting the door to Mark's office leave her peripheral vision.

"Well, since you're here, do you mind covering for me while I go into the back for some ketchup?"

Eve nodded, still focused on the box and the door. They had a refrigerator behind the counter, but the majority of food and condiments were stored in a huge walk-in unit in the basement, accessed through the common room.

"I'll only be a minute," Heather said as she grabbed a set of keys from the pocket of her apron and disappeared around the corner to where there were couches, a collection of poorly tuned guitars, and a few aging desktop computers with Wi-Fi. Despite this cozy ambiance, the common room usually sat empty. The regulars at the drop-in preferred the stark Arborite tables and hard chairs in the eating area, more in keeping with the institutional feel to which they'd become accustomed.

Harold stepped up to the counter. He pointed at the carafes behind Eve with one of his long pointy fingernails. Today, they were painted with red nail polish instead of the usual black.

"Coffee," he grunted, pushing a quarter toward her. Eve put the cardboard box of lost things back in the cupboard and poured him a coffee. She spooned three helpings of sugar into the cup, knowing if she put any less he'd complain. Harold took the mug and poured in a generous dollop of milk and then remained standing there. Eve kept her eyes trained on the door to the counselling room. She didn't see Harold reach into his back pocket and pull out a tattered leather wallet until he had extracted the photograph from it and placed it in front of her.

"Look," he said, bringing her attention back. Eve tore her gaze away from the closed door and looked down at the photo on the counter. It was dog-eared but still glossy. There was a white border around it, the kind film developers used before everything went digital. In the picture, a little boy was riding a toy horse that was suspended from springs on a metal frame. His hair was curly and slightly too long. She couldn't discern the colour because it was in black and white.

"That's me," Harold said. "Can you believe it?" He picked the photo back up and caressed the image with his thumb, as if he could make out the contours of the little boy he used to be through his razor-sharp fingertips.

"You look very happy there," Eve said. And then worried this was not the right thing to say. Harold was obviously not a very happy man, whatever he was as a child. She wondered if his mother took the picture, capturing the joy on his face as he rocked back and forth on the horse. She'd probably never envisioned a future for him that included shelters or twenty-five-cent coffees where he wasn't even allowed to have a spoon.

"Well," he said, still caressing the photo. "You never know how things are going to turn out, do you?"

The front door of the drop-in flew open and the little bell jingled violently. Harold quickly slipped the photograph back into his wallet, pocketing it before returning to his table. A dishevelled man ran past him to the counter, smelling of sweat and booze.

"Is the shrink in?" he asked her. His eyes were protruding and darted wildly back and forth, like a farm animal caught in a barn fire. Mark was not a shrink, but the people here thought of him in that way.

"He's not in today," Heather said, plunking a large canister of ketchup onto the counter. "Tomorrow," she told him.

The man continued to stand there, searching the room with his wild eyes. Heather repeated what she'd said, but more slowly this time. Her message eventually sank in. Without any further outburst, he grabbed a day-old Danish donated by a local bakery and went to sit by himself at a table in the corner.

Heather leaned in close to Eve's ear. "Mark was here," she whispered. "But he left to go back to his saner clients. Honestly, I don't know how that poor man does it. He's a saint."

"Yes," Eve said quietly, thinking sanity was in the eye of the beholder.

"Did you find your sweater?" Heather asked, getting out a funnel to pour the mega canister of ketchup into more manageable dispensers.

"What?" Eve said. "Oh, no, I didn't."

"Things have a way of turning up," Heather said, with her back toward Eve. She reached to the back of the cupboard, standing on the tippy toes of her orthopedic shoes. "Usually where you looked the first time."

By the time Heather turned to ask her taller friend for help, Eve was already out the door, the bell jingling in lieu of a goodbye. The wild-eyed man muttered questions to himself in the corner as Harold caressed the photograph he'd taken back out of his wallet. Each tried to figure out where they'd lost the things they'd been looking for.

WALKING ALONG GORDON STREET, Eve wondered how she'd come to be this desperate woman, roaming the downtown core and looking for a man she didn't want to see. But a mother's protective streak was a powerful motivator. It could take a woman to all sorts of places she didn't want to go.

She crossed at the intersection of Gordon and Yarmouth, cutting through the tiny triangular park that perched on its angled corner. An elderly woman with toothpick-thin legs sat with her dog on a bench next to an old fountain. It had been a watering stop for horses a hundred years ago, when it was built. The fountain sat dry and without purpose, much as the old woman who sat with her pet, watching resignedly as the cars passed by.

Once Eve reached the looming Italianate facade of the Wellness Centre, she stood and looked up. In a tiny window on the third floor, she saw movement. Mark's office. His metallic disk on the waiting room whiteboard would be moved to the *In* column now.

Eve took the back entrance, marching up what would have been the servant's stairs when the building had been a gracious home. Now it was subdivided into hushed carpeted offices used by massage therapists and other healing professionals who sought to knead the thornier knots out of their clients. Eve had come here to see Mark on the referral of a social worker at the hospital. She'd carried the address around in her purse for two months after Michael's death before gathering up the courage to mount these stairs. It took her that long to admit she had a problem. If crippling grief could be described as a problem and not a natural state of being for a woman who'd lost her only son.

When she reached the third floor, she saw the door stood ajar to Mark's office at the end of the hall. She walked past a room with a treatment table fitted in stark white linen. Flickering candles on recessed shelves surrounded it like a shrine. Eve took a heady inhalation of essential oils as she continued down the hallway.

"Hello, Eve," Mark said. He looked up from the small writing desk that faced the open doorway, not appearing surprised she was there. Behind him was a futon sofa, spread with a brightly coloured Mexican blanket — a funky alternative to the classic psychiatrist's couch. Two comfy armchairs faced each other by the window. Between them was a table holding a box of tissues and a pitcher of water with plastic tumblers. Eve had sat in the far chair dozens of times in her counselling sessions with Mark, sometimes making use of the tissues, more often the water. One to mop up her tears, the other to replenish the fluid she'd lost from them.

"Come in," Mark said. She considered her position in the safety of the doorway for a few seconds before taking one step inside. He'd have to find a way past her if he tried to close the door.

"I want you to stay the fuck away from my daughter," Eve hissed, mustering the courage of her outrage. "I saw you at the school yesterday." Eve flashed back to the memory of Mark's eyes as he stood on the sidewalk by the car, the dead black pits of them trained on Abbey like prey. She quickly blinked the image away. He was just a man after all. She mustn't project.

Mark leaned his chin in one hand, studying her, not used to her strong resolve or her swearing. She wasn't the depressed and sorrowful wreck she'd been that first time she'd entered his office. She knew now that the bastard had used that vulnerability to draw her into his arms and his bed, and she loathed him for it.

"I was at the school as part of the trauma team, Eve," Mark said, after he was finished studying her. "It's my job."

"Was it your job to follow Abbey to my car?" Eve demanded.

"I just wanted to see if you were okay," he said. "Are you okay, Eve?" He got up from his desk and Eve visibly stiffened. She cast her gaze around the room for something she could club him with if he got out of hand, but all she saw were soft, innocuous pillows.

"Hmm," he said, regarding her carefully. He was close, but not close enough to make her step back into the doorway. "You seem a little fixated on your daughter lately, Eve. It's concerning."

"The only thing you need to be concerned about is leaving my daughter alone."

"Oh, I don't know if I can do that, Eve." He smiled, exposing his perfect teeth. "Your daughter, I think, warrants a fair bit of concern."

"What the hell are you talking about?" She tried to maintain the tone of her earlier outrage, but her words were just that little bit hesitant. She'd been angry and frightened when she first came here, but now she was just frightened.

"I took a look at Abbey's school record. She's got a bit of a temper, doesn't she? Of course, we've talked about her anger issues before, you and me. There were those unfortunate incidents with the mice. I lied to you when I said you had nothing to worry about there. I think you have a lot to worry about." Mark walked over to the table and poured himself some water before taking a drink.

"And then this terrible business with Selena Patel occurred." He shook his head. "What a tragedy. Selena's a good friend of Abbey's, isn't she? Rivals as well, it appears." He put the empty tumbler back on the table. "I asked around the school about them. You know, just as part of my job. The two girls were even up for the same scholarship, I believe. The principal told me about it. Although it looks like Abbey will get the award now, what with Selena's accident. Lucky girl."

Eve was trembling now. Every word he said seemed to cut her, and he could sense the blood in the water. She felt him circle around her before he closed the door and went in for the kill.

"You understand that as a therapist I'm legally required to report any situation where I feel a person may be a threat, a risk to themselves or others." He pulled back her hair from one side of her neck while standing behind her, brushing his lips gently behind her ear. Eve started to cry.

"Don't, Mark," she pleaded, and she meant more than the unwanted kiss. If he reported his suspicions about

Abbey, it could lead to a deeper investigation into her daughter and possibly into Michael's death. Eve might not know for sure whether Abbey had put the glass in Selena's drink, but she couldn't take the chance that she had.

When Mark pushed her roughly down on the futon sofa, Eve tried to feel nothing, except for the scratchy Mexican blanket that grated against her skin. The ache from her rib came in waves, as Mark pushed himself inside her again and again. No magic left to save her, she bit her tongue and let the blood fill her mouth like a salty salve. Deals with the devil were not only made within the chalked lines of a pentagram. Sometimes they were made on your back, with a man who held the power of your family's destruction in his hands.

After it was over, Eve went to her mother's house. She knocked first, then walked in through the unlocked door. Her mother sat in the chair she wouldn't leave, watching the second season of *The Handmaid's Tale*. Eve said nothing, only sat on the floor at her slippered feet and put her head in her mother's lap. The tears fell onto her polyester pants and left beaded trails there.

Eve's mother patted her head with one veined hand, the only part of her body that betrayed her age besides her bad hip.

"Oh, Eve," her mother murmured, using the remote to turn off the TV. "Don't let the bastards grind you down."

TWENTY-SIX

I got called down to the office today. I thought it was about skipping school in the morning to go to the funeral. But they wanted to talk about the basketball game and what happened to Selena. Even though I had talked to the cops already. Even though there was nothing more to tell. The police weren't in the office, just my principal, Mrs. Anderson, sitting at her big oak desk with the school social worker beside her. I guess the team of Michael Cera look-alikes had all gone home or moved on to another traumatic teenage event. When I came in, Mrs. Anderson was dictating into one of those old voice recorders you hold in your hand. Who the hell uses those now that everyone's got a cellphone?

With no cops there, they didn't have to call in my parents, but they did anyway. First they tried to call my dad, but he wasn't in his office. So they had to phone my mom. She didn't pick up her cell. Typical! So Mrs. Anderson left a message. After that, I had to sit in a chair for half an hour while the social worker grilled me on how it felt to see my best friend blow chunks of her esophagus out onto the gym floor. How does she think it made me feel? *Not too fucking good*, I wanted to say. But instead, I dug my fingernail into my thigh again, where they couldn't see me from behind the desk. Just like I did that time Stephanie Roberts made Matthew Crenshaw hack up French verbs.

I told them what I thought they wanted to hear. That it was hard. That I was devastated. That I was coping. But it wasn't enough. They wanted me to break down and sob like those idiots at Dylan Penske's funeral. But I wouldn't give them the satisfaction. The social worker was lecturing me on some bull about "processing my thoughts and feelings" when Mom finally showed up. She flew into the principal's office stuttering apologies, looking like shit. Mom was so jittery the social worker had to go get her a cup of tea. When I looked over, I noticed her eyes were all red. I wonder if she's on drugs.

Then old Mrs. Anderson let on the real reason for the meeting. She'd spoken with the police over the lunch period. There had been other incidents reported of glass shards in bottles of kombucha. A woman in Toronto and some guy in Ottawa. Mrs. Anderson wanted us to know about the other cases before it was made public, due to the close connection between Selena and me and because we'd bought her the drink. Before I could say anything, Mom started choking on the cup of tea she was sipping as if she'd swallowed some glass herself. Honestly, she's such a total wreck. Can't cope with anything.

It was like that Tylenol case, Mrs. Anderson said. Mom told me later that this was a thing back in the '80s — some freak was spiking pills with cyanide right in the stores. That's why everything has a plastic seal on it now that tells you not to ingest anything inside if it's been broken. But I looked it up, the freaks just started using hypodermic needles to inject poison into things after that, like through the skin of an orange or the walls of soft packaging. So I guess they're choking the landfills with all that extra protective shrink wrap for nothing. I don't know how they got the glass in the kombucha though. Probably someone in the factory that bottles it did it, so damn bored sitting on an assembly line all day that they decided to add a little excitement into their dead-end-job lives.

After she finished telling us what the police had said, Mrs. Anderson told us that Selena had moved out of the ICU. That she might even go home this week but that her mom was requesting no visitors. Selena still hasn't answered any of my texts. I bet her bitch of a mother won't let her. That woman never liked me.

The social worker asked us to keep all this information to ourselves, but by the time we got out of the principal's office, it was already all over Instagram. Kids were taking selfies of themselves next to bottles of kombucha with stupid captions. *Close Call! Could have been me! Kom-gotcha!* One asshole had stuck a yellow Post-it to his bottle that said *Drink Me*, like in *Alice in Wonderland*. Really, there is no limit to the fuckupedness of people. I don't know if anyone knows that Selena is doing better, or that she might come home from the hospital soon. I wonder if she'll have to go back for follow-up surgeries. Dad said there was a possibility of that.

School was almost over, and Mom offered to drive me home. But I said I wanted to go back to class so I could take the bus later with my friends. She picked me up yesterday and embarrassed the shit out of me, speeding down the street like a maniac. She probably *is* on drugs, driving around with her kid in the car under the influence. I wouldn't put it past her. I thought maybe I should tell Dad about it, but when he got home tonight, he looked like crap himself. I decided to just go to my room after dinner to think about my next move.

I waited a while and then opened my bedroom door and listened to him and Mom talking downstairs in the kitchen. Dad had been told to take some time off work because of what happened to Selena. That's why he wasn't at the office today. I guess they expected him to break down like a sobbing schoolgirl as well. But there was more. He'd broken up with Julia. He told Mom it was over. I listened to him try to explain himself to my mom. But he couldn't seem to come up with one decent excuse for cheating on her. He just kept saying Julia had meant nothing to him, that she was a mistake he'd made, as if he'd stuck his dick into her by accident. I didn't hear what Mom said after that. Which wasn't surprising because she'd been walking around like a zombie all night barely saying anything. I kept thinking about all the times I needed my mom to be strong instead of catatonic. About how my dad was screwing up our family with his pathetic mid-life crisis. I pictured that stupid Julia in my dad's office trying to be my friend and it made me want to puke. So I closed my bedroom door and went to watch YouTube videos on how to apply liquid eyeliner.

Because a slut like that Julia doesn't deserve thinking about.

TWENTY-SEVEN

Richard pulled into a spot in the parking lot across the street from his work. He'd arrived late — after waffling earlier over whether he should show up at the office or not. As a result of that delay, the inner parking lot was already full. Devon had told him not to come back to work until tomroow. But Richard couldn't spend another day in coffee shops, muzzled, unable to respond to his email. He marvelled at how the unemployed must spend their time during the week. The movie theatres didn't even open until late afternoon on a Tuesday. He'd gone to see a film that he thought was about vice cops, expecting the usual reassuring clichés. Heart-of-gold prostitutes. Evil drug lords. But it turned out the film was a biography of former vice-president Dick Cheney, full of political commentary on the Republican right. There was not a heart-of-gold prostitute to be seen. Although Richard figured there must have been a few inside the White House during the Bush administration. They just didn't make it into history. Not like that intern who blew both the president and the whistle during the Clinton years. The Democrats never were any good at putting the lid on a sex scandal.

He shifted the car into neutral and pulled up the parking brake of his wife's Mazda. Eve had bought this car after she'd scored a three-book deal for her crime fiction series. He'd been surprised when she'd chosen a standard transmission. Perhaps she thought with her new success that she was ready to live a less automatic life. One where she could savour her control of the gears, reacting to the road beneath her instead of just going through the motions. But though the car was registered to her, she had rarely driven it since Abbey got her licence. Most kids didn't learn to drive stick these days. Richard had offered to teach his daughter, but she wasn't interested. So he took the Mazda to work each day, leaving his own beloved Bimmer with the automatic transmission at home, in case Abbey wanted to take it to the mall.

He dodged the traffic as he jaywalked across the street with his laptop bag, narrowly escaping a black Toyota that honked at him. The blare of the horn faded in pitch with the Doppler effect as he touched down safely on the curb.

He was prepared with arguments for Devon if he questioned him about being in the office today. He'd tell him he had no time for his sensitivity training bullshit. He was not a man in need of coddling. When Michael had died, he'd only taken a few days off to make arrangements.

Sitting with Eve in that shitty funeral home, where they'd been forced to pick from the abomination of child-sized caskets, he'd longed for the distraction of spreadsheets and PowerPoint presentations. As soon as the funeral was over, he was back at work, so early people made comments. Abbey was more like him, asking to go back to school the following week. Eve had said that wasn't good. But the approach seemed to work for his daughter and him. Even if he did have an occasional fall from grace that drove him to consult a medium named Collette.

When Richard stepped out of the stairwell, he saw the blinds were closed in Devon's office window. No one looked up from their desks to acknowledge his absence yesterday or his presence today. Devon mustn't have said anything. That was one point in the asshole's favour. Richard didn't want or need the concern of others. He wasn't interested in inquiries into how he was doing or good-natured pats on the shoulder. He'd been down that road of weak condolences before. *We were so sorry to hear … Such a terrible tragedy. How is Eve holding up?* The rare one had asked about how he was faring. Most avoided the question though. His work-as-usual attitude set a certain tone that discouraged questions about his welfare. Or maybe they just liked Eve better. He knew they thought he was an unfeeling bastard, coming back to the office the day after the funeral, leaving his wife at home to cope on her own with her fresh grief. But they hadn't seen him in his car at the end of the day, as he sat for twenty minutes behind the leather-clad steering wheel — waiting for his hands to stop shaking.

He walked past Julia's desk. The hook over the cubicle wall was still missing her blazer. He noted her tidy desktop as he went past, saw the photo in a white frame of her and some college friends all dressed up and smiling for a night on the town. The manila file folders were stacked up neatly in one corner, untouched since she'd left the office on Friday. He was glad that he and Eve had talked about her last night, getting that hurdle out of the way. But he still needed to earn back her trust, as well as Abbey's. And his daughter wasn't an easy touch. As she proved when she threw Eve's wineglass against the back deck railing. He was the one who'd had to clean up the glass. He was prepared to clean up this mess as well.

Richard opened the door to his office and slung his bag on the floor next to the empty garbage can. He sat down heavily in his padded desk chair and saw the door to Devon's office open. His boss came out and made a beeline straight for him. Richard sank more deeply into the chair. He anchored himself in its ergonomic lines in defiance, like those protesters who chain themselves to trees. He didn't care what Devon said. He wasn't budging. He'd refuse to go home to take his enforced time off. Devon could go fuck himself.

"I need you in my office," Devon commanded as he stood in the doorway. He didn't seem to care if people heard Richard being called to the mat. *Sit, Richard. Fetch, Richard. In my office now, Richard.*

"Listen, Devon, I'm fine to be at work, and I don't appreciate you —" But his pipsqueak of a boss cut him off.

"It's not about that," Devon said, shifting his eyes. He looked nervous for the first time Richard could remember.

"Then what the hell is it about?" Richard asked him, still refusing to leave his chair.

Devon stepped in and closed the door.

"The police are in my office, Richard," he said. "They want to talk to you about Julia."

THE VISITOR'S CHAIR WAS UNOCCUPIED when Richard walked into Devon's office, accompanied by his boss. A stocky older man and a younger woman, both in plainclothes, stood by the waxy leaves of a rubber tree plant potted in the corner. Richard never was able to tell if it was real or a fake. The woman detective wore a pair of tailored grey pants and a blazer like Julia's. The man had a proud beer gut that strained the buttons of his cheap suit. Both of the cops flashed their badges at him in unison, introducing themselves. He didn't have time to see whether their IDs were any more authentic than the plant. But he assumed like most people in such situations that they were. The woman indicated with a pen in her hand that he should sit down. It would have been awkward if he didn't, so he took a seat. He immediately regretted it. With everyone else standing, it felt like they were all looking down on him.

"We just wanted to ask you a few questions," the woman said, putting on a waxy smile to rival the rubber tree plant's leaves. Her dark hair had a red sheen to it and she wore slender high heels. Richard would have been thinking she was easy on the eyes if his balls weren't shrinking up so far between his legs.

"I'm happy to help, Detective ...? I'm sorry, I didn't catch your name."

"Malone," she said.

"Detective Malone," Richard repeated, using his most reasonable professional voice. "What can I do for you?"

"What's your relationship with Julia McCabe?" the other cop asked. Up until now, he'd been leaning his sturdy frame against the wall, saying nothing as he glared at Richard after the introductions. Richard guessed he was the bad cop to this Malone woman's good one. Richard found himself caught off guard by the question, despite Devon giving him a heads-up. He couldn't recall this cop's name either, but he'd be damned if he was going to ask.

"Ms. McCabe and I work together," Richard said, still keeping his cool.

"According to your co-workers, you do a hell of a lot more than that," Malone said, her smile having vanished. Maybe she was the bad cop after all.

"I'm sorry," Richard said, stalling. "What is this all about?" He started tapping one of his casual loafers on the carpet floor, abruptly stopping when he realized he was doing it.

"Julia was reported missing on Sunday," Malone said, consulting her notes. "By her roommate."

Damn that nosy Rachel. She and Julia shared a small walk-up apartment in the south end of the city. That's why he and Julia always had to rent hotel rooms or have trysts in the car. Rachel didn't like Richard, couldn't handle the noises coming from Julia's room the one time they'd used it for sex when she was home. And Rachel was always home.

She was a shrinking violet, in direct contrast to Julia's more gregarious sunflower personality. That girl never went out, only waited with the cat for Julia to return like she was her goddamn mother.

"She failed to return home on Friday night," Malone continued. "And she never sent a text to explain. Hasn't been answering her phone either. Her roommate says that's unusual."

Fucking Rachel.

"Maybe she just went away for a few days and forgot to tell anyone. You know how those twentysomethings can be." Richard looked over at the other cop in search of some middle-aged male solidarity. The man only scratched the paunch beneath his shiny suit jacket and continued to glare. His hooded eyes looked to Richard as if they didn't get a lot of sleep.

"We thought that, too, at first," Malone said, drawing Richard's attention back to her while donning her patient smile again. "We'd like you to tell us more about your relationship. To see if you can shed any light on her whereabouts. You do want to help us find her, don't you, Mr. Knight?"

"Well, of course," Richard stuttered. "It's just, who knows if she wants to be found. If you know what I mean." He'd heard of situations like this. There'd been that devoted wife and mother who everyone had been searching for last year. *She'd never just disappear*, they all said. *Totally out of character*, her husband insisted. They'd eventually found her shacked up in Vegas with a boy toy. She claimed later she'd been kidnapped, even though witnesses had seen her at the roulette wheel every night that week having a ball.

"Where were you Friday night?" the other cop asked, tired of restricting himself to glaring.

"I was here," Richard told him. "Working late."

"All night?" asked Malone.

"No, not all night," Richard admitted, as he tried to figure out how much to divulge. He didn't want to tell these cops where he'd gone after he dropped the burner phone in the office garbage can. Or that he'd been at Collette's later on. Both situations incriminated him — in different ways.

The fat cop moved away from the wall to stand behind Richard. He couldn't see the guy's face, but he could feel his protruding gut rubbing against the back of the chair.

"You know we've already put together a subpoena for her phone records," he said. "She probably didn't make many calls — none of them do that anymore — but I bet she did lots of texting. And the great thing about texts, Richard, is you can not only see who they're from ..." The jackass paused for dramatic effect. "You can also see what's being said."

Richard knew they couldn't trace the burner phone to him, but the contents of his texts to Julia might give away who they were from. And that would include the text Friday night where he'd agreed to meet her in a small park overlooking the Elora Gorge. He realized with horror that he might have even sent her a photo of his junk once. Although he couldn't remember if his face had been in the frame. But he'd heard of cases where they'd been able to identify men from such pictures, using a telltale mole or a characteristic bend of the shaft. He wasn't just an unfaithful bastard, he was an idiot.

"She wanted to meet, and I had originally agreed," he said. "But I didn't go."

"You didn't go?" Malone asked, one eyebrow raised in suspicion.

"No, I didn't," Richard lied. "I even sent her a text message telling her it was over," Richard said. They could check *his* phone records for that one. He'd used his regular cell after throwing out the burner. "Then I went home." Another lie, but he didn't see any reason to mention his trip to see Collette. He could only imagine the look on Devon's face and the office gossip that would follow. Guarded whispers that Richard was not only a lech, but a nutjob who thought you could talk to the dead.

"So, you didn't meet with Ms. McCabe?" Malone asked him again.

"No," Richard said.

"Can anyone verify that you were home Friday night?" The male cop stood in front of him now, blocking his view of Malone. "After you got home from work?"

"No," Richard said. "My wife and daughter didn't get back until late."

"How late?"

"After midnight, I think." It had been well after that time, but he didn't want this cop judging him on curfews when it came to his daughter. Or his wife.

The male cop moved his bulk back to lean against the wall. He and Malone exchanged knowing looks in a way that made Richard want to tap his foot again. But he refused to be intimidated. He was tired of these two messing with him. They didn't know jack shit. They were just fishing, fueled by office gossip and the nonsense reported by that cat-loving agoraphobic, Rachel. He kept his mouth shut.

Perhaps to fill the uncomfortable silence, Devon finally piped up from behind his desk and asked a question of his own. "What did you mean by *at first*?" he asked the cop named Malone.

"I'm sorry, sir?" she said.

Oh sure, Devon got 'sir' but Richard only got Mr. Knight.

"When Richard suggested that Julia might have gone off somewhere," Devon explained to her. "You said you thought so too. *At first.* What did you mean by *at first.*"

"Back on Sunday we thought that," the male cop answered. "Before." He reached under one of his suit lapels, retrieving a package of gum. Richard could read the flavour from where he was sitting. Spearmint.

"Before what?" Devon asked.

"Before we found Julia McCabe's car abandoned up by the Elora Gorge," Malone said, frowning.

The fat cop popped a piece of gum in his mouth and smiled.

TWENTY-EIGHT

Eve lay in the big king size bed with the blinds drawn against the early afternoon sun. She longed for sleep, but her racing thoughts wouldn't allow it. They flew about unbidden in her mind like dark birds, a stark contrast to the inertia she felt as she hid under the heavy duvet.

Her mother had not been able to help her yesterday, notwithstanding her new affection for Margaret Atwood quotes. "Don't let the bastards grind you down" was a loose translation of the subversive Latin carved into a doomed Handmaid's wall. The one whose tale her mother watched compliments of Crave TV. Everyone seemed to harp on the author's grammar with that phrase, missing the point by focusing on the medium rather than the feminist message. But Eve could hardly fault her mother for not understanding or finding a way to kiss Eve's pain better like with a childish skinned knee. Eve had given up nothing except her hot tears, unable to tell her mother what Mark had done to her and why. Instead, she'd dried her eyes and blamed the whole thing on pre-menstrual hormones, a bad day, an unkind word from a shopkeeper. At what age did we women start hiding from our mothers the full extent of our injuries? Expecting them to heal the hurts we long ago had stopped allowing them to see.

But now Eve had more to worry about than Latin conjugation or metaphorical skinned knees. She had slept with Mark for nothing. Abbey's principal said there had been other reported incidents of glass in bottles of the brand of kombucha Selena had ingested, too far-flung and random for Abbey to ever have been involved. Certainly, the Ragman had been at play, as he was with all such senseless acts, but he wasn't acting through her daughter. Janet had told her she was wrong about Abbey, but Eve hadn't listened. Now look where all her doubts and suspicions had led her.

Last night, she'd only wanted to be left alone with her pain and disgrace. But Richard had sought her out. He'd been trying so hard to mend things between them, whipping up a special dinner of beef stir-fry with ginger, pouring her a glass of wine without being asked. He hadn't been at work that day, he'd admitted, after clearing the dishes. His boss had asked him to take some time off. At first Eve had been worried. Had Richard been downtown to see her come out of Mark's office? But her husband only knew Mark as her therapist. It could all be easily explained. She felt like a hypocrite, still hiding her own infidelity while Richard struggled to atone for his own.

It was over, he'd told her, and he'd shown her a text, thinking she needed proof. In reality, the message only saddened her. Would that be how their marriage would end a few years or even months from now? Eve pictured receiving the news on her phone. *Btw, I'm divorcing u. Contact my lawyer pls.* Rolling over in the rumpled sheets of her bed, she pulled a pillow over her head and tried not to think about it.

Eve was no stranger to days spent hiding under the covers. Before she was married, she'd only seen them as blips in her usual workaholic schedule, part of the rhythm of her busy life. One time, after a particularly gruelling month of seven-day workweeks, she'd slept the clock around, losing a whole Saturday in the process. Other times, she would call in sick and spend the day reading or watching old movies as she munched on chips by the bagful in front of the television. But back then she had always bounced back the next day. Now, one day in bed for Eve could often lead to two, and sometimes a whole week where she didn't wash her hair or dress in more than track pants and a T-shirt. Eve no longer saw such days as necessary rest periods from a hectic life, but as a slippery slope into the soul-sucking depression she fought constantly to keep at bay. But today, the fight had gone out of her. She should be up. She should be writing. She should be doing anything but lying here feeling sorry for herself. But the "shoulds" were not motivating, regardless of the guilt they induced. The "shoulds" were like a smothering blanket of regret that kept her buried under the covers.

When the phone rang on the bedside table, she didn't want to answer it, but she also didn't want to miss another call from the school. Eve had been mortified when she'd listened to the voice mail from the principal yesterday, left when she was in Mark's office. She pulled the phone off of the table and looked at the call display. It was Janet.

"Hello," she said, falling back down on the bed and closing her eyes. She only winced a little. Her rib was beginning to mend.

"Hey, Eve," Janet said. "I'm calling you from New York. Can't talk long, the roaming charges are killing me. I just wanted to see how you were doing."

With no regard for roaming charges, Eve let the whole story come out. She told Janet about how she'd gone to see Mark at his office. About his threats, and the gut-wrenching sacrifice she'd made on the futon. And then, about discovering later that Abbey had played no part in hurting Selena. She cried, something she hadn't been able to do properly until now.

"I swear I'm going to put a generational curse on that fucking bastard when I get home," Janet fumed.

"I shouldn't have gone to see him."

"It's not your fault, Eve. You get that, right?"

"I know, but if I hadn't believed the worst of Abbey, none of it would have happened. And the thing is, on Friday night, after you and I were at the Delta ..." She couldn't finish.

"What, Eve?"

"I went to see Mark then too, Janet. I slept with him on Friday night. Willingly."

"Oh, Eve."

"I know. Stupid, right?" Eve wiped a tear away with a corner of the bedsheet.

"It's not about being stupid. You know what consent is and what it isn't. Even if Mark doesn't." Janet sighed. "But shit, Eve, I thought you were done with all that?"

Eve had thought she was done with it all too.

"I don't know what I was thinking. I was just so upset after seeing Julia. I —"

"Wait, you saw Julia?"

"She came into the bar, just like you said she would. I followed her out into the parking lot. We had words." That was a bit of an understatement. Eve had knocked Julia to the ground with the manifested force of her own rage. She hadn't hurt her. But Eve had been frightened by her loss of control as well as her temper. She'd run off, leaving Julia and her cutting words behind.

"I walked around for hours after that, not knowing where to go. Somehow I ended up at Mark's apartment. I'm sorry I didn't tell you, that I wasn't honest with you from the start, Janet. I was just so ashamed."

Janet was quiet for a moment.

"Listen, Eve. The truth is, I wasn't entirely honest with you either."

"What do you mean?" Eve had been so busy trying to bury her own secrets, she hadn't stopped to think Janet might have some of her own.

"Well, you were so freaked out about Abbey, I didn't want to mention it. But now that all this business with Selena has been explained …"

"What is it, Janet?"

"When I came back to the table at the hotel and you weren't there, I went over to the window. You know, the one that looks out over the parking lot? I wanted to see if you'd gone back to wait by the car. The waitress told me you'd just left."

"What did you see?"

"I saw Abbey, Eve. I don't know why she was there, but I definitely saw her in the parking lot. And now that you say Julia was there as well." Janet hesitated. "I just thought I better tell you, in case the two of them might have run into each other."

"But why would Abbey have been at the Delta? She was supposed to be at the school that night. There was some sort of dance."

"I don't know, Eve. But I saw her."

Just then the muffled electronic melody of a cellphone drifted in from the hallway. Eve sat upright in the bed and listened. Richard only used a standard ring tone for his calls.

"Shit, Janet, I think Abbey's home. She must have forgotten something and come back for it. I'll have to call you back later."

"No problem. But about that generational curse ..."

"We'll talk."

Eve disconnected the call and put a robe on over her rumpled pyjamas. She ventured tentatively into the hallway and listened.

"Abbey?" she called out, but there was no answer. She followed the sound of the phone to her daughter's bedroom. But when she opened the door after knocking, Abbey wasn't there.

After going silent for a few moments, the cellphone started up ringing again. Calling with its bright tune from the direction of Abbey's closet. Eve opened it. The heart-shaped lock of Abbey's pink glitter strongbox seemed to wink at her from the shelf. As she took it down, she felt the vibration of the cellphone inside before it went silent again. Abbey had texted her today from her phone, asking again if they could go see Selena. If she had her phone with her, what was in the box?

Eve fetched a bobby pin from Abbey's makeup table to pick the childish lock. The heart sprang open easily. When she lifted the lid, she found Richard's burner phone hidden beneath a pale-blue notebook. The one she'd found in his desk drawer at work. Abbey must have found it too. A coincidence, perhaps. Although Eve understood enough about the way the hidden world worked to know there was really no such thing as coincidence. Eve pictured her daughter reading the crude text messages between her father and Julia. No child should have to discover such things about a parent. Poor Abbey. But why had she taken the phone?

Eve touched the message icon with her finger, hoping Richard had deleted the texts before Abbey had seen them. But they were all there, the same exchanges that had hit Eve like a series of sucker punches when she'd first seen them. The last message glared up at her.

Plans changed, meet me at the Delta.

Eve put one hand down on the mattress, steadying herself on Abbey's crisply made bed. Janet had been right.

Abbey *was* at the Delta Friday night. She must have seen this text and gone to the hotel to catch her father red-handed with his mistress. Had she seen Eve as well, and that horrible exchange with Julia? Eve cringed at the thought. She checked the cellphone for the recent calls. They were both from a private number.

Eve's own cellphone began to ring in the master bedroom, only slightly muted by the pillow she'd dropped on top of it. Eve hastily put the notebook back into the box and refastened the heart lock before returning it to the shelf. She slipped the burner into the pocket of her robe and ran back to her bedroom to answer the phone. Thick static assaulted her when she picked it up. She winced and pulled it briefly away from her ear.

"Eve? Eve, are you there?" Richard's voice chopped erratically through the static.

"Yes, Richard. Is something wrong?" Even through the interference she could pick up the panic in his voice.

"Something's happened, Eve," he said. "The police were at my work today." The phone crackled and spat. She couldn't make out all that he was saying, but she got the gist of it. Julia had been missing since Friday. The police were involved.

"You're breaking up, Richard," Eve shouted into the phone, not sure if he could hear her properly either.

More static and then, "I am so sorry, Eve." The poor connection delivered his apology in fragments. "Eve, I'm so sorry for ..." The static disappeared. The phone call dropped. Eve tried to call back, but it only rang a couple of times before going to Richard's voice mail.

Eve sat back down on the bed, shaking. Abbey had been at the Delta on Friday, the same night Julia had disappeared. Another coincidence for her not to believe in. Or was she making the same mistake as she had before with Selena and the glass? She needed to look within, to separate her fears from true intuition. But even with all the magic of the world at her disposal, the one person a witch couldn't see with any real clarity was herself.

When the doorbell rang, Eve didn't hear it. She was upstairs, pulling up her jeans over sticky legs still wet from the shower. She planned to go to All Saints and take Abbey out of school. She'd demand to know why she had her dad's burner phone. And what she had done at the Delta. Perhaps she'd only confronted Julia, driving the woman into hiding. But from what Eve had seen, Julia didn't seem like the type to be intimidated.

Eve called Richard's cellphone again as she ran down the stairs to the front hall, but it went straight to voice mail this time. She didn't believe he'd done anything wrong to Julia, other than break up with her by text. He'd never been a violent man. But she wanted to talk to him, to find out what was going on.

As she went to grab her car keys off the hall table, the doorbell rang again. There was a slim young woman and a heavy-set older man standing on the front steps looking impatient. Eve opened the door. The pair flashed their badges and asked to come in. These were different detectives than the ones she'd seen at the basketball game. Although the man and the detective who'd interrogated her and Abbey at the game shared a similar rounded paunch. Eve tried to appear calm. The burner phone she'd retrieved from Abbey's room felt like it was blazing a hole through her purse.

"I've already talked with the school principal, detectives. We know about the other cases of glass in the drinks," Eve said. This was a ploy, designed to buy her some time to gather information with her mind's eye. She focused on the man. He looked less intelligent than the woman. His thoughts would be easier to access. Eve was just beginning to draw out some images — an abandoned car, a flash of fast-running water — when the woman spoke.

"We're not here about what happened to Selena Patel," she said. "We're here about Julia McCabe."

"What about her?" Eve asked, keeping up her end of the conversation even as she worked hard to extract more images from the mind of the male cop. But it was like trying to remove a stubborn clog from a drain. Eve concentrated all her energy into one fiery pinpoint that bore deep into the detective's mind. Finally, the images broke free, bursting out of him into Eve in a gush. They washed her in a sea of river water and blood.

"She's dead," the male cop said, snapping a piece of gum in his mouth.

But Eve already knew. In the flood of images, she had seen Julia's lifeless body at the bottom of the Elora Gorge, a strappy Jimmy Choo stiletto lying twisted and broken beside her.

TWENTY-NINE

Mom and Dad are at the police station! When I came home, nobody was here, which wasn't that unusual. But then Mom called on her cellphone and told me where they were. I thought they were there to talk about what happened to Selena. But when I asked about it, Mom got all cagey and finally told me the real reason. They found Julia's body. She's dead and now they're asking my dad questions, thinking he had something to do with it. I know when a woman dies under suspicious circumstances they always look to the guy she was fucking first. But I'm more worried about Mom.

I was there that night at the Delta. I saw her with Julia. How she knocked her down outside of the hotel. Although she barely seemed to touch her. Julia had been screaming at my mom, looking around for someone in the street to help.

I pulled back in behind the corner of the building then, afraid they might see me. Then I'd have to explain what I was doing there.

I waited outside Dad's work in the car before I went to Zanax on Friday night. Until I saw him leave the office and drive away. Then I used the pass card they'd given me that morning to get in the building and up to his office. There were some cleaners there, but I told them I'd forgotten something. I wanted to get the burner phone I'd found in Dad's desk, to see if I could figure out where he was going. But when I opened the drawer, it was gone. That's when I saw it in the garbage can. I guess that's why he didn't answer it when I called from outside. Although I'm not sure what I would have said to him if he did. Anyway, I took the phone out of the trash and played with the ring tones a bit before I got up the guts to look at those disgusting messages again. There were a couple of new ones. He and Julia had arranged a meet-up at the Elora Gorge. The only way I figured I could stop it from happening was by sending her another message from his phone, to screw up their meeting place. After I sent the text to meet him at the Delta, I pocketed the burner and went to wait at the hotel. I wanted to watch the little slut get all upset thinking Dad had stood her up. Anyway, my mom didn't know about any of that, so I don't know how she knew Julia would be there.

If I saw what happened between my mom and Julia, then anybody could have. Once they're finished investigating Dad, they'll be looking for a different person to blame Julia's death on. And after Dad, who would be a better suspect than the wife of the guy Julia had been screwing?

Of course, they could come after me. I was there after all. But nobody saw me. I was careful. Unlike Mom. She should know better than to let people see her do shit like that. Although she is sneakier than I thought.

After Mom's phone call, I went up into my room to get Dad's burner phone from my strongbox. I figured I better get rid of it since it would be a little hard to explain. But when I opened the closet in my room, the phone was gone. That's when I saw the lock had been tampered with. I know it was Mom. Dad would never touch my things. Although she never said anything about it when she called. So that's kind of strange. But I guess she had to be careful what she said with all the police around.

The house is all quiet, and I'm more than a little freaked out. I wish the dog was here. Even though usually I can't stand the stupid mutt. He got all excited and pissed all over my bed once. Mom had to wash my duvet three times to get the stink out. I still made her buy me a new one. I'm particular about my bed. I like to make it in the morning, tucking in all the corners, smoothing out the pillows. Some guy said once that you can't go wrong if you get up and make your bed every day. The rest of the day's achievements just kind of flow from there.

I hope Mom and Dad come home soon. I was trying to pass the time playing with the voice recorder I lifted from the principal's office. It looks sort of like a lighter and I thought it was kind of cool, so I slipped it into my shirt pocket when they were all busy fussing to get Mom's tea yesterday. It's simple to work, and I like playing back my own voice, but I can't concentrate. There are all these crows outside my bedroom window, sitting on the hydro wire connected to the house. They aren't making any noise, but they won't stop looking at me with their beady little bird eyes.

I've closed my blind, but I still know they're out there, watching me.

THIRTY

Richard wanted to call his lawyer, Chuck Sinclair, from the back of the cop car when they took him in. But the officer in the passenger seat said he'd call Sinclair on his behalf. They knew the number. Richard guessed the cops had the contact details of most of the local mouthpieces.

After Malone and her gum-chewing sidekick had left that morning, Richard had gone back to his desk. After all, they didn't have anything to charge him with, just suspicions. He knew it was the best thing for him, to bury himself in the minutiae of meeting minutes and project plans. It also made him look less guilty, he thought. He hadn't even tried to fix the figures in the infamous spreadsheet. Some prostitute down in Aruba had hacked into Mueller's email after he'd passed out from a particularly good paid-for lay.

Client data had been compromised. Richard had decided to leave the budget as it stood, blaming Mueller for everything. That was the least of that horny German's worries.

But when Richard saw the two burly uniformed officers come onto the floor after lunch, he knew something had happened. He had just enough time to call Eve before they got directions to his office from a co-worker and marched up to his door, guns hanging conspicuously in their holsters. The connection with Eve had been shitty though. He and his wife hadn't been able to talk for long. The uniformed cops took his cellphone away after that. It was evidence, they said.

Now Richard sat in a dingy interrogation room, wishing he'd been allowed to call Chuck Sinclair himself. If only to impress upon him the seriousness of the situation so he could get his ass in gear. Most couples like Richard and Eve didn't have a criminal lawyer in their contacts, but Richard had retained Chuck when there'd been an inquest after Michael's accident. Having to defend himself and his wife from wrongdoing in their son's death was an added insult to their emotional injuries. But Chuck had been calm and reassuring and moved them through the process, ensuring there was as little added trauma as possible.

Richard's faith in his lawyer was beginning to waiver a little now though. He'd been waiting for hours in this sweat-encrusted box of a room. He knew Eve had been waiting too, somewhere else in the station. Malone had told him that much when she'd brought him something to eat around nine o'clock. She'd also told him that Chuck Sinclair had been on the golf course when they'd finally gotten a hold of him. He was at a charity tournament west of Toronto, where he was expected to make a speech after sinking his eighteen holes. *He might be a while,* Malone had said. *Was Richard sure he didn't want to start the questioning now? So he and his wife could go home?* He knew better than that.

With no cellphone to surf the net on, he was forced to read the half-illiterate graffiti on the interrogation room walls over and over again. Until he complained and one of the uniformed cops brought him a book to read. *Moby Dick.* He wondered if the cop and the old lady at the coffee shop knew one another, or maybe they just had the same taste in jokes. When Chuck Sinclair finally arrived close to midnight, Richard was ready to shove a golf club along with the half-finished novel up his ambulance-chasing ass.

"Where the hell have you been?"

"Oil spill on the 401, kept the traffic snarled for hours," Chuck said. But Richard didn't believe him.

Before they had much of a chance to talk, Malone and her partner entered the room. They sat down across from Richard and informed him of the usual bullshit. That this meeting was being recorded by video. That he was not under arrest. The cops still hadn't told Richard why they'd brought him in. Although he knew it must have something to do with Julia's disappearance. That's when they told him she was dead.

"Dead?" Richard said.

"Yes, sir. Does that surprise you?"

"Of course it fucking surprises me!" Richard reacted with anger, but it was only a shield to buffer his deeper emotions. He had cared about Julia in his own selfish-man way. He wasn't made of stone. She had meant something to him.

"Listen," Chuck said, breaking in. "I've read the report. The young lady was found in the Elora Gorge, miles away from my client's house. I'm not sure what we're doing here."

"Your client had a sexual relationship with the deceased. So I think you know what we're doing here," Malone's partner said. Richard had finally remembered his name. Saunders. Like the Kentucky Fried Chicken colonel. Or was that Sanders?

"My client hasn't denied that." This much Chuck and Richard had been able to discuss before the two cops came in. That, and the fact that Eve already knew all about the affair.

"Were you with Julia McCabe on Friday night?" Malone asked, getting back to the questioning.

"No," Richard said, still trying to process the news that they'd found Julia's body.

"Then maybe you'd like to explain why tire tracks matching your car's make and model were found at the scene," Malone said. Richard didn't know how to respond to that.

"Lots of people drive that make and model of car," his lawyer said.

"You know, cars with a few years on them each have a distinctive tire tread. Unique wear and tear. We can impound your client's car, compare the treads on the tires to those from the crime scene. See if they match." This was from Saunders.

"If you have the right paperwork, you can," Chuck said.

"We're working on it right now." Malone smiled, and Richard swallowed hard. If they checked his car against the tire tracks at the gorge, he knew they would match. He was sorry about Julia. But his survivor instinct was kicking in just the same. He couldn't let this disaster blow back on him and his family.

"When we interviewed you earlier, you claimed you didn't meet with Julia McCabe. That you went straight home from work." Malone pulled out a sheaf of printed paper from a file folder. Numbers, dates, and times covered the photocopied pages. They'd gotten Julia's phone records already. Malone pointed to the number of his burner phone which appeared repeatedly down the page.

"I called this number. Is it you?" Malone asked him. *She knows that it is,* Richard thought. *She's probably even seen the picture of my junk.*

"Yes," he said, and then clarified. "It's from a burner I bought." His face burned red as if to punctuate the admission. He decided he better admit to the rest now, before they checked his tires.

"Okay, I went to the Elora Gorge to meet with her on Friday," he said in a rush. "But —"

"What time was that?" Saunders interrupted.

Richard gave him the time. Saunders scribbled the response in a tattered black notebook. Malone checked the notes on her phone.

"But then she never showed," Richard told them.

Both cops looked up in unison. "Are you saying you didn't see Julia McCabe at the Elora Gorge Friday night?" Malone asked, looking genuinely surprised.

"I already told you I wasn't with her," Richard said, feeling the clamminess on the back of his day-old shirt. He'd been ashamed to admit he'd gone to see Julia Friday night and been stood up. He'd only gone to tell her that he was breaking it off, face to face. But after waiting an hour, he'd given up and left.

"You are telling us that you didn't meet with Julia McCabe on Friday evening?" Malone repeated.

"I think that question has been asked and answered, Detective," Chuck said. "Move on."

But Malone didn't move on. "You didn't see her at the Elora Gorge, and you didn't meet up with her at the Delta hotel?"

"The Delta hotel? Why are you asking me about the Delta hotel?" Richard and Julia had never met there. They'd stuck with a hotel on the outskirts of the city to keep it discreet.

Malone flipped through the phone records in front of her, pointed down to one of the final entries on the last page from his burner phone.

"Read the text," she said.

Richard read it. *Plans changed, meet me at the Delta.*

"I didn't send that," he said, legitimately confused. He hadn't. The last text he'd sent to Julia from his burner was when he'd agreed to meet her at the gorge, then he'd thrown away the phone.

Malone and Saunders stared at him from across the table.

"I swear to god," Richard said. "I tossed that phone after I texted her about meeting at the gorge. Then I went there to wait for her, but she never came." *Who the hell sent that message?* Richard thought. Was this some sort of trick? Was he being framed?

"And what did you do then?" Malone asked him.

"I went home," Richard said. He hadn't told them about going to see the medium, and he wasn't about to now. He swore he'd face life in prison before he admitted to that. Although if this didn't get cleared up soon, he might have to make that choice.

"Can your wife collaborate the time you arrived home?"

"No," Richard said. "She didn't get back until much later. I told you that."

"You know what I think, Richard?" said Saunders, interrupting again. "I think that's bullshit." Richard looked over at Chuck, but he wasn't objecting. Apparently a cop calling your story bullshit was perfectly legal. *Who the hell sent that text about the Delta?* Then Richard remembered that the arrangement to meet at the gorge wasn't the last text he'd sent to Julia.

"If you have the phone records, you know I sent another text to Julia on the weekend, breaking up with her. That was from my regular phone," he said. "Why would I send a text to a dead woman?"

"Because you didn't want us to think you knew she was dead," Saunders said, leaning in, his generous stomach pushing up against the table between them. "I think what happened is that you met your little piece on the side at the Delta, and then you convinced her to come up to the gorge with you for some action *au natural* in the out-of-doors. Then for whatever reason you pushed her off a fucking cliff."

Before either Richard or his lawyer had a chance to respond there was a knock on the door of the interrogation room. Malone got up and let in the uniformed cop who'd brought Richard the *Moby Dick* novel. He handed her a file. After a hushed discussion, she closed the door and came to sit back down opposite Richard and his lawyer.

Malone opened up the manila folder. "This is a signed warrant to seize your car, Mr. Knight," she said, tapping the file with her finger. Chuck grabbed the folder off the table and scanned the pages. Richard read the details from over his shoulder but was surprised by what he saw there.

"I think you'll find all the paperwork is in order," Malone said, leaning back in her chair. But Chuck wasn't about to let her relax. He closed the folder and pushed it back across the table.

"You may have the right to detain my client's car, but you don't have the right to detain *him*. As you pointed out, Detective Saunders, my client had no good reason to push Julia McCabe off a cliff. By all reports it was a …" Chuck struggled for an appropriate word for Julia and Richard's inappropriateness. "A mutually enjoyed relationship." Malone rolled her eyes.

"His wife was aware of the affair, as was his place of employment. There were no opportunities for blackmail. The tire tracks have been explained by my client. He went to the Elora Gorge, but he did not see Ms. McCabe there. He has been nothing but cooperative, despite having been detained here half the night. So unless you have some real evidence, we're leaving."

THIRTY-ONE

Eve and Richard barely spoke after they left the police station, sitting in silence behind the tinted windows of the BMW as they drove home through the empty nighttime streets. Eve had discovered a voice mail on her phone and listened to it. Pauline Henderson apologized in a tearful and lengthy message. Their dog had gotten out through the cat door. She couldn't find him, even though she'd laid out his favourite liver treats on the front stoop. Pauline's voice continued on in the same hysterical vein. Eve deleted the message without listening to the end of it. She slipped the phone back in her purse to sit next to the burner she'd found in Abbey's room.

Luckily, the police hadn't searched her belongings. The only thing they'd asked her about during those long hours of waiting was whether she could confirm Richard had been at home Friday night. Which of course, she couldn't. They knew that. They'd been hoping to catch her in a reflexive lie designed to cover for him, but she had stuck to a loose description of the facts. She'd gotten home late after drinks with a friend. Richard had been home when she arrived. She couldn't account for his whereabouts before that. The police didn't seem too concerned about an alibi for any other time. They must have strong evidence to suggest Julia's death occurred the same night she disappeared.

When Richard and Eve got home, they were careful to be quiet coming through the door, not wanting to wake Abbey. Eve motioned Richard toward the basement so they could talk somewhere out of earshot. As soon as he reached the bottom of the stairs, Richard walked to the bar to get a drink, pouring himself a large whisky. It was from a bottle of fifteen-year-old Scotch he'd received from the Patels on his last milestone birthday. He sat down on the couch and downed the drink in one go before putting his face in his hands.

"Where were you Friday night, Eve?"

She wasn't expecting this, having been prepared for his own claims of innocence rather than having to defend her own. He was the police's main suspect after all.

"I was with Janet. I told you that." Eve bit her lip. She didn't sit down with Richard, preferring to stand. She wasn't ready to give away more than she had to.

Richard sighed before looking up from his hands. "I saw your shirt in the laundry hamper. On Saturday when you were at your mom's. I thought those stains were from that night you were sick. But it didn't look like that, Eve. It looked like blood."

Oh my god. He thought *she'd* killed Julia.

"I wasn't even wearing that shirt Friday night, Richard." She glanced guiltily over at the airtight stove. "I drank a ton of Shiraz at book club on Wednesday. Before I threw it all up. It was red wine and sick on that shirt, not blood." Of course, Eve had burned the blouse in the stove thinking it was blood too, but from a cat rather than a person.

"They found tire tracks from the car up at the gorge where they found Julia," Richard said, interrupting Eve's thoughts. "I was up there. I may as well tell you that. I'd arranged to meet her, but I swear she didn't come." He put his head in his hands again. "Where were you that night, Eve?" he asked her again.

Jesus, Richard was at the Elora Gorge? Eve still didn't believe he was capable of murder, but that certainly didn't look good. Richard hadn't mentioned the Delta either and Eve was suspicious as to why. But if she wanted the truth, she probably needed to start with her own.

"I was with Janet, but later I was with someone else," she confessed, swallowing hard. She told him about Mark. How she'd slept with him Friday night and that it hadn't been the first time. She left out the part about her and Julia's run-in at the Delta for now. She wanted to see how he reacted to the news of her affair first.

Richard sat on the couch with a blank expression, staring intently at his drink. His eyes betrayed the mask he wore on the rest of his face. She could see the glint of tears held back. Despite his own betrayal, she knew it still hurt. He stood up to fetch another Scotch, then sat back down with the amber drink in his hand.

"Well, I guess I had that coming," was all he said.

"I'm sorry, Richard." Eve sat beside him on the couch. They both looked straight ahead at the clock on the wall rather than at each other. It was after one in the morning.

"But Richard, where were you?" Eve needed to know. "You say you didn't see Julia at the gorge that night. But didn't you see her later, somewhere else?" She meant to lead him with this question. Now that she'd admitted her own hookup on Friday night, she thought he'd be more likely to reveal his own.

"Did the police show you that text too?" Richard shook his head, then took another belt of the Scotch. "I swear to god, Eve. I didn't send it. I wasn't anywhere near the Delta Friday night. I threw out that burner phone before I left the office. I told you it was over with Julia, and I meant it."

She tried to think of a reason he would lie about sending the text. He'd admitted to being at the crime scene. What possible reason could he have for lying about being at the Delta?

She took the burner phone from her purse and placed it on the coffee table.

"Where did you get that?" he asked, stunned.

She didn't want to tell him.

"Did you send that text, Eve?" He looked at her in alarm. "Oh Jesus. The tire tracks."

"What are you talking about?"

"The tire tracks the police found up at the gorge. They were from a BMW, Eve. I was driving the Mazda. The BMW was at home with you. I'd hoped maybe it was a coincidence when I saw the warrant, but —"

"I didn't have the car Friday night, Richard," Eve broke in. "Janet drove." But her heart was beginning to race.

"Then who did?" But even as Richard posed the question, the colour drained from his face.

"Richard, Abbey was at the Delta that night. Janet saw her. And I found your burner phone in her room."

"Wait, Janet was at the Delta? I thought —"

But Eve was up and off of the couch now, switching into full crisis mode. "We've got to tell Abbey to say she wasn't there, that she wasn't driving the car." She looked at the burner phone still lying on the table. "And we've got to get rid of that fucking phone."

"But Eve —"

"I'll tell them I was driving the BMW," Eve said. "We've got to throw suspicion off of Abbey." Someone was bound to have seen Eve arguing with Julia before following her out of the hotel bar. She didn't have time to explain it all to Richard. He would find out soon enough. But the incident would serve to focus the police's inquiries firmly on her and away from Abbey. She would take the heat, and if necessary, the blame. A mother protects her daughter at all costs. And besides, whatever Abbey had done, at its core, Eve knew it was her fault.

"What are you saying, Eve? That our daughter killed Julia? That's ridiculous."

"Wake up, Richard," Eve hissed. "Abbey was at the Delta. She's the one who sent the text so she could wait there for Julia. She had the car. Even if she wasn't involved, they're going to think she was."

"I still don't believe —"

But Eve was already rushing up the stairs to talk to Abbey. They had to get their stories straight. Just like they'd done after Michael. It couldn't wait until morning. The police had no trouble pulling a person out of bed in the middle of the night when it came to murder.

Richard followed Eve up the basement stairs and onward to the second floor. He was standing behind her when she opened the door to Abbey's bedroom, and when she switched on the light. He was there when Eve saw the crisp turquoise duvet tightly tucked into Abbey's bed, the pillow fluffed and undisturbed. Her cellphone lay discarded on the floor, next to a pale blue notebook.

But Abbey was gone.

THIRTY-TWO

Mom? Dad? I'm making this recording because I don't have my cellphone. I can't tell if this recorder thing is working in the dark, but I can see the little red light, so I hope so. I want you to know what happened to me. I want you to know that Mark took me, and it isn't my fault.

I thought it was you Mom when he pulled up in his car outside the house. It looked the same, a BMW with tinted windows. I know that's Dad's car, but you usually drive it. It was dark, and I couldn't see inside. The upholstery was different, red instead of black. But I couldn't tell that at first. I was so worried about Dad, I got in before I realized who it was. He told me you were both waiting at the police station, that you'd sent him to pick me up. He was Mom's therapist and he'd been at my school, so I believed him.

But he drove the wrong way. I know that now. I thought maybe he was going to a different station than the one downtown. I didn't want to ask. But once we were out of the city, he pulled onto a dirt road and forced me into the trunk. Momma, he had a gun. Why is he doing this?

I tried to get out, Daddy. With that little lever that you showed me, that lets you out of the trunk from the inside. Remember when you showed me? But I pushed and pushed on it and now my hands are bleeding. I tried with my feet too. But it won't budge.

I'm sorry for getting in the car, Dad. And for stealing your phone. I'm so sorry, Mom, for being such a bitch all the time. I didn't mean it. I didn't. If you find my diary later, don't read it. It was just stuff I made up to make myself feel more important, like some sort of badass. It's fiction, like you write, Momma. I wanted to be like you. If anyone reads it, tell them everything in there is made up. Please tell them that.

I don't know where he's taking me. We've been driving for a while. I'm so frightened … (Crying)

Momma, I'm sorry about Michael. I'm sorry about everything. You are so good at seeing things, finding things. I love you so much.

Momma, please find me.

THIRTY-THREE

Eve was totally losing the plot. Richard watched as his wife ran back down the stairs from Abbey's bedroom to telephone Janet. Janet was in New York. She'd told him that earlier. How would she know where Abbey was? She didn't leave a voice mail, just slammed the phone back down on the table. When Richard picked it up, the screen was cracked like a bad luck mirror.

Then she disappeared into the backyard with her garden shears. He looked out the window and saw her bent over in the moonlight. She was cutting branches away from the burning bush, the one where he'd found the Patels' cat. When she was done, she came in and dropped the branches on the floor. Then she fetched a black leather book and laid it out on the kitchen table, running one finger hurriedly down the page. He'd seen the book before when he was in the attic looking for Christmas decorations. It had Eve's name on it forged in red wax. He'd put the book back where he'd found it, assuming it was personal. Some childhood relic she'd held onto as a keepsake. He hadn't been able to make out any of what was written in it anyway.

Richard wanted to call the police, but Eve had convinced him not to. He was worried enough about the police finding out Abbey had the car Friday night to go along with her, at least for now. Abbey had probably just gone to a sleepover at a friend's house anyway, to get away from what was happening with her parents. Although Selena was the only friend Richard could remember her staying with, and she was still in the hospital. But he figured his daughter must have other friends.

He still couldn't fathom the idea that Abbey had anything to do with Julia's death, even if Janet had seen her at the hotel. Even if she had taken his phone and sent that message. It all had to be some kind of misunderstanding. Maybe the police would find the tire tracks matched a different BMW. In any case, they were wasting time here. They should be out looking for Abbey.

"What are you doing, Eve?"

She put the branches in a large metal bowl on the kitchen table. Richard had to jump back when she took a lighter from her pocket and set them on fire. As the flames caught, she mumbled to herself a string of meaningless syllables he couldn't make out. The woman was having a complete mental break. *For Christ's sake,* he thought. *She'll set the smoke alarms off.* He knew he should stop her, whatever she thought she was doing. She clearly wasn't in her right mind. The police would be showing up at the house any minute, once they'd gone to his office and discovered the car in their warrant wasn't parked there. He couldn't let them see his wife like this. But even as he thought this, he found himself unable to act. He was becoming mesmerized by the flames glinting off the metallic silver of the bowl, by the low guttural chanting coming from deep within his wife's throat. He hardly reacted when the first heavy crow hit the kitchen window and slid down the glass. It was followed by another and another, fast and furious, like the steady retort of a machine gun fire, each smearing the pane of glass with their slick avian blood.

Eve's phone rang on the kitchen counter, knocking them both out of their trances. She answered it, speaking in a low voice. Richard watched her as the flames died down in the bowl. Then he heard the scream.

Eve grabbed the keys to the BMW parked in the driveway. "We've got to go, Richard," she said, still holding the phone. "Do you understand, Richard, we have to go!"

Still feeling strangely docile, Richard followed his wife where she led, into the hallway and out the front door. Eve was the strong one now. He sensed that. The one with the power. He did not question his wife's instructions, nor her motivations. He got in the car. *This is what shock feels like,* he thought. *I'm in shock.*

Because the scream he'd heard had not come from Eve. It had come from her cellphone.

And the scream had been Abbey's.

THIRTY-FOUR

Eve had her hands clenched tightly on the steering wheel as she sped up the country highway out of town. She kept her mind focused on road conditions and the accelerator rather than thinking about where she was headed. When she pulled down the dirt road to the abandoned limestone quarry, the hard bumps of the ride told her the ground was rutted but bone dry. The car wouldn't get stuck. The heavy storm of last Sunday must have passed by this rural area north of the city. A mature forest, dense with soaring pines, hemmed the car in on all sides.

Mark stood in the full moonlight of a clearing, just up from the unfenced edge of the rocky drop into the quarry. Eve could hear the hush of water below, sourced from the river that coursed through the Elora Gorge. She'd come here as a teen to swim in the shivering cold pool that accumulated when the powerful restlessness of the river had tunneled its way into the quarry's hole. People said there was old mining equipment lost beneath its dark surface. But the water was so deep no one had ever found the bottom to confirm the myth. They were only a few miles upriver from where Julia had been found.

"Thank you so much for coming," Mark said, like she had simply accommodated him by showing up for a rescheduled session. As if he wasn't standing in front of a car that was parked precariously at the quarry's edge. A car that looked almost exactly like the one Eve and Richard had just driven up in. Except this one, Eve knew, held her daughter locked in its trunk. She could hear her kicking and scratching inside.

"What do you want, Mark?" Eve said, noting the menacing black grip of a handgun sticking out the front of his jeans. He rubbed the pebbled handle of the pistol with one thumb in an absentminded caress. She hadn't considered the possibility he'd be armed. But she should have anticipated that Mark's violence would escalate. With men like him it always did. Abbey started yelling from the trunk of the car at the sound of her mother's voice. Richard, standing beside her, stiffened. But he knew better than to act. He'd seen the gun too. Mark turned briefly to shout in the direction of Abbey's cries.

"Shut the fuck up, bitch, or I'll shoot you right through the trunk!"

The trunk and her daughter went quiet.

Mark returned his attention to Eve. "Remember how you were shocked that I didn't own a car, Eve? How fucking admirable you thought it was? Isn't it ironic? That I would buy the same kind of car as your *beloved* husband. A Bimmer, for god's sake. Such a fucking pseudo-status car."

What the hell is he talking about? Eve thought. She hadn't had time to divine anything with her chanting and fire. If that were even possible for her anymore with her limited powers. She was in the dark as much as anyone would be in that moment.

"Of course, I knew it would come in handy with Julia. That similarity." Mark chortled to himself before turning to Richard. "She thought it was you, Dick, when I pulled up in front of the Delta. Silly, silly girl. Got right in without looking. Easier than shooting fish in a barrel. I went back and got her car later. I'd been following her for a while of course, waiting for my opportunity, but I never thought she'd be such a pushover." This time, he broke into hoops of laughter. They echoed off the quarry's steep walls.

"Pushover, that's a rich one, isn't it Dick? Since I *pushed* your little slut into the gorge."

"You killed Julia?" Richard said.

"You really are not the shiniest tool in the box, are you? Of course I killed her. But they think you did it, don't they? And tomorrow, when it's light enough, they'll find your wedding ring not far away from her body. That'll clinch it. I snuck into your garage a few nights ago to find something to point the cops in the right direction. I couldn't believe it when I found your fucking wedding ring on the tool bench. What kind of husband does that?"

"Just let us have Abbey," Eve said. "Please, Mark." She took a tentative step forward. Richard tried to come with her, but she held him back before she leaned in to whisper. "I've got to be the one," she told him. "He won't hurt me." She wasn't sure if that was true, but she'd already endangered the life of her daughter by letting this man into her life, she wasn't going to risk the safety of her husband as well. Mark was capable of anything to get what he wanted. She knew that now.

Eve edged closer toward him.

"Stop!" Mark commanded, pulling the gun out. Eve froze.

"You," he said, using the pistol to indicate Richard. "Get in the car." He pointed to his own car, the one he'd used to fool poor Julia. The one Abbey was trapped in at the brink of the quarry.

"Fuck you," said Richard.

Mark smiled. While still keeping an eye on both of them he trained his gun on the trunk of the car.

"Get in the car or I'll shoot your goddamn daughter."

"Richard," Eve said. "Don't do it." She'd offer herself up. Mark would have to be satisfied with that. But her husband was already moving forward with his hands held high. Mark patted him down roughly when he reached him, confiscating the phone from his jacket and throwing it over the lip of the quarry. Then he opened the driver's door of the car. When Richard bent down to get in, Mark slammed his head twice on the metal frame in quick succession. Eve watched Richard slump unconscious as Mark pushed him inside and shut the door. He walked over and sat down on the trunk, rocking the car slightly. Eve's throat tightened.

"Now, that's better," he said. He indicated a spot beside him. "Now, you and I can talk, Eve."

Eve stayed where she was. "Why are you doing this, Mark? Why have you done any of this?"

"Isn't it obvious, darling? So you and I can be together." He ran one hand through his hair to tame some flyaway strands let loose during his violent attack on Richard.

"At first I thought all I needed to do was to get your shitty cheating husband out of the way. But it would look a bit suspicious if he got killed just before you and I rode off into the sunset together. It was so much better to think of him rotting in a jail cell for killing his mistress." He sighed.

"But then you couldn't seem to get over this obsession with Abbey. Abbey this and Abbey that. And then, in the garage that day you said you couldn't be with me because she needed you. Remember that, Eve? I thought we had come so far in your therapy. I thought you had learned that a woman could be so much more than her children."

"But Mark —"

"No buts, Eve. The girl's a burden. She's been holding you back all this time, keeping you from moving on. Trust me, once you're free of her, things will be better. You can start a new life. A new life with me."

Eve was trying hard not to cry. There would be no cavalry riding in to save them. They hadn't called the police after Mark's phone call. He'd warned her not to, saying he was holding Abbey because he had evidence she'd been involved in Julia's murder. After swearing she'd never suspect her daughter again of wrongdoing, she'd broken her promise and played straight into his hands. And now both Abbey and Richard were paying the price for it. Thinking of this made the tears come unbidden.

"Don't cry, sweetheart." Mark made hushing noises that set her teeth on edge.

"Everything's going to be okay, Eve. Pretty soon we'll be rid of both of them. One good push and this car will go right over the edge and into the quarry. No one will ever find it. They'll figure old Dick's done a runner to avoid being arrested and he took poor little Abbey with him. Then nothing will stand in our way, will it, sweetheart? If they ever do manage to float up to the surface, it'll just be another sad story for you to tell. One where your husband took his own life and his daughter's in a guilt-ridden breakdown. That'll get you way more sympathy than Michael's death ever did. I mean, after all, that was on your watch."

Eve heard Abbey sobbing softly from the trunk. Richard's unconscious body was still slumped against the steering wheel of the car. She felt as if she were waking up from a sleepwalker's fog, wondering how she'd ever ended up here. But of course, she knew how. Five years ago, she'd believed the worst of a twelve-year-old girl. She'd decided the Ragman had been at work in her daughter and in doing so she'd let him into her mind. He'd been allowed to grow and fester there, fed by her grief and her guilt. She'd wanted to assign a malevolent reason for the monstrous depravity of her son's death. When, as with most tragedies, there had been no reason at all. Her daughter was not a monster. She'd been a child. She was still a child. Looking at Mark, Eve knew now who the monster really was.

Mark beckoned her to him. "C'mon Eve," he said. "You know you want this as much as I do."

Mark was insane, and his plan was full of holes. The biggest one being that Eve would step off the edge of the quarry herself if he pushed the car over with her family inside. But she couldn't risk upsetting him by pointing that out. The situation stood on a knife's edge, as precarious as the rocky lip of the quarry. She needed to use what little magic she possessed to keep it in balance. Focusing all her energy, she affected a glamour like the one she'd used at Richard's office. Except instead of projecting youth, she cast an appearance of adoration and love. The illusion hid from Mark her shaking hands and the sour grimace on her face as she swallowed down bile.

"Darling," she said, sitting down beside him on the trunk of the car. Knowing Abbey was so close almost broke her resolve. She could hear her daughter's breathing as she listened for what was to happen next. Eve rested her head on Mark's shoulder. He put his hand on her knee and Eve had to focus even harder on her illusion to disguise the cringe.

"You don't need to do all this," she said, tracing a finger playfully along his chest. "We can just leave them here and run away together. I understand now that I don't need either of them. You were right. Let's just go."

"Oh, Eve," he said. "You always did live in a dream world." He brought the hand without the gun up to her face, pushing back strands of her hair to gaze at the lie of her face.

"No, really," she said, fixing him with her eyes. She was using everything she could muster to draw him into the

the delicate web of skin at the base of his thumb. Mark wrestled with her, but she was like a vicious dog clamped down on a fleshy chew toy. With his free hand he went to choke her. Together they moved toward the sharp drop-off of the quarry. Her healing rib shifted and popped, shooting her through with exquisite pain. But she didn't let go. Eve was ready to go over the edge with him. Ready to sacrifice herself to end it all. But instead of feeling her body pulled over the cliff, she felt her teeth clamp down one final time to meet each other. Mark released his grip from her throat, screaming as Eve fell to the ground. The gun dropped out of what was left of his hand. Eve spit out his thumb onto the grass.

Crawling away from the cliff of the quarry, she struggled to pull in oxygen that he'd robbed her of. If she could only get to the cellphone she'd left in their car, she could call for help. But Eve feared help wouldn't arrive in time, before Mark made good on his threat to push his own car into the quarry with Abbey and Richard inside. She remained crumpled halfway between the two vehicles, gasping for air. She was torn between the promise of the phone and the fear of leaving Abbey and Richard undefended, and her hesitation created a window of opportunity for Mark. He shouted and swore as he wrapped his jacket around his bleeding hand and clubbed her with a brutal blow to the back of the head. She sank to the grass where he kicked at her, favouring her injured side. When he finally stepped away, he howled, and his body and face began to waver and change, as if he were affecting his own glamour.

"You're going to pay for this, bitch. I'm going to make you watch your daughter beg for her life. I'm going to kill that fucking husband of yours right in front of your face."

Eve groaned, clutching her rib as she tried to protect herself from another crippling blow. With her eyes squeezed shut, she didn't see that Mark had moved away to stand in the full clearing where he was becoming something else. Or perhaps becoming what he'd been all along.

At first, she didn't register the cool blue light that steadily grew beside her either. It started off like a tickling breeze that teased at her skin but soon expanded until it had matter and form. She was fully enveloped in its brilliant blue glow before she felt the small steady hand reach out to lie on top of her trembling one. She opened her eyes.

Michael.

He knelt in the grass beside her, her little boy, bathed in blue light. His aura spread and surrounded them both, charged with an electricity that crackled in the night air. She reached out with both arms and pulled him to her, breathing in the scent of his hair — a mixture of baby shampoo with that indescribable essence only a mother can detect. She wrapped his small body in her own and inhaled his sweet perfume, perfectly intoxicated.

"Michael," she said, drawing him closer. "Michael, where have you been?"

He didn't answer her, only nuzzled deeper into her neck. She rubbed his back in circles like she'd done when he was a baby. She didn't need anything more than this, she thought. Nothing more than to hold her boy to her and forget everything else in the world. He could take her with him, to wherever he'd been, and she would go willingly.

A crash sounded above them, and Michael squirmed and pulled away from his mother. Her arms reached out, aching for him. But he stood up and held out his tiny hand to her again. She wondered at the sight of him, her boy full and whole. His tousled dark hair reminded her so much of Richard's when they'd first met and fallen in love. The serious look on his face was so like Abbey's when she studied at the kitchen table. In her son, surrounded by the blue light, Eve saw not only what she had lost but what she had allowed herself to forget she still had.

Eve took hold of Michael's hand. Her body seized from the jolt as her lost powers raced up her arm like liquid fuel. In her chest, they exploded and flared to fill the rest of her, veins and arteries set ablaze. Her silhouette burned a scorching red in the icy blue light. She struggled to open her mouth, to discharge some of her powers even as they threatened to cook her flesh from within. But a cunning magic kept her lips sewn together, unable to release the fire.

Eve worked to stand, never letting go of Michael's hand, even as the searing heat and pain coursed through her body from his touch. She bent on one knee in the moonlight's shadow and looked up at the man she'd known as Mark. What he'd become now towered over both of them, reaching the height of the tallest trees that banked the quarry. His clothes were torn strips of cloth that seethed and pulsed with a festering filth. Crows shrieked as they flew in and out of the tattered folds. His face was that of a snake's, a fierce black cobra. But when he opened his mouth to laugh, Eve saw the double-rowed teeth of a shark. A bolt of lightning shot down from the sky sending a hundred-year-old pine to the ground in a fiery crash. It narrowly missed the car that held her husband and her daughter inside.

Eve pulled herself up in the protective blue light of her son and stood tall against the monster of her own making. And in doing so, she readied herself to fight the Ragman for all she still had.

THIRTY-FIVE

Mommy, Daddy! I can smell fire! Why aren't you getting me out of the trunk? Why aren't you saving me? Oh god, I can hear the flames. They're crackling. I can feel the heat.

(Banging)

I'm not going to burn to death in here, I'm not! I'm hitting the little lever with my foot, Daddy. I'm hitting it so hard. I don't want to die! I don't want to die! (Cries out)

(Sound of trunk opening)

Momma?

THIRTY-SIX

Richard came awake in the driver's seat in the midst of chaos. Flames danced wildly in the clearing behind him. The sky had erupted into a storm with winds strong enough to rip branches from the lofty pines. Eve was in the midst of it all, awash in blue light. A little boy stood beside her. It took only a moment for Richard to realize the little boy was his son. His real son, not the charlatan's version conjured up using raps under the table and a faked falsetto voice spoken through a medium. Michael held his mother's hand as he stood strong and silent in the eye of the storm. A towering monster covered in rags thundered blows down on the two of them. Their blue aura shuddered and threw off sparks with each strike. He couldn't be seeing this. He wasn't seeing this. Richard turned away. But he could still catch reflections of the impossible scene in the rear-view mirror before the trunk popped open and obscured his view.

Abbey!

Richard battled with the door of the car before he found and released the lock. He stepped out onto the grass, shielding his face from the smoke as he raced to the back of the car. Lightning filled the sky. A fallen tree was ablaze only a few feet away. Abbey was curled up inside the open trunk, clutching at her ankle. As he picked her up in his arms, she cried out, then buried her face into his chest. The heat of the burning tree blasted the back of his legs, penetrating his clothing, singeing his calves. He turned toward the clearing, willing what he'd seen to be gone. But Michael still stood with his mother as the hideous giant with a serpent's face fought the blue light that surrounded them. Eve's body was taut, her head thrown back as if to howl. Red flames licked the back of her neck as she struggled to remain on her feet.

He wanted to run away with his daughter in his arms, as far as he could get from the scene in the clearing. To run away from his wife and his son and their struggle, his sanity still intact. But Richard had wasted enough time running away from what he couldn't understand.

He staggered toward Eve and Michael with Abbey in his arms. The ground shook beneath him with each of the monster's blows. As he stepped into the protective circle of blue light, he felt a blast of cool energy along with the searing sensation of raw heat that emanated from his wife. He lowered his daughter from his arms and placed her at her mother's feet. Thus, his family lay arranged before him in a completed tableau. Abbey on one side of Eve. Michael on the other. Richard stood behind his wife and closed his eyes before he wrapped her in his arms, clutching both his children fiercely to them. The bonfire of Eve's body burned him when she leaned back into his strength. As he fought to hold them all together, he heard a roar rising from deep within her chest, building with such force that he felt her rib snap. He looked up. From his wife's open mouth rose an astral arc of fire. It pierced the blue light and the sky above to set the rags of the monster aflame. Richard watched as it screamed, an unholy caterwauling that echoed off the steep walls of the quarry before the giant fell to the ground and disappeared into swirling black smoke. When the moonlight shone through and the thick sooty cloud dispersed, there was nothing left of the snake man dressed in rags. Only the prone body of his wife's lover remained, unmoving under a blanket of ash.

Richard continued to hold onto his family as the blue light began to fade. He could feel Michael slipping away from them, off to wherever he had come from and where Richard knew now he must remain. As his son left, Richard drew Eve and Abbey all the closer to him, though his arms ached in the act of letting go.

A man's love for his family holds its own powerful magic. Even the love of an imperfect man.

And Richard's love had held just enough to tip the balance.

EPILOGUE

Eve slapped the doctor's hands away when he pressed too hard on her rib.

"I'm all right," she insisted.

She sat in a plastic chair in the hospital emergency's inner waiting room. Richard was beside her. He took her hand as he waved the doctor away.

"She'll be all right," he said.

"I still want her to go for an X-ray," the doctor said. "Wait here." He stood up from where he'd been examining Eve and walked over to the nurse's station to scribble out a hasty requisition. He'd already checked out Richard's head wound and pronounced him concussed. Something you couldn't do a lot for, just like a broken rib.

"What happened back there, Eve?" Richard asked her.

She didn't answer, only squeezed his hand firmly in her own.

Eve couldn't make Richard forget what he'd seen. Janet's binding spell stopped her from erasing his memories. There would be no going back. The veil had been pulled aside. Her husband knew who and what she was now. When she had more time, she'd explain this part of herself that she'd kept from him. Although not all of it. She wouldn't reveal how Abbey had been conceived. There were some confidences a woman kept to herself, as did her husband. If all marriages were open books, not many would survive the reading. But as long as there was enough good material there, it didn't really matter.

Abbey came down the hallway on crutches, escorted by an orderly. Her foot sported a new walking cast. She'd broken her ankle kicking at the lever to release herself from Mark's trunk. She sat down beside her parents and rested her head on Eve's shoulder. Her icy-blond hair shone almost blue in the harsh fluorescent light.

"They told me I could go up to see Selena today, Mom."

"I'm so glad, honey."

In her mind's eye, Eve could see Mark strapped to a bed in a far wing of the hospital. He was covered in black soot but only injured with superficial burns. He ranted and raved to the two detectives who stood solemn at his bedside, blaming his crimes on the voices in his head, the prescription drug habit he'd developed, and the devil. In that order. The usual suspects. They'd found Julia's purse stuffed under the carpet of his trunk next to the spare tire. The female detective was reading him his rights, despite fears that he was too far gone to comprehend them.

When Janet came crashing through the double doors chased by the triage nurse, Eve's mother followed behind her leaning on a brightly bedazzled cane.

"They're family," Eve told the nurse. That and the power of suggestion she planted was enough to send the nurse back to her desk.

"How do you like my new stick?" Eve's mother held the cane up, proudly displaying the faux jewels and glitter.

"I made it for her," Janet said.

"It's beautiful." Eve lifted her hand toward the cane and a swirl of glitter danced around it like spinning stars.

"I left them both voice mails when we got to the hospital," Richard explained.

Janet leaned in to whisper in Eve's ear. "I heard you calling."

Richard didn't understand that Janet had been summoned long before his voice mail. The two women shared a frequency, transmitted more strongly than a signal from the loftiest of towers. He went to help Eve's mother into a chair. But with the help of her cane, she managed to get down on one knee to kneel in front of her daughter.

"Sweetheart," she said, holding both of Eve's hands in her own. "I'm so sorry. I had no idea." Eve planted a kiss on her lightly lined forehead.

"Check out my cast, Grandma," Abbey broke in. She bent down to help her grandmother up. Eve's mother took a seat and listened as her granddaughter relayed the details of her harrowing escape. How brave she'd been. How Richard had saved her. It didn't bother Eve, this retelling of the story without her role in it. She'd worked hard to delete certain memories from Abbey's consciousness, especially the one where she'd watched Eve burn with fire. But she wasn't sure if she'd managed to get them all. Her daughter was capable of throwing up walls that even Eve's reinstated powers couldn't penetrate.

Richard convinced his daughter and his mother-in-law to investigate the hospital vending machines with him. It had been hours since any of them had eaten, and the hospital cafeteria wouldn't be open for another hour. Eve watched as her husband held the double doors open for her daughter and mother. She remembered the strength of his arms wrapped around her, lifting her spirit up so she could find her power again. They had a long road ahead of them through the betrayal and the hurt, but they could still make their way back to each other. Eve had enough of her own strength for that now.

"I took the red-eye out of JFK," Janet said when the others had disappeared down the hall. "But by the time I touched down, I could tell it was over. I *knew* you still had your powers."

"Michael might have had a part in that."

"Michael is a part of you, Eve. That's what he's always been."

Eve thought about that and smiled. Then gave her friend a playful jab. "I can't believe you brought my *mom*."

"There are times a girl needs her momma," Janet said. "*And* her best friend." She wrapped one arm around Eve's shoulders. The air sizzled with the combined energy flowing between them.

A little boy walked by holding the hand of his mother. His tears still fresh from a tetanus shot. The mother picked him up, even though he was too big for that sort of affection. She kissed him on the cheek before leaving through the double doors. The scene tugged at Eve's heart but didn't break it as it would have done before. She understood what she had and what she didn't anymore. And what was more important, she'd made peace with it.

"Do you think he's gone, Janet?" They both knew she didn't mean Michael, despite the little boy reminding both of them of him.

"Don't worry, Eve," Janet said. "The Ragman's like a vampire. You got to let him in before he can do you any harm. Now you've shown him the door, he won't come again — unless you call." Janet lifted one high arched brow. "And I know you won't be foolish enough to call on him again."

Eve smiled. "No," she said. "No, I won't." Eve knew now that the Ragman hadn't lived in Abbey but in her own worst fears. Eve would never let the long shadow of her daughter's conception cloud her judgment again.

Janet stood up and stretched. "I'm going to check out that vending machine too. I can't eat that shit they serve on the plane. You want anything?"

"I'm fine."

Eve turned her attention to the TV bolted on the wall as Janet went in search of food. The news was on. A photo of Julia next to one of Mark floated above a ticker tape headline. Eve narrowed her eyes and the screen switched to snow just as Richard and her mother emerged through the double doors.

"Where's Abbey?" Eve asked after Richard had sat down.

"Janet picked up her cellphone at the house," Richard said. "She gave Abbey the keys to her Volvo so she could get it from the car."

"On crutches," Eve said, alarmed. Her restless mind's eye searched outside the confines of the hospital waiting room. She saw Abbey with Janet's key ring held between her teeth as she hobbled alone out to the parking lot on her crutches. Eve held her rib and prepared to stand so she could go and check on her.

"Honestly," her mother said, plunking down beside her. She lifted her bedazzled cane to bar her daughter's way. "You worry too much."

Eve pushed the cane lightly away but remained seated. "Didn't you worry about me when I was seventeen, Mom?"

"Of course. There's always something horribly wrong with all teenage girls. You can't help but worry about them. But they all come out in the wash," she said. "You did."

Eve smiled and took a breath as she allowed her mind's eye to rest. There was no need to watch anymore. Abbey was beautiful and bright and just as horrible and wonderful as the next teenage girl. She'd make her own choices, live out her own fate. She was her own person, so much more than how she was made, separate from Eve and her past mistakes.

SHE DIDN'T SEE ABBEY AS she reached the car in a far corner of the hospital parking lot. Didn't see her lean on the hood of Janet's Volvo to pull the recorder out from where she'd hidden it down her jeans. Abbey deleted the voice recordings she'd made in the trunk, especially the one about Michael and her diary. She couldn't afford any misunderstandings.

A small white fluffy form emerged in the greying light of the dawn, trotting toward her across the lot. The dog built up speed as it recognized Abbey. It jumped into her arms as she bent down to scoop him up, balanced precariously on one crutch. She leaned back against the hood of the car, whispering in one floppy white ear.

"Where have you been, little guy?" she said. "I thought you'd run away."

Then she grabbed hold of his furry neck and snapped it.

It was so much easier than the Patels' cat, who'd fought her unfamiliar hands. Abbey had only managed to paralyze the animal with the manoeuvre before she dissected it in the garage. Science camp had made her very curious about the insides of living things. She planned to become a doctor after all. There'd been a lot of blood, and she'd ruined the borrowed shirt she was wearing. She'd stuffed it in the laundry hamper, knowing her mother could always be counted on to clean up her messes.

"There's only room for one familiar in our house, puppy," Abbey said, dropping the dead dog to the pavement. Abbey didn't understand about familiars, that she couldn't really be one. But she wanted to understand. After what she'd seen her mother do at the quarry, she was eager to learn. She hopped down from the car hood and kicked the dog's body with her good foot. The animal skidded to a rest under the wheels of Janet's Volvo. Later she'd be horrified to think she'd run over him. Abbey opened the passenger door with the keys and extracted her phone from the glove compartment. Taking several selfies of herself with her crutches, she decided on the perfect one before posting it on Instagram.

Eve didn't see any of this as she waited patiently for her X-ray, secure in her belief that her daughter was like any other. Horrible and wonderful and filled with her own fate. Eve would no longer be watching all the time. And maybe that was a good thing.

Because there were some things a mother just wasn't made to see.

ACKNOWLEDGEMENTS

THIS BOOK WOULD NOT BE possible without the many special women in my life. My mother, my daughters, my dear friends. I am so grateful for all of them, and for the unique magic that each of them possesses.

I am also grateful for the seemingly normal, well-adjusted women who told me all the worst things they did as teenage girls — just because I asked. Many of their stories contributed to the character of Abbey. And, needless to say, they make for a harrowing read.

Of course, there are men to thank as well. My publisher, Scott Fraser, who first believed in me (and to my shock, apparently still does). My editor, Dominic Farrell, who patiently and professionally dodges the fury of a corrected writer's scorn. My dad, for never letting me forget about this book.

But most of all, I want to thank my husband, Marcus, for everything he does. His magic, like all great loves, is the strongest of all.

ABOUT THE AUTHOR

C.S. O'CINNEIDE WAS BORN IN Toronto, Ontario. In 2015, she walked the Camino de Santiago, where the disappearance of a female pilgrim inspired her first dark thriller, *Petra's Ghost*, a semi-finalist in the 2019 Goodreads Choice Awards. In 2020, she followed this success with *The Starr Sting Scale* and, in 2021, *Starr Sign*, both tongue-in-cheek noirs starring a hardboiled former hitwoman. *Eve's Rib* is inspired by her personal experience raising three daughters successfully into adulthood. Luckily for her, there was not a murderer in the bunch. O'Cinneide lives in Guelph, Ontario, with her Irish ex-pat husband, who remains her constant muse.